SERPENT SONG

Published by Brolga Publishing Pty Ltd
ABN 46 063 962 443
PO Box 12544
A'Beckett St
Melbourne, VIC, 8006
Australia

email: markzocchi@brolgapublishing.com.au

Printed in Australia
Cover design by Brolga Publishing
Typesetting by Alice Cannet
ISBN: 9781925367805

National Library of Australia Cataloguing-in-Publication entry
Creator: Grant, Toni, author.
Title: Serpent song / Toni Grant.
ISBN: 9781925367805 (paperback)
Subjects: Criminal investigation--Fiction.
             Detective and mystery stories.
             Romance fiction.

BE PUBLISHED

Publish through a successful publisher: national distribution, Dennis Jones &
Associates & international distribution to the United Kingdom, North America.
Sales Representation to South East Asia
Email: markzocchi@brolgapublishing.com.au

TONI GRANT

PROLOGUE

Clyde Fletcher tracked the high wire fence dividing the dockside shed from the foul water lapping his boots. Through the holes in the mesh, he scanned the area for any unwanted witness. Satisfied with his assessment, he allowed his mind to settle on the water's edge.

The biker smiled thinly, circling back to the road bike parked between the corrugated iron structure and the torn fence. In the riverbank silence he waited. Impatient.

Addiction gnawed. He walked around the bike again. Briskly rubbing his hands, Fletcher breathed warm air onto his rough palms. For hours he'd denied the need. Preparation required clear thinking. This close to the end, with everything in place, Clyde Fletcher had time and he might as well enjoy it.

Dirty fingers rolled the joint and in a languid sweeping motion, Fletcher's fat tongue licked the paper's edge. Greasy lengths of hair and unlikable features briefly lit up in the flame's glow. He drew fully upon the sweet contents.

In a slow outward breath, the biker's face turned to the ink-coloured heavens. Inhaling deeply again, he let the smoke fill his lungs. The insidious vine rapidly spreading and easing his growing tension. Calm, measured actions pulled at his impatience.

Any minute now.

From behind ominous clouds, the full moon showed itself, creating a mysterious blue underworld. Stepping instinctively into the shadows, Fletcher organised his mind for the next move.

Tonight, he'd make his own deal and exit his two-world existence. Gone for good before they realised he'd double-crossed his way to a tidy pay packet. Bunkered down by the coast, shaven, clean and sipping on a beer or three. Hell, he'd even pay some little slut to be at his beck and call, day and night. Subconsciously he grabbed at his crotch. And he wouldn't even have to share the mole.

He reached into the pocket of his leather coat with a grubby hand. Checking the mobile phone, he took another long drag on the joint, precariously stuck to his cracked, bloody lips. In the dampness, its sweet, sickly smell hung about him.

Again, his world was cast in blackness as thick cloud cover disguised the low gleaming orb. His eyes adjusted to the change and he listened.

The dim sound of a motorized dinghy begged an approach to the secluded area. Fletcher strode to the noise, the colours of his tribe, stitched visibly to the back of his leather coat. He waited on the shore impatiently.

"You're late," Clyde warned.

"We had some trouble at the dock," the Italian replied smoothly. His congenial expression showed genuine regret. "Do you have it?"

Clyde nodded. "I want the money first."

The Italian reached down and clumsily dragged a sports duffel bag from under the bow. Wads of neatly stacked cash exposed as the zipper released, tearing along the stitching.

At the rear of the small vessel, another man remained watchful. In his right hand, a semi-automatic pistol gleamed in the moonlight; the left one held the lever of the small motor. He stumbled slightly as the wash gently rocked the small tinny. Beside him fishing rods clacked together against a small blue esky.

Clyde eyed the pistol, noticing the attached silencer. His own assurance was secured at his hip, wedged in the waistband of filthy jeans. Any new business deal required extra precautions. With one assessing glance he dismissed the clumsy pair. The biker had nothing to fear here.

He spoke slowly, delivering the instructions in demeaning sarcasm.

"Good. You give me the money and then you can have the 'gift'. Capisco? Now get that boat a bit closer to the bank Signor, otherwise we'll all end up in the drink."

The two Italians glanced silently at each other. Following the biker's directions, the first stepped ashore, dropping the bag at Fletcher's feet. A whispery scent of damp earth and bank notes drifted upwards into the night air as the duffel spilled open again.

Fletcher drew sharply on his joint, attempting to mask the rising anticipation within him.

The Italian stepped back, collected the bag of pills and in a precise movement, threw it to his assistant in the boat. The skilled action caught Fletcher by surprise.

He shrugged, ignoring the Italians and snatched the load of cash. One long, last draw on the joint and the remaining butt flicked into nearby bushes.

"Nice doing business with you," the biker called conceitedly, pushing the bag into a secret compartment behind his pannier and exhaling another putrid breath.

"Sir," the Italian spoke clearly, his thick accent emphasizing his message, "I have another message for you."

"Oh yeah. What would that be?" Fletcher stopped. Arrogantly the biker turned to face the Italian and the revolver targeting his forehead.

"Time to die, traitor".

CHAPTER 1

" I'll see your $50 and raise you another $50." He placed the notes between them and waited.

"Aww. Come on. You're bluffing!" The other looked from his hand directly across the table into the hardened face. He searched the grey eyes for a sign of emotion. A weakness. A give-away.

"We'll see." Cold eyes stared back at the new kid and felt nothing.

On the overhead platform, Detective Francesca Salucci pressed her body uncomfortably against the iron structure. Through the grimy window of the small room, she made a quick assessment.

"I have a visual. There are two, I repeat, two offenders in the room," Francesca said quietly into the mouthpiece. "I see five handguns, three assault rifles and ammunition." She drew a mental picture of the shed. "On a bench. South facing wall. Behind internal door. Target has direct access into warehouse. Through open window."

"Copy," a voice buzzed in her earpiece.

Francesca pushed against the steel. In the centre of her back a tubular prong dug into the bulletproof vest. Another beam pressed against her temple, jutting dangerously out. It was about three inches in both length and width. She filled her nostrils with the smell of dusty steel, relishing the childhood comfort it recalled. The third was in line with her shin, a real bruiser at a length and width that could do some serious damage should she move forward carelessly. Sliding silently down the wall, she crouched in the darkness.

From here, she could provide cover for the team on the ground. And she had a bird's eye view of the whole interior of the warehouse. But those steel beams allowed limited movement and despite her agility, this section of the overhead walkway was too narrow to be truly effective. Likely she would fall and kill herself. She decided to leave her post and move to a more satisfactory location.

"Come on, make a decision Rick. The boss will be here in ten and I need to do another round."

Francesca froze as a metal chair slid along the concrete. She was now in direct sight of the doorway to the room. If he opened the door of the staff room and looked up, she would blow the whole operation. She fought the urge to move. Movement attracts attention. People only see what they want. Concealed in the shadows, the detective controlled her breath and through the window watched him walk to the fridge. He grabbed a beer and flicked its cap, which went skittering across the concrete floor. He sat back at the table.

"You're a bastard. I know you're bluffing but if I lose tonight the missus will nut me. I'm out."

Francesca breathed out slowly. She moved quickly, contorting her body to fit between a second set of steel bars. Today was not the day to watch from afar. She had to get closer.

For long minutes, she dodged the bars with careful steps and kept an eye on the suspects below. As the top of her head clipped another steel prong, Francesca grunted quietly. She stopped mid-way through the manoeuvre, listening intently. Piles of rat poo dislodged and fell as her bare hands found purchase on the narrow ledge. The solid pellets of shit hitting the gas cylinders directly below, in a musical plink-plink rhythm.

She gagged. The smell was incredible.

Satisfied she'd remained undetected, the detective proceeded along the ledge, standing fully and easing closer to the small room. Here the tight ledge opened onto a viewing platform. Directly above, a large hook and pulley system covered in dust-ridden cobwebs hung menacingly. From it, in silent wonder, a chain made from impressively large linkages dangled.

She was too exposed. Silently she climbed down; the lower level gave her protection as well as visual awareness. She nodded to herself. She was almost directly above the room and behind the open doorway.

"I'm in position," she whispered into the mouthpiece, giving them an update of her new post. Again a mental picture of the building layout filled her head as her earpiece buzzed. Each of her team had reached their designated post, checking in their locations with a central command.

"Copy. Stand by."

Any minute now she would receive the order to go. Any minute now their target would arrive. Any minute now the chopper would be overhead, giving her team back up and support. Francesca wrapped long fingers around the handle of her standard issue pistol.

She waited in the dark. Silent. Poised. Still.

"Got you!"

Francesca's scream of surprise caught in her throat; she felt his familiar warmth pressing against her bare skin.

Night turned to day and the warehouse interior morphed into a magnificent mansion basking in an Italian Riviera summer. Around her, laughter and instructions echoed as two teams took each other on in a game of tactics. Water fight tactics.

Girls versus boys. Winner takes all.

"Nicholas! What the hell?" Francesca disengaged from his hold, turning as her friend Justine squealed a loud entrance.

Bursting through the house at pace, Francesca cleared the sandstone steps in one almighty jump. She landed heavily, rolling commando-style, hiding behind the twisted trunk and dripping heaviness of a flowering crepe myrtle.

Close behind, two young men followed, hands raised in anticipation of a direct hit as they breached the doorway. Beside them, hidden by the lush foliage of a potted clivia, Mel readied her aim. In both hands the bright yellow glow from two dangerously full water bombs. At her feet, a pile of backup ammunition was ready.

"3 o'clock! Look out!" Nicholas yelled, warning his team as the girl landed on target, hastily following through with a watery barrage.

"Now, Miss Francesca. What am I to do with you?" the Italian said, wedging his prisoner firmly between an abundant garden and the white colonnade of the wide veranda. The boy stepped closer, blocking her only escape path.

Francesca instinctively stepped back, her buttocks pressing against the sandstone edge. Discreetly reaching behind, she grasped the yellow water-bomb resting on the stone.

Nic smiled menacingly.

With one arm he reached behind her, grabbing her wrists tightly together. The other was raised above her head squeezing the liquid contents tightly, willing the latex bubble to burst.

"No Nicci!" Francesca squirmed in his hold. Her team's narrow lead hinged on her outmanoeuvring this foe. "Please."

"Nic! Incoming!" Paul yelled to his brother. The boy weaved slightly as a yellow missile landed close beside them, splashing against the stone wall of the mansion. Using the distraction Nic secured his prisoner.

Discarding a blue cannon in the direction of her friends, he snatched the yellow balloon from her grasp. Victory was sweet. All the better for dousing the girl in her own watery ammunition.

Capturing Francesca, aside from his own personal pleasure, heralded the added enticement of a resounding win. Nicholas anticipated the gleeful gloat to his team that he had secured a hostage and won them the game.

He cocked his head, raising a questioning eyebrow. Why shouldn't I? He demanded silently.

Her soft eyes pleaded. She held her breath as his eyes travelled across her features. She felt him relent a little.

Struggling against him was pointless. At the realisation, Francesca stood still. She looked at him face-on in surrendered defiance.

His expression changed again. "You're mine," he said, his black eyes boring into hers as his mood intensified. Francesca caught a short husky breath. Only wit would save her now.

"Oh yeah? Prove it," the girl goaded, her own green eyes sparkling with delight as she prepared to escape his capture and join her friends.

Nicholas met her challenge. In one swift movement he released her hands and pulled her to him, pressing his lips to hers in a passionate kiss that left her breathless.

"Francesca! Where are you? Ring the bell! Ring the bell!" Mel cried from a distant place.

Francesca awoke with a start, temporarily disorientated, as the tolling bell called from her cell phone.

"Pronto? Salucci." She cleared a sleepy throat.

"It's Johnno. We have a floater. Pick you up in twenty." Her work partner's voice slurred with sleep and he coughed to clear his throat. "Your old friends are back. It's Chi You."

Francesca glanced at the bedside clock. 4.30am.

"I'll be ready," she said, flopping heavily into the pillows. She hugged at herself, wrapped in the imaginary warmth of her lover's embrace; caught in that mysterious place between dreams and full awareness.

At the silent briskness of her small Sydney bedroom the detective sighed wearily. That dream. Haunting again, weaving within her psyche. Again commanding unwanted attention.

"Nicholas," she whispered his name in the darkness. "Always Nicholas."

CHAPTER 2

The tiny ensuite bathroom, on the same mezzanine level as her bedroom and walk-through wardrobe, carried a black and white theme. Francesca had tempered the classic combination with the soft colours of the Italian Riviera, adding scented candles and subtle lighting to create the lush feel of an urban day spa.

In the steady, steaming water, Francesca gazed at the foamy water swirling around painted toes. This was not the time to become absorbed in a future that did not belong to her and a past she couldn't change. Regardless, she stood, in the middle of the thinking box, letting random thoughts control the conversation. For just a moment. And she turned her attention to that dream.

It was her eighteenth year. Two friends enjoyed the compulsory three-month backpack tour around Europe. Francesca and Mel visited all the must-see places, indulging in the culture and pleasures to be found in each. Italy was their last stop. The Delarno summer residence in the little township of Rapallo, the final destination.

Not as touristy as other stops on the Italian Riviera, Rapallo rhymed with old-fashioned glamour. Its lovely boardwalk flirted with the protected harbour; rows of pastel-coloured terraces leaning against the harsh hillside. The town trimmed with bright floral displays and towering palm trees with long, slender necks.

At one end, an emerald parkland complete with marina hosted a dazzling array of yachts dancing in the waters of the Ligurian Sea. At the other, rugged and handsome, a jutting outcrop was home to the Castello del Mare, Rapallo's symbol.

Perhaps its lure could be likened to the backdrop of a classic movie set. At any moment Francesca expected Audrey Hepburn to take to the crowded streets on a Vespa. In that sense of innocent surprise, it appealed to Francesca. Not to mention, the town's romantic atmosphere created the perfect stage for her teenage crush.

Ten years ago, Francesca was a very different person. Shy and protected, she was enchanted by the storybook glamour of the Delarno family; the special relationship she shared with them aided by Cristiana. Encouraged by the matriarch's warmth and thoughtfulness, Francesca learnt the traditional ways of a dutiful wife and mother. It was a role that Cristiana paid particular attention to, the tuition of Francesca Salucci.

It was Cristiana's eldest son that now held Francesca's attention. Nicholas Delarno.

Even as a boy, he knew what he wanted and how to get it. Blessed with devastating looks and a boisterous personality, his self-assurance could only be assumed.

Five years her senior, he would become Francesca's childhood protector, dispelling her worries and influencing her choices. During the dark months following the loss of her own mother, it was his security and compassion the girl would seek.

He had kept this part of him hidden from friends and family; moments of gentleness he shared only with her. To reveal himself to her in this way would have lifelong implications. It bound Francesca to him, still.

She stood for a moment, dripping in the small shower recess, wondering. Hoping. Francesca shook a heavy head. Time to shift focus. Distraction was a tool that walked a well-trodden path and

Francesca stepped gingerly through the process. The detective reminded herself gently: forget the past.

Wrapped in a soft towel, she chose the clothes that now defined her detective status, and threw them on the bed. The contents of her antique armoire caught her attention and prompted a slight smile. The restoration of that particular piece had taken months.

Thick layers of colour from bright red to the obligatory shades of white celebrated the creativity of previous owners, but her own efforts had been rewarded upon the discovery of the beautiful wood patina. Francesca decided it was time the timber took centre stage, laid bare in a coat of clear varnish.

One particular door of the piece refused to stay shut, opening itself regularly to reveal quilts and cushions, pillows and throws and various collections of odds and ends she couldn't part with. In the bright moonlight that streamed through the bedroom's French doors, Francesca considered it, tut-tutting at its cheekiness. Tonight the cupboard door had again mysteriously opened during her slumber.

Absently twisting her unruly hair into a tight knot at the base of her neck, she pushed the door shut and turned to go. A small hall table neatly arranged with a collection of photographs, her mother's silver mirror and an intricate jewellery box butted against the iron balustrade and half-wall of the mezzanine. Here, her eyes rested. That box stowed some of Francesca's most valuable and cherished items. The most special being a prized photograph.

With a defeated sigh, Francesca gave way to the yearning that taunted her again tonight. She sifted through the contents until she found the faded yellow picture. Once again she was lost in him. The detective gazed at the treasure, her finger tracing the outline of two people, their heads close together, searching for the next puzzle piece. In that captured instant, two smiling faces, relaxed and happy in youth.

Under the colonnade veranda of the Italian home, a small timber table held court. The area offered a cool respite from the afternoon heat. Here, as the sea breezes gently nudged, a daily ritual took place as two childhood friends took turns to talk, laugh and test their logic. Cherished moments together wrapped in a changing friendship. That precious time before life becomes complicated by sex. And secrets.

During that last night, after the water fight, Nicholas had been different. Possessive. Confident. Francesca knew she would belong to him by sunrise. The stolen moments of intimacy that had dotted her life since her sixteenth birthday would be replaced with an honest relationship.

As the three-month tour of Europe ended, an impromptu farewell party had turned the grassy straights between silver-leaved olive trees into a dancefloor. Under fairy lights strung from heavy boughs, the sweet, damp air shimmered with romance.

She'd been wrong, and it hurt. Francesca returned home, used and betrayed, and swore she'd never see him again.

Six months later Francesca found herself wrapped in his arms and bed sheets after an alcohol-fuelled venture. And so the cycle began. For the next five years Francesca vowed to never see him again, only to find herself back in his arms at the end of every failed relationship.

Finally, her mind and heart determined to rid him from her system. Francesca removed herself once and for all from his reach, building a formidable reputation in the back blocks of western Queensland. She'd worked every celebration, stacked up her leave and buried herself in law textbooks. The sacrifice had been worth it.

Last year Detective Sergeant Francesca Salucci was seconded to one of the most revolutionary organised crime investigative teams in the country and settled into a new life in Sydney.

Working beside the NSW Police Organised Crime Squad, this specialist team focused on infiltrating and investigating international organised crime syndicates. It possessed enhanced statutory support and was well funded.

The work was stimulating and dangerous. Its heady combination determined Francesca's life. She lived for her work, relished the intensity and most of all, the long hours.

In this investigative role, Francesca had a family and the focus she needed. Francesca dragged her thoughts back to the present. *I need to forget you.* She nodded to herself. Yes. This obsession with him had to end. In every other way she was strong. But him. A secret kept hidden from their families and pushed deep inside herself underneath the many layers of her success.

CHAPTER 3

Francesca searched the empty street below for Johnno's vehicle. A delicate wrought iron balcony extending from her bedroom overlooked a small entrance garden. Reflections on the pond below gave the marble and concrete fountain an eerie, translucent glow. Across from her, a majestic eucalypt spread its limb like protective arms, dispelling a slight lemon scent into the damp air. She breathed it deeply.

The cosy apartment in Sydney's Inner West was discrete and secure. A solace from the intense pressures of work and far enough away from the Delarno family, their money and their heartbreaker of a son.

Ten years on from that Rapallo holiday, she had professional credibility and options. Now she needed a way to emotionally be rid of him once and for all.

It's time Francesca. Time to clear him from your heart for good.

A framed replica of van Gogh's 'Blossoming Almond Tree' leant against the mezzanine rail. She looked at the print fondly as memories of the street markets in rural France steered her thoughts. From that market alone, she'd packed and shipped a whole suitcase of trinkets home.

And here is the start, she said to herself. These particular memories from your past need to go. No more reminders.

The large eucalypt lit up by oncoming headlights caught her attention again, its branches bobbing in the brisk breeze. As it cast distorted shadows over the footpath, Francesca shuddered involuntarily. She walked to the small table, reverently placed the photograph in the music box and closed the lid.

She'd kept that photo for all these years. *Was she such a fool?*

Her heart ached.

Briefly checking her appearance in the full-length mirror, she straightened her uniform of well-cut pants, silk blouse and soft knit jumper. Handcuffs sat snugly in the small pouch at her hips. Work. And company. At last. A new focus, although she doubted Johnno appreciated the early wake-up call.

Chi You. Not so slick this time, thought Francesca, rubbing her hands together in anticipation as she descended the steps two at a time to the kitchen and dining area below.

~

This organised crime group of triads, known as Chi You, still fascinated Francesca. Their origins were as complex and controversial as their namesake, the Chinese mythological God of War. Ancient sketches of the God depict a bronze bull-like head with two horns and four eyes. The body, taking human form, possesses six arms wielding weaponry.

The modern day Chi You group carried out their actions in the true sense of their namesake, with a ferocity and cruelty matched only by their greed and tyrannical style of leadership. They were a group to be treated with caution and respect.

Members carried bull-like symbols on their bodies, etched in ink, hidden in intricate designs. Initiation was not for the fainthearted and involved cruel torture tests as part of the rites of passage. Permanent, deep scars to the upper torso and limbs were hallmarks of tribe members. They wore dark long-sleeved clothing to hide the afflictions among the general public.

Survival of initiation meant lifelong protection for you and your family.

For Francesca this was now a personal quest. She remembered clearly her introduction to Chi You. It would haunt her forever. It started with a boy. He was no more than 13 years and brutally afflicted with Chi You markings; his lifeless body dumped in an industrial bin behind a warehouse. A hollow gaze of death had not hidden the terror and pain he must have felt in his last moments. The welted bruising splayed across his bony limbs, broken ribs clearly visible through his stretched skin and fingers bent in broken, torturous ways.

Then there were the deep, clotted cuts from knife wounds as he fought for his place in the tribe. Francesca's sickened dismay at the brutality of the initiation spurred her sense of justice. She would never learn this boy's name. It was the code of Chi You. But he had a mother who was grieving for her lost son. Francesca vowed then and there to bring this group to its knees. For him and his family she would get justice.

Francesca glanced at the dining table, beyond the island bench of her small kitchen. Johnno would arrive any minute now. She couldn't say she felt prepared. The table was littered with the Queensland Police Department Chi You brief. The scattered contents of the impending trial were spread for Francesca to search legal and technical loopholes within the statements and process. Amongst the papers an empty bottle of Campari and a small drinking glass sat in a puddle of melted ice.

To her left a large free-standing oven took space along the back wall. Francesca loved to cook. Sometimes she needed to cook. Thankfully the team were always appreciative of her contributions to the morning tea fund. For Francesca it was a far safer option than the alternative. She wasn't good in relationships. Since turning her back on the heart-breaking affair, she could never get the balance right;

work, the memory of Nicholas and the poor bastard who tried to fill his place. An appreciative team was by far a more satisfying option all-round.

Johnno was here.

"I'll get back to you later," she said at the Chi You brief. Casting a glance over a stack of dirty dishes in the untidy kitchen, the detective added, "you too."

Francesca grabbed a warm coat from the hook on the wall and locked the door behind her.

CHAPTER 4

"Any news?" Francesca climbed into the over-heated car, smiling at his wayward appearance. Ginger hair stood on end, ruffled by a restless night and dire need for a haircut. His big hands wrapped around the steering wheel. Francesca waited for his reply, studying the sinewy lines that defined his forearms. Some way along, almost at the elbow, the cuffs of his shirt were rolled in a tight bind. His shirt was ironed today.

Johnno insisted on wearing his shirt sleeves in this fashion; rain, hail or shine. It was the western way. Beneath the twisted fibre, she knew his powerful arms linked to muscled shoulders and back, still bruised with ruck marks from the weekend's rugby friendly.

At his waist, a two-ring plaited belt with an overlap of bonded leather would flap against his hips when he walked. On his feet, a pair of tan elastic-sided boots, polished and supple.

"Nothing much. Sounds like an execution. The boys took a phone call and rang me after they found the body. The caller was quite specific about mentioning Chi You and hung up."

"Do we know anything at all about the caller?"

"Not yet. But I've already asked forensics to analyse the recording."

Yesterday's stubble formed a dark shadow around his mouth and jaw, making a sandpaper sound when he rubbed it. Her partner was loud, tall and broad. He had the biggest hands she'd ever seen. Safe hands his mates had said. They meant for the rugby ball but she knew it went a bit further than that.

Johnno loved his mates, sport and girlfriend, in that order, and lived each day to the full. His popularity compounded by a quick wit and equally wicked sense of humour. On the flip side, the Scot could be absolutely ruthless. Francesca loved working with him. She trusted him with her life; and she trusted his judgment more.

"Just get in, did you?" he teased good-naturedly, referring to her fresh appearance at the early hour.

"No!" Francesca tried to sound indignant, smoothing her damp hair. "Couldn't sleep!" She changed the subject. "Well can't say I'm surprised to be out on a job tonight. It's a full moon and you know what they say about full moons."

For emphasis, she pointed to the large disc slowly disappearing in the early morning light. Francesca babbled on feeling the nervous excitement build at the prospect of a new job. She smiled to herself. This new case was the distraction she craved.

"A floater! Hmmm!" She sobered suddenly. After ten years in the job the sight of death still made her stomach squish unhappily. "Execution style and Chi You. I assume there are no witnesses."

She turned to face him. Despite the early hour and bleary expressionless face, she knew his mind was already in focus preparing for the day ahead.

Turning sharply off the main thoroughfare to a dimly lit alley, Francesca reassessed her bearings. The first misty whispers of a wintery fog began to drop. At the end of the road, the reflective paint of the marked police car caught their oncoming headlights.

Outside, the dockside location breathed an eerie pre-dawn feeling. An overpowering stench of rotting fish joined with the foamy green water, splashing against the wharf pylons as the tide turned to make its way back out to sea. Its age-old rhythm of coming and going meant that eventually all sins would be revealed. Francesca gagged at the smell. Not a good start, she thought.

As they neared the first police officer Francesca scanned the isolated location. They were directed to follow a tight track skirting around shrubbery at the water's edge.

At the end, a large boggy clearing opened onto the back of an industrial area.

The detectives stopped at the body which was lying face down in the muddy wash, dressed only in jeans and socks. His bare back was covered in muck and tattoos. Hands tied securely behind with cable ties. A single bullet to the head was the only obvious injury. The wound indicated he had faced his fate. Indeed, it did show all the hallmarks of an execution-style murder.

"What are your first thoughts Francesca?" Johnno asked.

"Well, he's not bloated, so I guess it's a pretty recent occurrence. His hair is greasy and blonde. Pale skin showing an array of freckles and moles. Look at the fat distribution around the hips. All of it indicates Caucasian origins. Well, to me anyway. I have come across Chi You members from non-Asian backgrounds before, but it's very rare. Also I note that his tattoo style is not Asian."

She wondered about his lack of shoes and belt. His jeans wore the label of a low market brand. Thick socks would show he may have been wearing boots. In fact, she fleetingly thought, the socks reminded her of standard Police issue. As the moon slipped behind the clouds, Francesca reached for her torch and continued her observations of the body.

"Also, scarring typical of Chi You membership is not present."

She greeted the forensic police with a nod and a tight smile. Johnno turned his attention to the location to take a couple of photographs before facing the body prone in the stinking mud. He focused on the body through his lens, taking the necessary close ups that would help them get started later in the day.

"You're right to get in a bit closer if you need, Francesca." Johnno beckoned after a quick conference with the lead forensic police officer.

Leaning close to the body, Francesca's hands covered her mouth and nose from the foul stench of him as she tried to analyse the tattoos. Symbolic markings might give them some clues to his gang membership or allegiances. Bold tribal markings on his shoulders and upper arms indicated an islander affinity.

In the half light and thick mud, it was difficult to determine the detailing around the upper back, although it resembled the makings of a bird's claw. For this particular case, Francesca admitted any inference from the ink work would require a trip to the morgue once the body had been cleaned.

Stepping away, she turned towards the river bank. The Maglite strobe shone brightly across the muddy embankment. It was foolish to hope for obvious clues. Tracks from a beached boat, perhaps a foot or shoe print. In reality, she needed to distance herself from the body. Nausea built at an alarming rate after the close inspection. She whispered a mantra … breathe in through the nose, out through the mouth, trying to settle her queasy stomach. It would do her credibility no good if she started spewing now.

She shook her head to try and clear the dreadful smell of him from her nostrils, the smell of blood and death. Wondering how long it had been since his last shower, another distinctive smell permeated from his hair. The results of a toxicology report would let her know exactly the mix of drugs he was taking, although she was almost sure it was weed. That meant the body hadn't been in the water. He was either murdered on this spot or dumped.

The moon hung low, paling in the emerging dawn light. Focusing on the last of it bouncing off the small white crests on the Parramatta River, Francesca shivered. Swirling water made her jumpy and the detective was glad to have the team around this morning. She glanced behind to Johnno, reassuring herself she was not alone. The fog that had threatened earlier was dissipating, withdrawing in a wet mist as the dawn broke across the sky, splitting the dark clouds with yellow colour wash.

She shivered. Someone was watching her. Francesca felt the hairs on her neck prickle in agitation. She checked again in the direction of the boys who were engrossed in their analysis and searched along the river bank beside her before diverting across the water. Here, where the river narrowed, she scanned the row of parked cars facing the bank. A black SUV stood alone facing her. Was she paranoid?

The detective quickly grabbed the mobile from her pocket to take a picture. It was quite a distance. The bright flash issued a warning to the vehicle. Francesca swore.

Hastily she reached for the tiny night vision binoculars attached to her hip and in a partial read wrote the numbers by memory in her notebook. The lights of a garbage truck shone momentarily through the back windshield. The driver's large head and bulky frame were revealed in the backlight. And he was looking directly at her. He blew her a kiss.

Francesca blinked and shook her head in disbelief. Her immediate reaction was to drop the binoculars to her side.

"Johnno," she squeaked, turning her head momentarily to alert her partner. Francesca returned focus to the spot across the river. The car had disappeared. She examined the roadway, tracking side to side through the binocular lens along the river bank avenue.

"Francesca," Johnno said, drawing out her name by syllable. "You'd better look at this." The detective coughed discreetly. The distinct smell caught in his throat as the body was turned over.

Morning light broke across the sky. The small group of police exchanged looks over the motionless body. Staring plainly for all to see, the numbers two and five scalded the victim. Upon the left pec, sealing his flesh, the burn was similar in size to a cattle branding iron, the type used to determine stock ownership.

"And you're positive the caller mentioned Chi You?" Francesca spoke first. No triad group she'd ever known had ever claimed a murder.

Johnno nodded as she continued.

"This is really unusual. I mean the whole set of circumstances are odd. Chi You are particularly careful in this area. In fact, this is the last thing I'd expect from them." She turned to Johnno. "You know how they operate."

"Yeah," Johnno agreed.

"Twenty five. It's the triad number for undercover cops and traitors." She looked back at the body.

"Well … this message is a warning of some sort," Johnno concluded after a few silent moments.

Francesca nodded and focused on the tattoos. More specifically on the wings of the eagle that wrapped around his upper shoulders and chest. Its story seemed out of place with the heavy black markings on his back. Was this dead man searching for a new identity by covering up old allegiances?

"You see here," she said pointing to his torso, "he's not part of Chi You, not in the traditional sense anyway. There is no evidence of blade work." After a few moments, she continued, "What do you think about the placement of that brand? It's centred on his heart. To me that indicates he is a traitor at the centre of something."

Johnno nodded but it was pure speculation at this point. He spoke after another long silence, "Thanks boys."

Francesca glanced around at the scene in the morning light, imprinting the whole picture in her memory. For her own records, the detective snapped a couple more location photographs and followed Johnno along the muddy bank back to the car.

CHAPTER 5

The Five Dock café bustled in morning activity. Francesca greeted the owner with warm familiarity and found a private table at the rear of the small room.

Over breakfast, the detectives explored Chi You habits and the creep in the car across the river in low, private voices. Their hushed but intense discussions went largely unnoticed until the second round of coffee. By now the place was beginning to fill with groups of mothers and small children.

Francesca switched subjects when she realised one of the groups was paying more attention to them than to the whining children.

They stood out like dogs' balls anyway. Cops have a look about them and Little John with his messed-up ginger nut lit up like a beacon amongst the dark-haired crowd of well-dressed customers.

Johnno leaned back in his seat, causing it to stretch alarmingly under his bulk and surveyed his partner of 12 months.

She was a looker all right. Physically a beautiful specimen of average height with curves in all the right places. Her dark hair fell in waves down her back and stopped midway to shapely hips. Startling green eyes sparkled with vitality, emphasized as they were with thick black lashes and heavy eyeliner. During the summer months her skin turned a deep golden, a tribute, he supposed, to her Italian heritage.

The boys in the squad called her Movie Star and she took it in her stride. Everyone in the team had a nickname. Usually it related to an unfortunate mishap on a job, or an obvious character or physical trait. His was Little John because there was nothing little about him.

The coffee had been delivered and he watched her sprinkle the sugar over the top. She seemed absorbed in the process, waiting and watching as the sugar perched high above the tight foam before slowly descending.

"You know …" she started.

"That's the sign of a great coffee. Made to perfection. When the sugar can sit on the top like that it means the milk has been agitated to …" Johnno finished the sentence of the girl he'd come to regard as a little sister.

"Smart arse," Francesca responded her lips forming a playful pout. "I don't say that every time."

"Have you ever tried to sit the sugar on the coffee crema? Now when that happens you know the coffee is good," Johnno continued to bait her.

She looked into her coffee as a playful smile tugged at the corners of her mouth. She composed herself enough to look directly at Johnno and smiled sweetly revealing pearly teeth and a surprising fullness to her face.

"Alright you've had your fun," she said simply, returning her focus to the coffee, creating patterns in the milky froth with her spoon.

Johnno watched her. He couldn't put his finger on it but recognised the cracks behind the stylish clothes and façade, signs that she wasn't coping. Distraction and agitation replaced by a 1950s housewife. A fresh homemade treat every morning tea accompanied by obsessive fussing over process and court preparations. The lucky dip of emotional outpouring that the team bore daily.

"How are you going with the Chi You brief?" he asked casually.

Whether the cause was work-related or chick's business made no difference. Every detective on Johnno's team was subjected to the same scrutiny. They worked a deadly game. Knowing the importance of this, Johnno employed numerous tactics to help each member stay on form and focused.

"Good," she lied, thinking about the papers scattered around her home. If she missed something in the brief and Chi You walked, she'd never forgive herself. In one month, the pressure valve would be released enough for her to relax a little and get a decent night's sleep. Subconsciously she stretched her shoulders, flexing and prodding the tight muscles with her fingers.

"Do you need a hand? I can organise for someone else to handle this new matter if you like," he persisted noticing again the hollows under her eyes that makeup couldn't hide.

"What? No way. I'm good Johnno. Besides, we all have massive case loads, there's no one else available. Truly, I'm good. Just a bit flat at the moment, that's all." She reached across and squeezed his arm where it rested on the table. The girl smiled reassuringly.

"Coming to Ruthie's tomorrow night?" He changed tack. "Great band, good food, great blokes. You never know, you might pick up! That drummer you hooked up with last time, what was his name, Peg Leg Pete, is playing."

Francesca shook her head in disbelief. "You're an arse, you know that. His name was Van Peart. We didn't hook up."

"Bullshit!" Johnno cupped his hands over his mouth, pretending to sneeze. "I saw you leave with him."

"If you must know, I caught a cab. Alone. After he offered me a joint."

Francesca burst out laughing at the memory of his stunned face as she left him at the curb with a warning.

"What! No way! You never mentioned it before." His rumbling laughter caught the attention of the mothers' group again.

"Shut up Johnno. And you will never mention it again. It was frigging embarrassing. So, yeah I'll come but I'll sort out my own love life thanks very much." Francesca played with the spoon, licking the cold froth from the handle.

"Right. So now I know your type. You've expanded your repertoire. Potheads and arse-holes. Why don't you hook up with one of my mates? They might not be as classy to look at as your latest and greatest, but they're decent blokes. And they know how to treat a lady."

Francesca blushed as the whole café turned their attention to the unlikely pair and the topic of their conversation. She looked into her empty coffee cup, hiding bright red cheeks.

"Thanks Johnno, you are really sweet and I love your mates, but you know me. I don't mix business with pleasure. If it all fell to shit, well, it would be awkward. Besides, my taste in men is not THAT bad! I agree, in the past, I've made some bad choices."

She paused, sobering. "To be honest, lately I've been so wrapped up in work I haven't had time for relationships. When you're a cop ... think of it from my perspective. Our profession doesn't turn men on to me like the women turn on for you. Besides, I have my work cut out keeping all of your team in line!"

She tried to sound light. The truth being every guy she ever met was invariably compared with Delarno. Forget the glass ceiling, no man could get close enough to her to bust through the Nicholas Delarno ceiling.

"Let's go," the detective said abruptly, not wanting to get trapped in her head again. She pushed the chair back and stood before Johnno had a chance to respond. "The boss will be chaffing to talk about this morning's call out. I bet the Minister's been on the phone already. He's a pain in the arse. I hate election years."

She switched her phone off silent to find five messages from the boss. She shoved it in Johnno's face, emphasizing her point. He would have the same if not more. The boss rarely phoned her.

"All right sister, let's get rolling." Little John stood, dwarfing her. His chair scraped loudly across the tiled floor. He got the hint... personal life off limits. Again.

Francesca glanced guiltily at his hurt expression. "Thanks for looking out for me ol' buddy. Hell, I dunno know where I'd be without ya, an' all," Francesca said, mimicking a wild western drawl that sounded more like goofy on the drink. She finished the display with an exaggerated wink and a dramatic fluttering of her long eyelashes.

"Come on you dag. That's the worst accent I've ever heard." Johnno resisted the urge to flick her across the arse with the napkin as they headed out of the café into the sunny winter day.

CHAPTER 6

Two detectives entered the small rectangular room that had been divided into a glass-fronted office and six work stations. Inspector Goodwood raised his head from the stack of paperwork surrounding him.

In the corner behind him a framed photograph of his grandchildren, a happy crowd of blonde-haired angels, beamed at him from their position on top of the four-drawer filing cabinet. Beside the photograph a wobbly clay construction glazed in ghastly mud-green was marked 'Pa'. The top drawer was opened displaying a fanlike construction of papers shoved in all directions.

One wall showcased his achievements with certificates and merits framed identically. At his overcrowded desk a trio of small flags poked in a stand. Australia, New Zealand and Fiji.

Closely shaved and dressed immaculately, he met their noisy entrance with an intense gaze over the rim of his reading glasses. In his grasp and poised mid-air a Waterford pen indicated he was mid-way through a tick and flick process on the pile of briefing papers in front of him. Behind him a large window looked over yet another CBD building, his blinds angled so that the morning sun created shards of slivered light.

"Detectives," he greeted them, motioning for them to enter.

"Good morning Sir," Johnno began, launching into a summary of the morning call out and finishing with the comment. "Francesca seems to think the placement of the brand on the body could be significant."

"Oh?" He looked directly at the detective. "Why? Have you seen this before Francesca?"

"No Sir. The number twenty-five is significant to the Chinese. But identification of any kind is not common practice. I believe a brand over the heart is more symbolic. In a weird way, I guess, romantic. Chi You is too clinical."

Goodwood nodded. "Well you are the expert where that group is concerned. Who do you suggest is behind it then?"

"Branding is also used as an intimidation tactic between rivals and followers. So we thought we'd check recent mob activities," Johnno answered.

"Good. You think Italian or Middle Eastern?" the inspector enquired.

"We're not sure, Sir. Branding and burning flesh … I believe it's more Italian. Old-school Italian," Francesca responded.

"Keep me informed. Who else do you need on the case? I want this sorted a.s.a.p. Fucking elections. Eight months can't come soon enough. Francesca get me something on paper by 2pm so I can get it to legal."

Francesca shifted uncomfortably at the inspector's penetrating gaze. "The Minister in all his wisdom has called a press conference for 3pm today. He wants to set up a task force."

"Yes Sir," she responded.

"I think a task force is a bit of a waste of time and resources at the moment, Sir." Johnno's response drew an arched eyebrow from the inspector. He continued, "We really have nothing but speculation to show that it is the beginning of anything much. If it turns out to be Middle Eastern mafia we can link up with the boys and their current operations. Francesca and I can handle the preliminary investigation at present."

Goodwood thought about it for a moment. "You have until the end of the day."

"Thank you, Sir."

"And another thing, keep your bloody phones switched on! You're no good to me if I can't talk to you and don't give me that out-of-range bullshit."

"Yes, Sir," they replied in unison.

~

Francesca stretched her arms high, arched her tired back and shoulders and rested her hands behind her head. Shutting her eyes to the data tables swimming on the computer screen before her, her head momentarily relaxed forward to her chest. She knew the places and names like the back of her hand and still no connection to this morning's murder.

Johnno yawned loudly as his stomach let out a hungry growl.

"My thoughts exactly," she said, her eyes remaining shut. "I need food too." The thought of a hot dinner had her salivate instantly. "Coming?"

Her partner simply stood and grabbed his coat. "I know a great place," he began, already at the door of their shared office.

The contrast of the cool night air and the rush of the hour nipped at her senses forcing her to step back momentarily. People and traffic streamed everywhere, racing like ants in the hours before a western rain storm. It was bumper to bumper this time of night.

Francesca observed the rush, double stepping to keep pace with Johnno. Office staff darted amongst the stationery cars scurrying to meet train and bus timetables. A small family of disoriented tourists checked a map huddling together in the set back doorway of a vacant shop front.

Booths of food outlets were crammed with school girls, noisily vying for attention and texting endlessly. Everywhere Francesca looked an entire city was tired and hassled.

The red-headed detective strode towards the corner pub.

They chose a booth that had a view of the television. "My shout, what would you like?" Francesca offered. Tonight's $10 menu was homemade rissoles, gravy and vegetables.

"Sweet," Johnno replied. "I'll have the special."

Francesca wandered to the bar, ordered the drinks and food and turned to watch the news. The Police Minister was struggling.

"He looked like a wanker tonight. Does that mean I'm in for it tomorrow?" Francesca asked, concerned about the repercussions.

"Nah, the boss is good. Just keep Goodwood in the loop."

"Yeah that would be easy if I had something worthwhile to report," she said as Johnno's phone sounded the ACDC classic Thunderstruck over the bar room noise.

"Jonathan McCrae." He listened intently as the caller spoke, madly nodding and taking notes on a serviette. Finally he replied, "Yes. Thanks mate. I'll let the boss know. No worries. Cheers."

"Sir. It's Johnno. Lab says the body found this morning is a known member of the Ares Outlaw Motor Cycle Gang, Clyde Fletcher."

There was a pause.

"Yes Sir. I'll let Francesca know. Thank you Sir. Good night."

Detective Jonathan McCrae turned to his partner, who was staring at him. Her eyebrow arched a question. He grinned at her, his freckled face split like a watermelon.

Francesca thought Johnno was about to burst. "Well?" she enquired.

"You're looking at the leader of a new taskforce ... Operation Serpent." He grinned again. "When we get back to the office, I need a detailed summary of the relevant information on hand at the moment. The groundwork for this investigation has to be solid. Your role is to keep an eye on the legalities of every aspect of this operation as well as taking on a key investigative role. Don't be afraid to show initiative. Copy?"

"Copy." Francesca couldn't hide her own enthusiasm. Another

case to sink her teeth into and she beamed across the table at him.

"We'll be joined by key members of the OMCG taskforce tomorrow morning." He pushed out from the table. "Ready? I want to make a decent start tonight."

~

"Here, Johnno, the rap sheet for Clyde Fletcher," Francesca said. "Assault police causing grievous bodily harm, possession of prohibited substance to supply, armed robbery. Spent some time in Long Bay but released on good behaviour ... huh ... weird. Only lasted eight months on a five year sentence. Stabbing offences. Firearms offences. More drug offences. Current warrant issued for his arrest based on latest armed holdup at the TAB on the South Coast last month. And that's only NSW. I haven't even started on the other states."

Francesca continued to read the intelligence summary.

"Became a member of the Ares in 2000 after Long Bay stint and has risen steadily through the ranks. Sits at the round table. Sounds like a dedicated follower to me. Wonder why he was a traitor? Could have been patching over to Chi You, I suppose. It would explain the public exposure and the lack of initiation markings."

"Yeah…. Could be possible." Lost in thought, Johnno tapped out a percussion beat. "Ares setting up Chi You over one lost follower? A bit over-dramatic if you ask me. There has to be more to it than that."

A chart projected onto the wall created a grid pattern, within which, known illegal activities and key persons of interest were listed. On a detailed map of Sydney beside it, green circles highlighted areas of known Chi You activities. A blue X marked the location of Clyde Fletcher's body and another dotted the approximate location of the suspicious SUV. An arrow directed the view of the driver who'd faced Francesca.

Known links to the Melbourne-based Italian mob were cross-referenced with Middle Eastern organised crime syndicate activities.

This grid and map system provided a quick visual of any correlations between the groups.

Along another wall, Francesca had begun pinning close up photographs of the tattoos found on Clyde Fletcher's body, as well as some location shots.

The pair sat staring at the boards in front of them. Not one overlapped in boundaries, which was hardly surprising. As expected, vested interests in drug and arms trade weaved through every crime syndicate.

"Hey Johnno, an Ares Motorcyclist, an Italian mobster and a Triad gang member walk into a bar…" Francesca said, aware of her bad joke.

"Ok. But they wouldn't walk in together. So who would walk in first and what would they be looking for?" Johnno countered.

"I think Triad would walk in alone. Remain in the shadows. Away but present," she responded.

"Yes I agree. I think Ares and triads meet at the bar. I think Chi You is partnering Ares to sure up supply. Well-established drug routes and systems. Manufacturing. We know that Clyde Fletcher was a member of Ares. Ordinarily the murder of a chapter leader would spark a fairly rapid response. There would be talk of some sort of action within the group by now. I think the real question is more along the lines of: why are the two groups working together. Is it narcotics or cash or something else?" Johnno responded. "I can't come at a third party at this point. The link is too tenuous."

Francesca knew at times outlaw gang members assisted other criminal syndicates. Usually recruitment came by individuals on a contractual arrangement rather than the gang as a whole.

"I see your point. Assuming Clyde opposed the move, I can see that publically calling him a traitor would maintain and boost leadership power within a bike gang structure. And we'd have to assume the hit would happen in-house," she said. "I just can't see a partnership between Chi You and anyone to be honest. Chi You always worked alone. I think we're dealing with a partnership between Ares and another syndicate. But it's got me stuffed why our killer would call out Chi You."

"Let's talk about Ares for a minute," Johnno replied. "Have you had much to do with them Francesca, in particular, their president, Robbie L?"

Francesca shook her head. "Not really. Any altercation in Queensland between bike gangs was handled by a dedicated team. I never had the chance to work with those guys. Although I do know our biggest concern was the Warlords."

"A quick history lesson. Ares took the Greek God of War as their mentor. Possibly the most despised amongst the ancient Gods, Ares lived by a code of rebellion - bloodthirsty rebellion. His behaviour apparently represented manliness and courage. Ancient Greeks described him as savage, dangerous and militaristic; qualities the Ares Motor Cycle group relish. You would recognise their symbol, I imagine."

"Large hands holding the leads of a fierce looking dog and a wild pig with the words Phobos, meaning fear, and Deimos, meaning terror, branded on each beast," she said.

Johnno nodded. "Also, the flag with the combination of blue and white stripes and the southern cross in the background."

"And we have branding again. Maybe you're right. Ares and Chi You."

"Maybe. Where are you up to? In relation to cross-referencing outside of Sydney district."

"Western region and then I am finished with NSW. Do you want me to keep looking or start something else?"

"Stay with western region. Finish the job. I'm going to start on Ares." Johnno responded. "Tomorrow I'll get the team to look into the Warlords, just to be sure."

Francesca shrugged and nodded, methodically going through the data when something caught her attention. A charred body had been found in a mineshaft at Lightning Ridge, a mining town in the far west of NSW. The report stated there was a single gunshot wound to the head and at some point the hands and feet had been bound. The body, found two weeks ago, was yet to be identified.

"Johnno," she said, unable to contain her hopeful voice. "Come and look at this. Listen." She read the file to him. "What do you think?" she asked, looking up at him questioningly as she finished reading the brief summary.

"Could be something," he said cautiously, sniffing loudly at the air. "The Ridge though? That's a long way from Sydney. What would they be doing out there? Here is Sydney," he said pointing to a digital map of NSW, emphasizing his point. "That's Lightning Ridge."

A raspy sound interrupted the silence as his rough hands rubbed chin whiskers thoughtfully. "We have a dead Ares gang member with a triad number system. Anything about the guy at the Ridge?"

"No, no markings, no number, just burnt," Francesca replied, thoughtfully adding, "Remember that article in the Australian Federal Police Newsletter? That one on mob activity in Sicily. It talked about a resurgence in Italian mafia traditions. Traditions like burning or branding traitors." She glanced at Johnno and continued, "So, our connections are symbolic indicators of traitors. I know I keep talking about the Italians, but I can't help thinking of that branding as symbolic. To me it screams a message. Bike gangs and Chi You are more methodological. Brutal without emotion."

She continued, "Think about it. We've assumed Clyde Fletcher was getting in the way of some new deal. Nero is based in Melbourne right? What if the deal has already been made and the bodies bind the contract. They point to Chi You. Why the Chinese? To throw us off track." She stopped and thought for a minute. "Unless, of course, it's a three-way pact, in which case there is another body somewhere."

Francesca placed her hands behind her head and stretched, looking up at the ceiling thoughtfully. "So then you have to ask, is Australia big enough to hide and sustain such a huge crime syndicate."

"Wait! You know what I think?" she almost shouted. "Chi You is pretty much nutted now. Cairns. Melbourne. Gold Coast. It's all but over for them. They're under the pump with the court matter in Brisbane next month. They won't react now. They simply can't. That creates time and opportunity. Time to create new partnerships with lower-level Chi You members. The Melbourne chapter had the strongest leadership. Nero would be licking his lips at this opportunity, you have to agree." Francesca faced him, her face glowing with resolution. "We know he's into symbolic gestures. You saw that report from the Victorian Cops about those three murders last year."

She looked at him earnestly.

"Next month's court matters will bring convictions I'm certain. Without an active figure head, the group will dissipate. It has happened before with other triad gangs. That's a whole lot of talent and connections down the tubes, unless the members can be coerced to patch over. Maybe, just maybe, Ares and Nero are looking to expand membership, increase supply … in effect take over Chi You. So they put any gang members not wanting to comply on notice with the symbolic twenty-five."

She sat back, nodding in satisfaction at her conclusion.

Johnno processed her theories for a long minute. "We need to get identification on that body in the Ridge," he stated. "I still think you're drawing a pretty long bow with Nero."

Francesca looked across at him incredulously.

"However, we know the highway between Melbourne and Brisbane is the main narcs' courier route," he continued. "Drug supply is the common denominator between them all. I'm almost one hundred percent sure, but here," he said pointing to the outskirts of a small town in the central west, "that's a Warlords clubhouse. I have a mate out there. Might give him a call, see if there's been any rumblings, off the radar so to speak."

"I know," he continued at her doubtful look. "They wouldn't organise the hit from there. That type of instruction comes from the main clubhouse, but they could deploy the runners from there. Do you see the Ridge? Not too far away.

"And if someone has been making enquiries on behalf of Ares or Warlords, my mate will know. I want to cover all our options at the moment. A dead body found in Warlords territory under those circumstances is something we can't ignore."

"So you think the murders bind a new agreement?" Francesca asked hopefully.

Johnno shrugged. "Considering drug demand exceeds supply at

the moment, OMCG could be contracting out the manufacturing to other syndicates. Unless, of course, another shipment is due. Quick distribution. Alternate couriers would spread the risk, for a hefty price. I don't think Italian mob terms would wash with Ares. Nor Warlords for that matter. Fletcher got in the way. Maybe he was too greedy. Maybe Chi You aren't as undone as we thought."

Francesca glanced at her partner. "Are you telling me we're now looking at four syndicates – Nero, Chi You, Ares *and* Warlords?"

"You know what, we could sit and speculate all night. As I said, we won't know anything more until we get some results on that body at the Ridge. Tomorrow I want to double-check that information and then take a look myself. You'd better come too."

CHAPTER 7

"Lightning Ridge is a small town in the NSW outback. No one knows exactly how many people live there but there are over 9000 post boxes. Can you believe it? People sort of go there to get lost," Johnno commented as they landed in Dubbo. "It's a funny little place, very quirky. You'll probably like it."

He continued as Francesca looked out the small window surveying the country airport before her. "Most of the itinerant residents move out in the summer. Too hot. The Dubbo cops are picking us up at the airport. The Ridge is about 4 hours drive north west of here. The camp is another half hour drive out of town apparently."

Francesca nodded.

"The guy who owns the camp is a bit of a character. Poor bastard has mental health issues. Something to do with a war. Anyway, we know he's in camp. He was seen in town earlier this week stocking up on supplies." He paused. "It's cooler this time of year, you see."

As they stepped off the plane, Francesca relaxed in the huge sky surrounding her. From horizon to horizon, 360 degrees, it was big, blue, and she couldn't help feeling like she had been transported to the inside of a snow globe. Smiling, Francesca relished the marvellous familiarity of western life in the big blue shed.

The drive to the Ridge was long and dusty. Those paddocks visible from the air surrounded her now. Massive gum trees, their white branches spreading out, almost stretched in the morning winter sun.

As the temperature rose Francesca ditched her heavy jacket and scarf in favour of her t-shirt. It showed her athletic build enhanced from years of ongoing training. She leaned forward slightly to stretch her arms behind her head, linking her fingers at the base of her skull. Her back arched releasing the strain of sitting for so long.

Detective Harry Jones, a local operative, eyed her in the rear view mirror. His eyes followed the line of her bunched biceps and lean arms to her rounded breasts straining against the flimsy fabric of that silky top. Dark Fiorelli sunnies masked her eyes and her lips, clearly visible, were etched in a half smile. He couldn't keep his eyes off her. The girl's head was turned towards a wheat paddock that had attracted the attention of a family of emus. Dad and kids in stripy pyjamas were clustered near a stand of native acacia.

For hours, vast paddocks rolled along, every now and then giving way to a series of small country towns that had plenty to say about their past.

As they neared Lightning Ridge, the landscape changed dramatically. Stands of eucalypts, river flats and paddocks gave way to a flat red and white powdery moonscape. Scattered upon the hill, mullock heaps of wasted white rock and dirt surrounded shanty homes.

Lightning Ridge township emerged from the tree-lined highway, its wide streets flanked with an endless array of signs and directions scribed on any vertical surface. It was a town brimming with personality. Francesca scarcely knew where to look first. The whole place promoted sensory overload.

After collecting the local sergeant and grabbing something quick to eat, they headed north east along a back road to Angledool.

Francesca couldn't hide the satisfied smile. She was instantly at home on the dirt track leading to the mine and leaned back into the seat to enjoy the sparseness and the billowing dust.

"Told you this place was awesome." Johnno gazed out the window, his body twisting in the seat as he assessed the state of the paddocks. "How long since you had rain?"

"Eight months. We had about 2mm. Could do with some more," the sergeant replied, keeping an eye on a small mob of straggly stock camped close to the road.

~

The vehicle stopped amid the piles of excavated dirt. In the middle was a small camp comprising of an open tin shed and a small fireplace. A generator hummed behind the shed operating an ancient-looking fridge, its blue enamel stained with dust and age. A small room attached to the shed housed what Francesca imagined to be a bedroom and bathroom. The set-up was very basic, with a bunk bed and an array of sparse furnishings, and Francesca wondered what kind of person would choose to live in such desolate, primitive fashion.

The sergeant strode over to the mine entrance and cupped his hands over his mouth.

"Enzo! Enzo! It's Sergeant Tom. How are you doing today? Come on up mate I have some friends who want to meet you."

A long ladder stretched from the floor of the hole to the reinforced opening where a rickety piece of machinery was used as a hoist. Tom stepped away from the hole, as Enzo made the slow and seemingly painful journey to the surface.

"Enzo, this is Francesca and Johnno, from Sydney. They want to ask you a few questions about the other night. Just tell them what you told me and anything else you may be able to think of. I'll be right here with you." The little old man squinting in the bright sunlight, looked towards Johnno and Tom. His gaze fell to Francesca.

"Mamma mia!" he exclaimed suddenly falling to his knees at Francesca's feet, speaking in rapid dialect Italian, his head bent in respect.

Francesca was so shocked she took a moment to start translating. Sicilian dialect. The kind she'd heard as a young girl. The other detectives stared in open amazement.

"Santa Maria, Santa Maria," he was saying and blessing himself over. He began praying in Latin, the Hail Mary, remaining on his knees at Francesca's feet. He reached a grubby hand into his pocket and pulled out a piece of paper. He looked down at it and continued to speak in Italian.

"Mother Mary, please forgive me. I have taken the oath a long time ago but I paid for my sins. Please, grant me forgiveness. Please spare me, I do not wish to die."

He kept his head bowed, not daring to look at the woman standing before him. Mother Mary, the Holy Mother of God. Stunned, Francesca translated the prayer for Johnno and Tom.

Tom quickly strode to the old man and knelt on the ground with Enzo.

"Come on old mate, show me what you have there." His voice was gentle and reassuring.

Enzo's aged eyes beseeched Tom. After a nod of reassurance, slowly, Enzo opened his fearful fist to reveal a faded holy card. There was blood smeared over the dress and feet but the face was still visible.

Tom gazed at the picture in amazement and then at Francesca. The resemblance was uncanny. He looked at the card again. "Unbelievable!"

"What? What has he got?" Francesca whispered, almost too afraid to ask.

"Enzo may I show Francesca your card?"

"Si! Si! Santa Maria." He was motioning in Francesca's direction but never met her eyes, his head bowed in respect.

Johnno and Francesca examined the holy card, exchanging glances between each other. It could be Francesca painted on that card. It was certainly unbelievable. They handed the precious card back to Tom.

Francesca shuddered. She'd seen this card before, a long time ago—a childhood memory that came flooding back. It was a holiday in Sicily with Nic's family. After church, one bright Sunday morning, a young child had wandered into the hillside garden, picking flowers to make a daisy chain necklace. The soil had been turned and it smelt divine, wet and musty, and new flowers were planted. In the damp, the corner of the holy card poked temptingly out. Francesca pulled at the corner and brushed the dirt from the picture of the Virgin Mary.

The painting was beautiful and the gold around her head and hands shone in the morning sun. A corner was missing, but this was a picture of the most beautiful woman Francesca had ever seen. Eavesdropping later that day in the commotion and hushed tones of the housekeeping staff, Francesca had learnt the truth. Although at her young age, she'd never fully understood the meaning.

There was no such luxury today. With burnt edges and the bottom corner missing, Enzo's card showed the hallmarks of a Sicilian mafia card. A tangible reminder given to new recruits as a sign of their pledge.

Enzo started speaking again as in the confessional. "Mother Mary forgive me for I have sinned. My family was in danger, my beautiful wife, my children; I had to take the oath. I had no choice. I broke commandments out of protection for my family. It was many years ago. I have paid my dues to them, many times. Why are they punishing me now? Again. First with the dead body and now they send you."

Francesca felt sorry for the old man. He thought she was the Mother of God in person sent by the mafia to punish him.

"Enzo," she spoke gently in Italian. "The Lord understands your story and on Judgement Day you will be able to talk about it with him. I'm not here to hurt you. I just want to talk for a bit." Then quietly, "Tell me, is this the Sicilian Mafia holy card?"

"Si! Si! Sicilian."

"Enzo, this is important. Can you tell me about the burnt body?" she insisted.

"Oh Mother, I was hiding. The person was already dead and burned and they bought him in a big black car and put him down one of my mineshafts. I did not know what to do. For weeks I stayed hiding until Sergeant Tom came looking for me and I showed him. Will I have to leave now? I have nowhere else to go."

Francesca glanced at Tom. "No, you should stay here. Tell me Enzo, did the men speak? Did you hear what they said?"

"No they did not speak. Two. There were two men." Enzo looked at Tom for reassurance.

"Enzo, last questions, have you ever seen these men before? If you saw them again would you know them?"

"No I have not ever seen them. It was very dark, very late. The fire was out. I saw the lights of the car and I hid. It is not safe to be alone and unprotected out here. I thought it was ratters. I hid behind the mound over there, near the tree." He indicated the area with a turn of his head.

"But, now I remember Mother, one man had blue light. Yes, it was strange like a blue torch. I am sorry Sergeant Tom, I have just remembered that." He looked at Tom who was transfixed by the exchange between Francesca and Enzo, yet not understanding a spoken word.

"Thank you Enzo, you've been very helpful."

"Thank you Mother Mary. Thank you."

Tom helped the old man to his feet and led him away from the detectives. Francesca translated the entire conversation to Johnno adding, "Triad initiation involves lighting a blue lantern. These days it's usually symbolic."

Johnno leaned against the bulbar of the wagon and pulled a folded map from his back pocket. He placed it across the bonnet. After a few moments he marked the location of the mine. This was not a random act, but in fact a reminder to an old man of his lifelong duty to the Sicilian mob. It was becoming clearer that they were now locked in a three-way contest between the country's biggest crime gangs.

"Johnno, did I cross the line?" Francesca stood beside him, lost in her thoughts. She felt weird about playing on the old man's fears and illusion that she was the Holy Mary.

"No mate. You didn't give him false hope and you put an old man's fears to rest. Poor guy." He returned his focus to the map. This track linked with another back road into Queensland.

CHAPTER 8

Chief Inspector Goodwood gazed blankly out his office window onto the roof of the building alongside. He was facing mounting pressure to resolve this matter without fanfare. The media were asking questions, which meant the police minister needed answers. So far, everyone was on his side, understanding the process, but that wouldn't last. Thank goodness the trip to the Ridge was successful.

In another event the Warlords and Ares were engaged in public warfare. Decidedly more visible to a majority of the population and more accessible to the media, that problem required a different policing approach. Two pressing matters, not enough information. They needed a lucky break and more time. Goodwood was confident he could manage the bike gangs himself.

At first, he'd been sceptical of Francesca's contribution when she joined his new team. But thanks to her fresh approach and recent experiences with the triads, she'd actually brought about good results. The girl thought differently to the men on his squad. She processed information in a very perceptive way and yet presented that same information in a factual, court-ready format.

At the moment, he needed her research skills. Goodwood checked her biography. Her specialty was Triad but her background and family history was Italian. She understood the culture more than anyone on the squad. A lifelong immersion in her upbringing and regular family holidays to Italy. He told himself it was cliché to expect her to understand the workings of the Italian Mafia. That she would possess innate connectivity to the cultural aspects behind their actions.

Goodwood was desperate. This matter had to be shut down. The Inspector contacted his Roman counterpart, a fellow he'd met during a police envoy to Australia once. Francesca was fluent in Italian, she'd worked brilliantly with Enzo in Lightning Ridge and she was experienced enough to get herself around the protocol of the Italian Police Force, get the required information and get home.

"Salucci I want you to go to Rome." Chief Inspector Goodwood stood in the doorway of the detective's office, his face set with determination.

"What? I mean, I beg your pardon Sir?" The Italian's stunned expression was comical.

"I want you to go to Rome. You have the language skills. I have a contact in the Police over there; he will put you in touch with the right people in their international crime team. I don't believe the Melbourne group is working alone. I assume you have a current passport?"

"Yes." Francesca could not believe her luck. She held her breath, waiting for the last instruction.

"Organise it. I want you gone by the end of the week."

"Yes Sir. Thank you Sir." Francesca almost leapt out of her chair and kissed the inspector on the cheek.

Rome! By the end of the week! And then Rapallo! Francesca's mind launched into overdrive. Even she was surprised at how quickly she could mentally move from preparing to meet with an informant to Rome and Nicholas Delarno.

From that moment, she determined to work day and night in the Italian capital and earn four days off in Rapallo. This was the answer she'd been looking for. A farewell tour of a life that was never hers.

Francesca kept her emotions in check. This was her chance to say goodbye for good. Melancholy, hope and relief welled in her black-rimmed eyes. It was nearly over.

The trip to Rapallo would be easy to justify to Goodwood. She could always say that her investigations took her to the tumbling village town.

Goodwood turned his attention to Johnno. As the conversation continued, Francesca held her breath again.

"Johnno, keep digging here in Melbourne. I want you to focus on Chi You and Nero. The OMCG team at Operations can keep tabs on Ares and Warlords. Anything you need, support-wise, let me know. Don't work in isolation. I want to know if there is the slightest link between these bike gangs and the other two groups. This job takes priority." As an afterthought the inspector added, "Johnno, this is your operation. Do you agree with this approach?"

"Do you really think the Italian police can help us with this specific case? If the organisation was still being coordinated from Sicily we would have the information already. I mean the corro between the Melbourne mob and their overseas connections has not increased, in fact it's been quite the opposite," Johnno responded tautly, disgruntled at Goodwood's interference.

"Precisely. Makes me think they are waiting for something to happen. I think we need some distance. To look at it from a broader perspective as part of a bigger movement. Francesca will be able check first-hand with the Italian international organised crime team. She will immediately recognise patterns or connections with our investigations here. If the links do exist, she can set us up for continued co-operation. If this is the beginning of a new trend, I want us on the front foot."

"And you don't think the Italians can investigate it in Rome and send through any relevant information?" Johnno said, agitated.

"No. I don't," Goodwood responded in irritation. "I need someone there I can trust. We need to safeguard our information as much as possible until we work out who we are dealing with.

"Francesca, take fourteen days including travel time. Keep me informed every step of the way."

Francesca released her breath, avoiding Johnno's astonished glance in her direction. The awkward moment was interrupted by another phone call as the boss turned on his heel, leaving the room as abruptly as he'd arrived.

CHAPTER 9

Nicholas was late. The negotiations had lasted longer than he'd expected and as he raced to the waterfront venue he hoped his cousin would understand. A tempestuous bitch, she was likely to cause a dramatic scene regardless, ensuring she remained the centre of attention.

To his pleasant surprise, she was so caught up with the half-naked men gyrating around her on the dancefloor she almost forgot her manners and who was, or not, in attendance.

He slid into an isolated booth at the far end of the club, downing a good measure of scotch. Neat. No ice. Happy to be alone for a few moments, he watched the humping scene of partygoers moving as one on the dance floor with the bass beat.

He saw her watching him from across the room, her smoky black-rimmed eyes assessing him. Nic averted his gaze. He could spot a high-class hooker from a hundred yards. He'd never had to pay for sex and he wasn't about to start tonight. Nonetheless, she made her way to him, standing close and facing the band. His cousin teetered over and collapsed in the booth across from him.

"Allora, Bella. Happy 21st birthday, little one." Nicholas leaned in to kiss each cheek.

"Nicci! How do you like my party? Isn't it awesome?" Allora scanned the crowd of heaving bodies through a sweaty haze. "This DJ is the best. And even though it is MY birthday, I have not forgotten you, my cousin."

Nicholas furrowed his brow in question. "I'm not sure what you mean." He sucked in the last mouthful of his drink, beckoning the waiter for another.

"Well, my darling cousin. Daddy says you've been working too hard. I thought I'd buy you a present." Allora gestured to the hooker standing nearby. "When she found out you were the client, she said no payment necessary." She raised a pretty questioning eyebrow. "Now, I had better get back to my boys. I see they're waiting for me. Ciao Bello. Enjoy."

Allora kissed him on both cheeks and tripped across the room to 'her boys'.

Nic eyed the hooker. His gaze travelled between Allora and the girl as the conversation filtered through. He shook his head. Allora turned to face him, blowing a kiss in his direction from the dance floor before disappearing into the centre of the crowd.

Nic shook his head again. He should be insulted by such a gesture. Allora obviously thought he needed a good fuck after his intensive work load. It was her answer to everything.

Maybe she was right.

He watched the hooker's tight arse as it moved rhythmically to a tribal drum beat. His fascination roused as she pushed it in his direction. She moved closer to him and he noticed the skirt of her short gauzy dress did nothing to hide the skimpy lace underwear. Heavy breasts pressed against the deep V of her neckline. He wasn't mistaken. Maybe he would take that fuck after all.

He remained seated, sliding is hand up her lean thigh, beneath the flimsy skirt. He felt the quiver ripple through her as he traced her tattoo, his fingers following the outline of the lace underwear. As she spread her legs to take him, those five inch heels anchored into the floor. He stood, taking his place behind her, so she could feel his cock pressing against her arse. He felt her hold her breath.

Pulling her hair to one side, practiced fingers slid around her neck tracing the valley between the silk top and skin at her breast. She leant against him. It was too easy. And he wasn't in the mood.

His thumb traced the circular tattoo. Three bent legs centred by the head of the Gorgon and crowned in snakes with corn leaf ears. The Trinacria. The ancient symbol of Sicily.

The girl belonged to Nero. The tramp stamp proved her ownership.

"Not tonight honey," he said and stalked towards the exit.

~

Nic punched the alarm code and made his way through the apartment's plush interior to his favourite room. He poured another drink and settled into the high-backed single chair facing the eastern seaboard. A slight sea breeze ruffled the gauzy curtains revealing the lights of the Gold Coast horizon glittering beyond the dark window frame.

Resting his head against the leather headrest, he breathed out deeply. It had been another taxing day at the end of an equally manic week. He wondered how much longer he could withstand the pace. But he'd expected nothing less after issuing the aggressive challenge. Deliberately he'd pushed his father into a corner and true to form, the old man had come out swinging.

Unrealistic schedules and near impossible business negotiations were only the start of a stubborn rebuttal. Nic closed his eyes. He loosened his tie and unbuttoned the top two of his shirt.

The son remained adamant. It was time to take control of the offshore business interests. He glanced around the apartment. He was ready to leave this place too. He'd spared no expense during the renovations. Vast spaces of masculinity gave the home a gentlemen's club feel. Rooms of grand proportions displayed rare finds and original pieces. A home dedicated to relaxation and pleasurable pursuits. The exclusive apartment was the envy of his peers.

And yet it was the smallest, most private room that gave him the greatest pleasure. Sparsely furnished with only essentials it overlooked a parkland which was studded with frangipani trees. On the damp air of the Gold Coast evenings, they gave the room a unique fragrance. He had insisted on the plants, they reminded him of a time when life was less complicated. At the heart of those memories, there was a girl he used to know. Francesca Salucci.

Feeling unsettled, he crossed the room to stand in the shadows of the balcony reaching over the garden. He breathed deeply at the salty air, slowly exhaling as he waited, watching the moonlight wash over the bare branches and thick trunks.

Predictably his thoughts were filled with her and his skin prickled. He wondered how often she thought of him and their secret nights together. She had distanced herself from him and his family some years ago. Resisting the invitations to events that would bring her close to him. He could find her if he wanted. A simple phone call would have her back in his bed. But he would never do it.

An old-fashioned ringtone roused Nic from his thoughts. He answered huskily, "Pronto?"

"Ciao Nicholas. It's Silvio. Come to lunch tomorrow. Sophia is here with the children and Paul will come too after he finishes at the church. We will see you, Si?"

"Of course. Yes." His father's tone underpinned their tension. As always with him, a phone call was a demand for mandatory attendance thinly veiled as an invitation.

"Bene. Your mama is cooking your favourite. See you at midday."

CHAPTER 10

The gentle clinking of the security gates was lost against the sound of an accelerated engine, gunning from an underground car park. Nic loved that sound. Relishing the power of the sports coupé, he sped along to the highway that linked the famous tourist towns, tracing the outline of the beautiful coastline until he could turn onto the Pacific Motorway.

Five years ago, Silvio Delarno announced semi-retirement from the family business. Nic took on the development and investment interests, establishing a Gold Coast office. His sister, Sophia, and her husband, Mark, managed the many farming interests, choosing to stay at the family homestead on a farm in North Queensland. At the time, it was the perfect arrangement.

Nostalgia filled the young man's head with memories of a carefree childhood. It was during this time of year that tradition dictated the family holiday in Rapallo, a town in the Italian Riviera, and the catching up with extended family. Nic loved being in Italy. He loved the food, the people and the freedom.

Like a faded Kodak picture show, he recalled the ease of the holidays past, swimming in the beautiful clear waters, cruising around the various isolated inlets on the family yacht. And the food. Even now, as an adult, he yearned for the annual Italian summer holiday. An intuitive body clock that chimed every August. And he yearned for Francesca who had holidayed with the family every year since childhood—at least until time and circumstances had taken her from him.

Nic grunted, accelerating out of frustration. One day that place he loved so much would belong to him. As tradition entitled it to be for the eldest son of the eldest son. And so would the girl.

He'd increased his personal financial position during the last twelve months in anticipation of obtaining the family business. A son determined to remove his father from the equation. Silvio's controlling ways would only hinder Nic's plans for the expansion of the Genoese shipping interests. One way or another, his father would relinquish his tight control. It would be given to the son or he would take it.

Nicholas craved the greater challenges brought on by international law and finance. His motives were no secret in the family-run business. The son's exasperation at his father's interference was widely known amongst the family and senior management team.

This year he was being truly tested by his father. Nic sensed the time was near. He'd virtually lived in the boardroom, successfully negotiating impossible deals on his father's behalf. Last night, it was the reason for his tardy arrival at Allora's birthday. Perhaps the family gathering would bring about the reward he sought. Perhaps Silvio had finally realised it was time to step aside.

The sports car purred along the freeway and, as Nic exited to Coolum, he glanced at the clock. He'd made good time whilst daydreaming about Rapallo and the new business arrangement. Turning sharply into a concealed driveway, he stopped at the security gate and pressed the buzzer, looking into the camera lens perched on the gatepost.

"Pronto?"

"Mama! It's Nicholas." The camera must be broken.

"Nicci! Come' sta? Un momento."

The ornate gate opened. Nic wound slowly up the steep driveway to the parking area next to the great home, turning to face the garage and guest quarters at that level.

His parent's home, although reminiscent of their retreat in Rapallo, boasted a modern twist. Pale apricot washed walls, behind white roses, gently contrasted with the hillside and lush surrounds. White shutters protected the windows of the summer heat and glare. Inside, a sweeping staircase and stucco ceiling designs gave the three-storey mansion all the elegance of a bygone era.

Outside, column pines lined the driveway making way to rolling green hills dotted with an assortment of fruit and nut trees. An extensive and well-maintained vegetable and herb patch could be accessed from the modern kitchen. This level also housed the living areas, study and led to a stunning pool deck.

Adjoining the lower level car park, a wide concrete staircase climbed to the ground floor of the mansion and was lined with magnificent concrete urns, each brimming with trailing flowers. In the centre, a large cycad, its thick stem rising about a metre to where the spiked dark-green leaves began.

A large Delarno crest mosaic marked the entrance to the home. All the family homes featured the emblem.

Outdoor living areas were as magnificent as the interior ones. Their spacious comfort meant that the family could gather, eat and talk while watching the children enjoy the infinity pool. Beyond, the vast Pacific Ocean glistened and sparkled.

Nic climbed out of the car, taking a minute to stretch as a yawn escaped him. Reaching back inside he grabbed the flowers he'd bought for his mother along the way.

"Uncle Nicci!" A three-foot-high missile came hurtling down the stairs and launched into his arms, wrapping its bony arms around his neck.

"Angelina!" Nic grunted as she kneed him in the ribs. "You grow more beautiful every day!" He planted a kiss on each cheek "Ciao Bella! Salve!"

Angelina giggled fiddling with her long dark plaits. "Salve! Did you bring me a present?"

"You bet I did. Do you want to see it now?" He was reaching into his pocket pretending to pull out a small gift.

Angelina nodded in excitement, large dark eyes shining in anticipation. "Yes please." Wriggling free she stood expectantly in front of him. Her impish face burst with life.

"Close your eyes. Hold out your hands." The little girl complied expectantly.

Nic reached down and started tickling the girl as she wriggled and writhed wildly.

"Stop it uncle Nicci," she screamed between fits of laughter. "Stop it! Stop it! I'll wet my pants!"

"Ok. Ok. I've stopped, but you have to help me with the flowers for Nonna."

"You have to catch me first!" The little girl scooted up the steps, little legs taking two at a time and feet slapping loudly on the concrete.

Nic bent to pick up the flowers that were now squashed on the ground and chased after her, shouting he was going to catch her as she squealed in delight.

"Uncle Nicci's here," Angelina announced as she tore through the house to the safety of her mother's lap.

"Nicholas! Salve!"

"Hello everyone!" Nic kissed his mother's upturned cheek and handed her the decidedly crumpled flowers. To her questioning expression, he answered, "Angelina."

The old woman laughed and nodded. She squeezed his hand.

"Thank you."

His brother and sister already relaxing on the outdoor deck overlooking the pool turned in greeting.

Marco, his nephew, gloated to his father as he scored another successful shot in a game of pool basketball. "Five–Nil. You're going down old man!"

"Where's Dad?" Nic asked. It was unusual that he would miss this chance to comment on his grandson's prowess over his son-in-law.

"In the study, taking a phone call. He shouldn't be too much longer. It's been like the telephone exchange here today. I think this is the fourth business call this morning," Sophia said, casting a quick glance in the direction of the study.

"This is what I've been saying," Nic began, leaning across the table towards Sophia. "Look at him. He's too old for this. I'm ready to take over that aspect of the business. I have the money and we're in a good financial position to move right now."

Nicholas gestured towards the study before throwing his hands in the air in exasperation. "He's too pig-headed. He should be retired, playing with his grandchildren, drinking coffee with friends. Not this. Not work like this on a Sunday."

His sister shushed him, casting a warning look at the others gathered to keep quiet as their mother, Cristiana, returned to the table briefly.

"Sophia, I need some help to carry the dishes. Your father is ready for his lunch." The woman turned on her heel, wringing her apron between tired hands.

"Let us help." Nic stood as well.

"Sit Nicholas. Have you learned nothing? This is women's work." Sophia spoke in a sarcastic tone, but the smile and twinkle in her eye suggested a tease.

Cristiana appeared with the beginnings of a sumptuous meal and Silvio took his seat at the head of the table, placing the telephone beside him. Nic noted his father's strained expression as he sat quietly, listening to the friendly banter between his children and grandchildren. It was unusual for him to be so quiet.

As the women went to make coffee, the phone rang again.

"Pronto? Si. Un momento." Silvio stood, excused himself and moved to the study, shutting the door.

The brothers exchanged surprised looks before returning their attention to the pool. Taking business calls on a Sunday during family lunch never happened.

"Zio! Did you bring your swimmers?" Marco's deepening voice yelled from the pool.

"No! Sorry!" Nic turned to Mark. "Looks like you are back on!"

"Me? Nah! I've had enough. Besides I'm so full I'll probably sink! But I have an idea. Marco, your skateboard's inside."

Marco nodded. He duck dived to the edge of the pool, giving his sister a friendly splash along the way.

Cristiana returned with the coffee and an array of biscotti and chocolates.

"Thanks Nonna." Marco grabbed a handful of the sweets, giving his grandmother a wet kiss on the cheek, and disappeared.

She waved her hand in his direction, playfully wiping the wet drips from her clothes. "Caffé? Where is Silvio?"

"Please coffee, yes please." Nic's headache brought on by an evening of melancholy reflection and an empty bottle of scotch was back in full force. Wishing he'd brought a change of clothes he eyed the soothing waters of the salt water pool. It looked so inviting. "Dad's in the study on the phone."

Cristiana's disapproving clicking noise preceded her comments. She shook her head to emphasise her unhappiness. "This must be the tenth call in two days. From Italy, is all I know. He will not say who it is or what's going on but I know it's not good news. Perhaps you boys will be able to find out. He refuses to talk to me." Cristiana held up her hands in a frustrated gesture before pouring the coffee for her son.

Dimples appeared as her lips pursed; her jaw tightened in a worried expression. Her son studied his mother closely. Today, her lively eyes were shaded in darkness and deep lines. For the first time Nic noticed her fragility. Her tiny frame stood proud, but she seemed smaller, more brittle.

"Uncle Nicci, when you get married, can I be your flower girl?" Angie's little voice roused him from worried thoughts. Nic looked down at his favourite niece, pulling her sodden body onto his lap.

"When I meet the right girl and I get married, I will definitely have you as my flower girl." The little girl beamed, reached for a chocolate and nestled her little body into his.

Nic looked up at Sophia and his mother. All hopes of the

conversation being unheard diminished. His mother had that look on her face. His marriage and more grandchildren were her favourite topic. He had no escape with Angelina swiftly falling asleep on his lap. Her body heavy in relaxation, eyes shut, she savoured the last of her chocolate treat as it rolled slowly around inside her mouth.

Cristiana took her chance at the wide invitation. Nic looked to Sophia for support. She smiled and launched into her own assault, as her mother opened her mouth to speak.

"You know mama, I was speaking to Stefano Salucci last week. I ran into him at the supermarket. He is holidaying in our area. He told me Francesca is doing very well. You remember her don't you Nicci?"

Nic's eyes flicked at her memory.

"Well, now she works in the Queensland Police, but she's living in Sydney. She was asked to go and work for some specialist crime department. Stefano showed me a recent photo. You would notice her Nicci; she has grown to be quite beautiful."

Sophia continued to wind her brother up, turning her attention to her mother for a moment. "And Mama, Stefano also tells me she is heading to Rome next week. The police have sent her there to work on some investigation. Of course he couldn't tell me about it but she must be doing very well for them to pay her to go to Rome!"

Sophia winked at Nic and mouthed you're welcome as he pulled a face.

"Francesca Salucci, she was always such a charming girl. God bless her mother." The old woman signed a cross over her chest. She frowned slightly. "Your father though … he would come around I'm sure." Cristiana gestured to her eldest son, her palms facing up and placed out wide before her.

"You would do well to marry someone like her, Nicholas. That girl knows our family and she would know how to look after you. I remember she did have a crush on you when she was a teenager. Such a difficult time for a girl, particularly without her mother."

"Mama stop!" Nic was laughing. "Help me Paul!"

"Mum's right! You should be thinking about settling down. Listen to your mama, Nicholas!" Paul chimed cheekily.

"Ok! Ok! I get it." He pulled out an imaginary notebook and pen. "Find Francesca Salucci. Marry her. Have lots of babies." He looked at his mother who nodded at him.

"Good! Sophia can get you Francesca's number I am sure." Cristiana smiled, clapping her hands together as her face lit up at the prospect.

"Mamma mia! You're all crazy. The poor girl lives in Sydney and I live on the Gold Coast. Whatever you're planning, it won't happen. Besides, she's more than likely already in a relationship," Nic said in exasperation. Why did every conversation with his mother these days revolve around him being in a relationship?

"Oh no. Apparently not, according to her father," his sister relayed helpfully.

"See Nicholas. She will move home for love." Cristiana nodded knowingly. "Look at you, my son. So tired and caught up in your work. You need someone special in your life."

Nic shrugged his shoulders. That may be the case, but another secret relationship with Francesca Salucci was a complication he didn't need. Particularly with his father breathing down his neck.

"Papa, you are back with us," Nicholas said, welcoming the distraction of his father's return.

"I will get fresh coffee." Quickly Cristiana rose, heading for the kitchen.

"Everything all right?" Paul asked concerned by his father's solemnity.

"No," he said quietly. The old man looked knowingly at Nic. "I need some fresh air." Rising from the table, he kissed each child on the head and left.

"I'll go," Nicholas said, gently placing the sleeping child on the padded chaise. He caught Silvio and they walked in silence.

"What needs to be done?" Nic asked as they reached the orchard.

"I need to go to Rapallo. Nero has some representatives based in Genoa who can help with this new business venture. They're called the Seta Group. I know them. You probably remember Carlo and

Bice Seta from years ago. I want to make a personal assessment. I don't trust Nero. He's greedy." The old man paused and looked out towards the sea. "And he's careless."

"I know Seta. But Dad, you can't seriously be thinking of going, what, within a month of heart surgery! Think of your health. Think of mum. It's time for you to start easing back. Let me go to Rapallo. I've taken the oath. The Commissions have already accepted me as your representative."

Silvio looked at his son, his hard eyes assessing Nic's motives.

"I'm not challenging you for leadership. But I am ready to take on the responsibility of the international operations. Under your guidance, of course. We work as a team." Nicholas paused. "Two strategic minds working together puts our family in a stronger position and we have the support of the Commissions. Nero has lost credit within the group. He's lost their trust."

Sensing a shift in Silvio's manner, Nic waited for his father to respond and when he didn't, he knew he'd been given silent permission to act.

"Now let's compose ourselves and get back before the others start to worry. Give me the details later, after the family have gone home. You will see, Capo. This way is better."

The old man turned to his son. "Salucci will be in Rome. Francesca. I'm going to invite her to stay at the villa in Rapallo. That won't be a problem for you, will it son?"

Nicholas cautiously searched his father's expression. "Of course not."

"Good. Use her as you see best. Then hand her over to Gino."

"What? Gino? No, I won't!" Nicholas objected. "Let me take her. I've managed her in the past."

Silvio scoffed. "Is that what you call it? Alright, you 'manage' her. Be assured, I will make the call if I have any doubts. And you'll have no say."

Nicholas paled and bowed his head. "As you wish, Capo."

CHAPTER 11

Francesca pressed 'send' on the email. Her work was done. Nine gruelling days in Rome had given her insight into the workings of the Sicilian mob and she was glad to be out of there. Adding to her exhaustion, negotiating a way around the Italian police service had tested the limits of her diplomacy.

Captain Cesare Augustus, her contact in the Roman Police, lived up to his pompous name in manner and looks. A crop of shocking black hair framed a bronzed face that was held high and with a good measure of disdain to all around him. His hooked Roman nose stood proudly over a pencil-thin black moustache that moved about comically as he spoke. It was so precise Francesca felt tempted to ask if he'd used a Nikko pen to draw it on. His thin lips were often etched in dissatisfaction, particularly when he spoke to her.

Despite a small frame, he was lithe and fit and wore his uniform with pomp and ceremony. Slightly shorter than Francesca, she sensed it irritated him immensely that he was forced to look up when he spoke to her. Francesca was sure that was why he insisted she remained sitting in his presence.

"Miss Salucci. Welcome to Rome. I hope that you can learn something from us. Your Mr Goodwood seems to think that we have information pertaining to your case." He'd greeted Francesca in rapid Italian as if to remind her that she was a guest in his country and she would speak his language. There would be no misinterpretation on his watch.

His intimidation made Francesca feel like she'd been called to the principal's office. She smoothed some imaginary crinkles from her suit.

"Thank you captain. May I say that the NSW Police Service and I are very appreciative of your time and help," Francesca responded, managing a sweet smile, to which Augustus shrugged mildly, suspicion guarding his features.

"Well, let me show you around and you can meet the men who will be helping you this week." He ceremoniously led her to a small room that housed the detectives. The room was hot and sweaty. A noisy air conditioner rattled away in the corner. The summer sun streamed through grimy windows that were laced with cobweb curtains.

Francesca smiled warmly as she was introduced to the team, which consisted of two young men who could hardly have been older than her. After the initial niceties, Francesca expected to be given the rundown on the situation but quickly realised neither of them had any intention of helping her let alone share any information. There was simply no reason to.

As she lay in bed that first night in Rome under a single sheet, having kicked the blankets on the floor, she wondered why she had been fed to the wolves like that. The men's suspicion and lack of response was not only disheartening, it frustrated the hell out of her.

It took a full three days of persuasive conversation and a good dose of old-fashioned charm to eventually convince the team that she was in Rome to learn. They revealed some historical nuances to her case. The friction was defined by two families who were once locked in an old-fashioned turf war.

She was told about a series of insignificant events that hurtled on and off until the 1960s. But any case files that may have been useful to her had been destroyed. The Italian detectives believed the family's influence was more embellished story-telling than fact. The aim was to bolster the reputation of a well-known crime family: the Nero clan based in Sicily.

Francesca focused on this evasive and powerful family whose relatives now dominated the Australian crime scene. Styling their operations to suit the changing political and economic climates, this crime syndicate had managed to almost evade culpability.

Francesca gathered every photo and piece of information she could from them and their known associates, filed it in a secure space on her laptop and stored a backup copy on a thumb drive which she hid in another bag. A third USB drive was posted back to Johnno.

In the end, when it was all said and done, she had nothing more than accumulated frustration and the family tree of the extended Nero clan. Another dead end for Operation Serpent. Johnno had been right. There was no real point in visiting Rome. Other than Francesca's personal quest, but no one knew about that.

And so, with five spare days Francesca said goodbye to Rome and turned her attention towards Rapallo.

~

During the hot train ride to the small coastal town, Francesca thought about Nicholas and the challenge she'd set herself. She mentally prepared for the disappointment of not finding him in Rapallo at this time of year. This town would forever mark the time and place she'd realised that there was a difference between love and sex. The beginning of the end, she supposed.

And that tourist seaside town in Spain would always be the starting point of their relationship. After that particular summer holiday her father would never allow her travel with the Delarno family again. The detective stood outside a memory, recalling the day her world had been tipped on its head. The first day her emotions had changed from friendship to the feelings that had guided her actions into adult life. The day of her sixteenth birthday.

It was early. She couldn't sleep, so, before the family awoke, she'd slipped out the bedroom's French doors and taken a secluded path to the beach. At that moment, Nic and Paul were returning home having spent the night clubbing with mates.

She conjured the images that were the catalyst for feelings that continued to haunt her for years. A sun-kissed torso, exposed, his shirt tucked into the waistband of his dress pants and trailing along behind him. A devastating smile of acknowledgement to an awkward Francesca.

Amidst the hazy glow of sunlight filtering through the morning air, his greeting in seductive Italian, "Good morning Francesca, il mio bel fiore. Happy Birthday." My beautiful flower, he'd called her.

Francesca blushed in teenage awareness as he kissed both cheeks in a lingering traditional greeting. And then her mouth. Strange emotions surged through her. The intensity of his eyes met hers as he stepped away, holding her hands. The lingering smell of aftershave, tobacco and sweat was intoxicating.

He tasted of the ocean. Francesca was mesmerized, bewitched by his sexual presence, anchored to the spot on that narrow pathway between the rock boulders.

The kiss had affected him too. She saw a strangeness cross his features and light his eyes with desire. His mind and heart had opened. He stepped again towards her, gathering her gently to him and kissed her, encouraging her innocent passionate response.

Paul arrived upon the scene, cast Nicholas a warning look and stepped around them. It was too late. The eldest son had already stolen Francesca's heart.

Later that day, when Giuliett Seta and her friends had fixed upon her in a sick joke, Nicholas had stepped in to protect her. That girl got the treatment she deserved and Silvio's friends and family members would never again bother Francesca.

Everybody knew she belonged to Nicholas. From that day on she would be referred to as Nicci's girl. It added another layer to the complex relationship she shared with him. Francesca would continue to bind her emotions to his as stolen moments turned into secret night-time visits.

The train eased to a standstill at the tired Rapallo station. Francesca stood and gathered her things. She was no longer a lonely lovesick teenager. Her adult life was filled with success and promise. This was her chance to prove it to herself. It drove her desire to visit his town again, to say goodbye and move forward.

Staying at the villa without him was the first step. Visiting their favourite haunts was the next. Next week at the Gold Coast she would end their protracted affair in person. Francesca felt a fissure of anxiety and excitement fill her heart. And then, the relief that it was almost over.

She stepped behind the crowd of tourists and followed them through the tunnel leading to the station doors. The sunlight burst through the glass, opening to the overcrowded car park and waiting taxis. In front, beautiful, tumbling Rapallo.

Nicholas! The shock of seeing him sent Francesca's mind into a spin and she stopped, transfixed in the middle of the walkway. Had she conjured him by magic in her daydreaming? She took a second look. No, he was real enough, leaning casually against a black Maserati.

My god he looked good. Oh my, was she blushing? Francesca pressed her flushed cheeks gently, brushing her wayward hair aside. She suddenly felt awkward about her resolution. Her steely determination hid behind her heart which was now sitting firmly in her throat.

"Nicholas! Hello! This is a surprise! I had no idea that you were in town." Francesca kept her voice calm.

"Francesca! Bella! How long has it been?" He leaned in to greet her in the traditional Italian way, holding her hands and kissing each cheek. The detective's heart back flipped to her chest.

About six years, thought Francesca, six long years. "I'm not sure," she said, shrugging casually. "Time gets away. How've you been?"

"Very well. And you?" he said, his eyes smiling at hers.

"Great!" she nodded enthusiastically. "Well, it's nice to see you again Nicci. I won't hold you up. Enjoy your holiday."

Francesca made her move to leave and catch a cab to the tourist centre. Time to find alternate accommodation and lick her wounds. So much for bravery. Tomorrow she would take the first train to Venice and get the hell out. Stuff the big long-winded speech saying goodbye and outlining why she would no longer be his girl. This was it and combined with a quick lap around the town she'd move on.

"Wait, Francesca." He reached out his hand to hold her wrist. "Don't leave," he said, with a small awkward laugh. "I thought you were coming with me to the villa. That's the arrangement, yes?"

"Well, I thought so. But Silvio didn't mention you'd be here. I don't want to intrude." Francesca blushed again and all she could think of was to run.

"No? I'm here on family business. I insist. You must stay at the villa." he said and released her hand. "We have so much to talk about."

Francesca tried to hide her reluctance. "Ok. But only for tonight. I really want to get to Venice before I head home." She was a terrible liar and he knew it.

"Let's just see how we go, shall we?" he changed topic. "Bella, is this your entire luggage?" he asked in surprise. "You travel light!"

"Yes only two little bags … one for business, one for holidays." Francesca flashed sparkling eyes at him.

"Andiamo! You'll be needing refreshments after that long trip. That train was crowded. I would have come to Rome, you know, to collect you and save you that trip." He smiled in genuine happiness, easing her into their old friendship and despite herself, Francesca relaxed after the awkward meeting.

She climbed into the passenger seat of the sports car. The space between them was small and personal. She drew a deep breath and gathered her thoughts as he closed her door.

"That's a very kind offer but I didn't know if I'd get away. Besides, the train was relaxing after such an intense fortnight," she said as he sat beside her.

Her heart trembled slightly at his devastating grin.

"It's good to see you again," he said patting her bare knee as they roared off down the hill to the town centre. The lingering warmth of his touch burned a hand print in her flesh. She smiled vaguely at him, placed her hand on her leg and looked out the window, absorbing herself in the surroundings.

They fell into an easy silence as Nic negotiated the heavy holiday traffic. His mind slipped to the demands of the day. This morning the Commission made it very clear. In pushing forward with the new business arrangement, Detective Francesca Salucci would be brought to heel. Particularly where Chi You was concerned. Nicholas reluctantly conceded his relationship with the detective was about to reignite. It was insane. And dangerous.

Nic would never hand her over to Gino, his father's cold, murderous consigliore. So he set his heart and head, determined to walk the tightrope between friendship and lovers. And then he saw her. And she reacted to him. And they were back at the start like ten years before.

The mobster raked his hand through dark hair and took the corner too fast. He had other things to consider. His father's clandestine operations were compromised. The finger firmly pointed to Nero. Frustratingly, the Italian connections remained sceptical. Old loyalties to Nero were not as easily divided as he'd thought.

Silvio's recent erratic behaviour only confirmed past beliefs. His father had always pushed the boundaries of their confidence. Nicholas faced their distrust with abject determination reasoning the detective's information about this current matter would help rat out the traitor in their ranks. And find friends in high places. Francesca would help them. Willingly or not.

Nic wanted more from his childhood friend. To learn everything he could about Robbie L, president of the Ares outlaw motorcycle gang. The outlaw biker his father had seconded to help bring about the changes. Despite Silvio's insistence, the young mobster knew their group didn't need outside assistance. From outlaw bike gangs or Chinese triads. Or the Seta Group for that matter.

Under his stewardship, the business would blossom with growth in the Middle East and Russia. And he would prove it once he'd exposed this current deal and Nero for what he was. Nic glanced across at her.

He was no stranger to using his sexuality to get what he wanted. It was going to make his job a whole lot easier knowing she was still attracted to him. The arrangement would not be complicated by the deeper feelings he still felt for her. He buried them and flashed her a warm smile.

The streets of Rapallo wound their way around the seaside hills, past the marinas and high-end apartments until they reached the majestic Delarno villa. The entrance to the great estate was clearly marked by a pair of marble lions that sat upon pillars of granite on either side of the gates. The base of these pillars was carved either with the family coat of arms or with a Fleur de Lys onto each side. As they neared the entrance, decorative iron gates opened automatically to reveal a steep cobblestone driveway flanked by ancient cypress.

Nic negotiated the narrow road and stopped at the row of pencil pines edging the car park. Quickly alighting, he walked to the passenger door.

"Welcome back. I hope my home still meets with your approval." He bowed slightly and held her hand as she stepped from the vehicle. Linking arms he suggested, "Let me show you to your room."

He caught the fragrance of her 'J'adore' and immediately recognised its distinct scent. She always wore it for him.

The exterior of the home was as Francesca remembered it, a Venetian style of paint render in soft apricot hues. White shutters on the windows were thrust open to welcome the summer breeze and the musky scent of the Cinque Terre filled the air.

Francesca gasped as she entered the hall. Since her last visit, it had been extensively modernised in a tasteful refurbishment. Intricate Turkish rugs had been placed over glossy marble tiles and antique Italian furniture featured throughout. Large portraits, landscape paintings and historical maps of Delarno strongholds lined the walls. The renovation was lavish and refined, yet honoured the essence of the historic building. It was a luxury hotel housed in an ancient Venetian castle.

The ground floor, with its entertaining rooms and large tiled balconies, overlooked the gardens to the ocean beyond. Francesca recalled the Delarno's idea of the perfect family time, starting with afternoon drinks on the balcony before continuing into the evening with dinner, music and games. All the time watching the changing shades of the waters on the bay as the sun set over the hills and the twinkling lights of Rapallo appeared.

An iron staircase symbolised the Delarno family regalement in its fretwork. Solid timber stairs inlaid with marble led to the upper-floor bedrooms and bathrooms. Each beautiful room featured aged oak floors covered with more silk rugs and a modern ensuite bathroom.

Francesca's room opened onto a balcony overlooking the bay with a potted olive tree thoughtfully placed in one corner. She admired the beauty of its twisted trunk and pointy silver leaves. In the middle of the room stood a four-poster antique bed covered in the finest linen. To the side a matching wardrobe took up one enormous wall. A writing table and chair were placed near an open shuttered window. The ensuite bathroom was crisp, clean and modern. Francesca breathed a sigh of gratitude and smiled.

"Thank you, what a beautiful room!" She turned to Nic who had propped her bags near the bed and moved back to her side.

"The view over the bay from the balcony is quite majestic, look," he said gently holding her elbow, urging her forward.

"Down there," he said pointing, "is a lovely little beach that has hidden alcoves and is quite unique. Only the locals know about it." He stood behind her, his arm protectively resting on her hips.

Francesca stepped away. She was not that easy. Not anymore.

"Sounds perfect," she responded. "It's quite warm today. I might head down there now."

"May I suggest instead we go to Santa Margherita Ligure for lunch? It's a short but beautiful drive. A lovely re-introduction to our area. And then perhaps a swim?" He looked at her pensive expression. "That is if you're not too tired from your journey."

Francesca wasn't keen for a swim as such. She just needed some time alone to process the change in circumstance. He was keen to reconnect, it was more than obvious. She was not naïve enough to believe she would be immune to him. At home in Sydney she'd made a promise to herself. A commitment to rid him from her heart for good. She'd spent a good part of the train trip convincing herself this was the only way to go about it.

Staring at the coal face of her decision, she was shocked to realise just how emotionally ill-prepared she felt around him. How exactly did she think she would go through with this plan. He had no idea she'd spent to last six years trying to get over their relationship. The very reason she was even in this place. He'd think she was a complete lunatic if she blurted out "I've come to say goodbye." She mentally shrugged. Why did she even care what he thought. She'd be gone tomorrow. God save me! Her brain was a muddle. At his close proximity she could hardly think. This afternoon she'd just have to wing it. After all it was only one night.

"Give me a few minutes to freshen up." She heard herself say. She was not sixteen years old. Or eighteen for that matter. She squared her shoulders. Toughen up princess and take control of the situation.

CHAPTER 12

After a short drive, Nicholas pulled into the Grand Hotel Miramare, a crisp-white art-nouveau hotel surrounded by manicured lush grounds and views across the harbour.

"Wow!" Francesca exclaimed, gazing around the entrance. "This place is pretty amazing."

He smiled and nodded. "I'm glad you approve."

He reached for her hand, absently pressing her fingers against his lips, as they were led to a private table set amongst tropical gardens. From here, the guests were afforded privacy and uninterrupted views of the majestic coastline.

"Nicci this is outstandingly beautiful and very unexpected. Thank you," Francesca said looking back at the hotel's impressive proportions. It positively gleamed against the backdrop of the stunning Italian Riviera hillside. Francesca felt like a princess in the Delarno world again. Transported back to the time in her youth where everything Delarno made her feel that she belonged with him.

"You're very welcome." He smiled at her, a knowing smile shared between former lovers.

He sat back in the chair and studied her in the afternoon sunshine.

Francesca masked her discomfort with a shy smile of her own as her gaze wandered to the magnificent coastal surrounds. "So…" she said, searching for a talking point within the romantic backdrop.

"Hungry?" he asked, deliberately drawing her attention back to him.

"Famished!"

As if on cue, an impeccably dressed waiter appeared with the first course and a bottle of wine.

"I took the liberty of pre-ordering. I hope you don't mind."

Francesca was dumbfounded. "That's hmm … that's very thoughtful."

"What are your plans during your holiday then, Francesca?" Nic asked, clinking his glass to hers.

"Sunshine, relaxation and perhaps some sightseeing." Francesca took a sip of her wine, it was regional and exquisite. "I need to shake off my Sydney winter blues. Thought I might head to Portofino. I didn't seem to make it there last time I was in Italy. It's my one regret."

"Only one regret?" Nic flirted, raising an eyebrow in question. Francesca blushed. "Well young lady, Portofino it is. It's the perfect place to start."

"And then I might head east. Maybe check out Venice and do the loop back to Rome." She added hastily, "I'll take off tomorrow afternoon. But don't rearrange your day for me. I thought you were here in Rapallo for work, right?"

"I am. But Francesca, we're in Italy. A day here, a day there, what does it matter?" He shrugged his shoulders. "A few niggling problems with the business can wait. I'm in no rush to leave. In fact, a few days off will help me recharge after such an intense couple of months."

"Tell me about it. I haven't stopped for a break in years. In fact, not since I joined the crime squad six years ago."

"So you don't mind if I crash your little holiday?" Nic asked, hopeful, with that boyish expression she'd never resisted.

"I guess not," Francesca said before realising that sounded ungrateful. "Of course not, be my guest," she added more enthusiastically.

"So where have you been Francesca all these years? What has kept you so busy that you've not been able to have a holiday?" Nic steered the conversation.

Francesca relaxed into the safe topic of work.

"Six years ago I joined the Special Crime Unit in Brisbane. I guess I must've done alright. They put me in charge of a team that brought down a major drug operation. It was pretty big. Made the news. I'm in Brisbane next week for court." Francesca's humble recount of the Chi You bust caught Nic by surprise.

"You mean the trial of the Chinese gangs?" Nic couldn't hide his disbelief at her pivotal role in the operation. Perhaps he'd been the only one to underestimate her abilities.

"Yes. That would be the one. Actually, it's only the initial hearing. Hopefully the Department are on the ball. God knows the amount of time and work I've put into that project to make it a watertight case for our lawyers." Francesca tried to sound nonplussed, but her voice raised pitch at the anxiety of Chi You walking free. She drew a deep breath and drained her glass.

"So now I'm confused," Nic responded, refilling the wine glass as the waiter arrived with the second course. "I thought you said you were living in Sydney."

Francesca waited for the waiter to leave before answering.

"Sorry. My fault. Last year I moved to a specialist Organised Crime Unit in Sydney. They asked me to come down and help out. I guess I'm doing alright there too. After all I was sent to Rome. That doesn't happen every day, let me tell you. The Italian police were almost helpful, in the end." Francesca mused, thinking about the unmasked joy Cesare Augustus expressed at seeing the back of her. She smiled secretly.

"You're working together on a project?" Nic probed.

"You could put it that way I suppose. But let's not talk about my work. This is such a beautiful setting." Francesca shook the last thought thread of mafia operations with a decisive flick of her hair.

"And how is Paul? What is he up to these days?" Francesca asked.

"He joined the seminary and is now working out of Brisbane in a poorer parish. My father, like any Italian, thinks it is a great honour to our family to have a son in the church. My mother, though proud, is asking for more grandchildren! You can imagine my dilemma!" He shrugged and laughed.

She pushed the thoughts of those long nights with Nic from her mind and said, "Paul would make an excellent priest. He's a very thoughtful person."

"Sophia is back in North Queensland, as you know," he said. "Shall we walk off lunch?"

Francesca nodded. "The renovations to your villa are amazing," she said, cocking her head as she changed the subject. "Elegantly masculine I would probably describe. Did you oversee the project?"

"Yes. Do you think it's not pretty enough?" he teased.

"Oh no," she protested. "That's not what I meant. I love the overall feeling of strength. When I walked inside today I felt very protected." She held up her hands defensively. "Not an intimidating way, more ... at peace and safe. You'll think I've lost my marbles." She laughed self-consciously and glanced in his direction.

He smiled at her comments, looked down at her and impulsively kissed the top of her forehead. "Thank you Francesca."

They climbed an old pathway through an olive grove. Wild thyme and rosemary brushed around them, releasing a refreshingly pungent fragrance. Sitting close together at the hilltop lookout, the pair faced the sea.

"Did you know that block of land has been in my family since the early 1500s and has been passed from generation to generation to the oldest son. It's hard for me to believe that place, that place I love so much, will be given to me by my father upon his death." Nic's thumb rubbed along her fingers as he spoke.

Francesca's eyes widened. "I didn't know that," she said, crossing her legs at the ankles as she shifted to a more comfortable position. She leant back into his shoulder. "I knew your family came from the Genoa area. That's an amazing legacy, considering the amount of turmoil this part of Italy has endured over such a huge time period."

"I agree. Our family has been very fortunate. My ancestors were bankers and sea merchants. When Genoa went into decline in the 14th century my family sidestepped the downturn. Lucky for me my ancestor fell in love and married the daughter of a Venetian merchant. In fact, in my home there's a tapestry depicting the story of their courtship. As a consequence, the bulk of our operations were temporarily moved to Venice meaning we were able to spread our trade interests and absorb the disruption."

"I remember reading that the Venetians were very powerful at the time. Wasn't it around then that all the beautiful palaces were built?"

"Yes, I believe it was. For us, having access to both ports at our disposal meant that my family were able to continue trading despite the wars, alliances and diseases."

"And you'd never have to cross the Italian interior and negotiate with the hostile kingdoms. Although there were the pirates to contend with," she said.

"Yes ... the pirates. But by the late 1500s, the Genoese port had resumed its success thanks by and large to the rise of Spain."

"Of course, the Spanish explorers would've needed funding from somewhere."

Nic nodded. "My ancestor, who'd started a small bank in Genoa, married a banker's daughter from Florence. Together, with the help of her family, they built a successful empire combining finance and shipping, capitalising on the huge growth in the area. In fact, my property once belonged to a Spanish merchant who traded from Genoa."

"Oh?"

"My family took the land as payment for monies owed when the merchant went bankrupt."

"I didn't know that. So when was the house built? I mean it's not 500 years old, is it?" Francesca asked.

"No. The original home was ruined by time and war although the foundations are still visible under the house in the downstairs cellar. Our actual home was built at the turn of the twentieth century and through a series of renovations and additions we have the present home."

"And you still have business in Genoa?" Francesca asked, curious about the family's local ventures, a topic her father rarely talked about. Quite a contrast to his extensive knowledge of the Australian-based industries owned by the Delarno family.

"Yes. Genoa is the largest port in the Mediterranean plus it has the airport and sufficient road links. These days trade is very accessible. The banking arm of our business was sold many years ago. We still deal with fabrics, high-end, namely silk and lace. That's my mother's family business. And of course the transport business, shipping cargo, works well with our family maritime insurance interests.

Giuseppe Zanda, my great grandfather, was a tremendous friend to many members of the royal families across Europe. At the time he supplied all the luxurious fabrics for the palaces and ceremonial dress."

He turned his dark head to look at her and asked: "How well do you know your recent Italian history Francesca?"

Francesca shook her head and shrugged. "A little," she replied truthfully. Nic nodded and continued.

"Mussolini marched on Rome in October 1922 persuading the Royal Family of Italy to give him the office of Prime Minister. My grandfather, Antonio, enjoyed the game of politics and in Mussolini he found a person of mutual understanding and political philosophy. He helped him in the south and was rewarded considerably, ensuring the Delarnos were not forgotten in such a tumultuous time.

"My father moved to Australia when he was fourteen. At the time, he and my grandfather were having some troubles. My father started farming and soon built a small empire. Later, they did communicate a little, but were never close. When Antonio passed, as was the tradition, my father received all that was rightfully his by birth, despite their disagreements.

"My father is still in control of the Italian transport and European businesses today; my sister and I have ownership of the Australian elements. Silvio is in his 70s you know, but he won't give it up … yet. I think he has been waiting for me to settle before he hands over."

He looked at Francesca, haloed by the setting sun.

"It may be sooner than I anticipated. I haven't been very interested, but fate has a way of placing you on your path." He pushed a stray curl from her face, bringing her fingers again to his lips.

Francesca blushed wildly. There was no mistake in his meaning. She swallowed hard and looked away. How the hell could she walk away now? She'd been wanting this kind of commitment from him for years. She had some serious thinking to do.

"Shall we head back to Rapallo?" Nic asked, breaking the silence. Francesca nodded quietly in the late afternoon light.

"You were very quiet on the way home Francesca. Is something on your mind?" he asked as they drove up the hill towards the villa.

Sex, Francesca thought. *How much I've missed making love with you. More importantly can I trust your new commitment to us?* She'd felt herself changing over lunch. The talk on the hill had sealed the deal. Before her very eyes she was becoming a part of his life again. The anxiety beat in her chest. It was happening way too fast. And she only had herself to blame—thanks to that bloody photo and a stupid pact. Tomorrow morning she would make an excuse and clear out. In the safety of her Sydney home, she would go about living her life and locking up crooks. To walk this path again with Nic would only end in tragedy and heart break. Namely hers. Enough was enough.

"No, just thinking about work," she responded vaguely.

"You can talk to me about your work. You know, if something is bothering you. I can keep a secret," he said with a mischievous twinkle in his eye.

The detective blushed. "As can I," she responded smiling.

They lingered in the villa courtyard that was lit by fairy lights and candles creating a dreamy atmosphere. Late 1960s love songs played softly on the portable radio. Inhaling deeply at the scented air, she stifled a yawn and stretched.

"I'm sorry," she said. "Long day. You must be tired too."

Nic watched her long shapely arms extend above her head. Her profile enhanced when her back arched as she stretched upwards on her toes. His desire was strong but he promptly ignored it.

"A little," he said stepping towards her, holding her hands at arm's length as he faced her. "However, I still have some work to do, so I'll see you tomorrow morning for that swim."

"I'm sorry, I didn't mean to interfere," she stifled another yawn, blinking long and slow.

"Not interference Francesca. More, a welcome distraction." He held her hand to his lips, kissing the palm before placing it back at her side. "Goodnight Francesca."

"Goodnight." Francesca flushed, kissed him briefly on each cheek and quickly made her way to the grand staircase and her beautiful room. Alone in her room with a head full of questions about him, she drifted off to sleep.

~

In the still night terrified screams roused Nic from his own fitful sleep. It was Francesca. Bursting through the door he searched for the intruders. Moonlight streamed through the open windows and doors. Silk curtains danced a romantic tango with the fragrant summer breeze of orange blossom and magnolia.

He saw her thrashing wildly in the centre of the large bed, she was crying out again. A glistening sheen of panic covered her. White cotton bed sheets twisted around her and she fought to break free. She held her hands up.

"Don't shoot! Don't you dare!" she screamed, tears sliding down her cheeks.

Her body heaved again, then she stilled. "Put the gun down."

He rushed to the bed.

"Francesca! Francesca! Wake up!" Rousing her from the nightmare, he gently touched her. Linking his fingers with hers, his soothing tone guided her to wake.

"Get off me!" Retching free from his hold, she pushed him against the wall behind the bed. Her forearm braced across his chest.

"What have you done to my father?"

"Francesca! It's me!" He broke her grasp holding her wrists tightly to her side, stilling her on the bed in front of him. "It's Nicholas. You had a bad dream. Come, we are in Rapallo. I'll never let anything happen to you. I promised. Remember?"

"Nicholas?" Francesca burst into tears. "I dreamed that my father was dead. Why?"

"Shh, love. It's just a silly dream. You'll see tomorrow when we ring your papa that everything is fine." He held her close.

"How can you be sure? It was so real. Are you sure everything is ok?"

"I'm positive. You've been working too hard. Everyone is safe." He spoke in a soothing tone, brushing her hair from her face as you would a child.

Slowly, her body relaxed into his. "Do you need anything? A drink of water?" he asked after her final shaking breath to relax.

"No thank you. Please don't go. I'm afraid. Nicci, don't leave me," she said.

"Of course."

Settling beside her, he pulled the sheets and blanket to cover her. He propped himself amongst the pillows, and stroked her hair, smoothing the worried lines of her forehead. He hummed a lullaby his mother would sing when he, as a little boy, had trouble sleeping. All the while he gazed upon her face as she relaxed into sleep again.

"Daddy. I'll talk to you tomorrow. You'll see. We're all safe," she whispered.

He looked at the dark curled eyelashes brushing her high cheekbones as she finally relaxed her eyes to sleep. He took in the details of her face: the curved eyebrows that framed her fine forehead, the long straight nose, the thin top lip and then fullness below, the small determined chin and that slender neck that was made for his lips.

His gaze followed the contours of her body slowly unwinding and stretching out under the sheets to rest beside him. Gathering his warmth to her, a deep breath escaped those lips. He slid into the sheets to sleep and her hand came to rest across his chest. Her fingers were long and decorated with a solitary ring on her middle finger, a delicate cameo with an intricate gold support.

Nic raised her hand and kissed her fingers lingeringly one at a time, and soon realised his mistake. Even in sleep she responded to him, murmuring and pushing herself closer, entwining her legs around him. Her lips brushed his chest. She may sleep tonight but he definitely wouldn't.

In the dark, he wondered about this strange place he now found himself in.

That night, his terror at what he would find, if she were to be hurt by those Nero bastards, kept him awake. His instinct to protect her had propelled him to act. Just as he'd done in their childhood.

That pathetic line about fate this afternoon. He could have kicked himself for being so stupid. Revealing his deepest desire with her. What was he thinking? He knew a serious romantic relationship could never work. She was a Salucci. The daughter of a Salucci and a Manfrin. That was suicide.

The Commissions only tolerated it now because Nic had assured them his influence over her would guarantee her co-operation. A necessary short-term proposal to take the heat off Chi You.

His own father had put him on notice about their secret affairs years ago. The son would never give her up to them. So he held her tighter the only way he knew how. By making her believe in a future with him.

He would find a way to get the information he needed and keep her safe. Keep her alive. He'd vowed to protect her when they were children. He would never let her down.

~

The morning sun filtered through gauzed windows. Francesca woke to the warmth beside her. She tried to think. Her wayward hands had different ideas. Snuggling into the body she knew so well, she explored the bare skin yielding in response.

Smiling, she pressed her lips to the muscular chest. His heart was beating steadily. Her knee slid up to rest across his thigh. Her fingers caressed the well-formed shoulders and slipped down his arm to take his fingers in hers. She raised her head, gazing adoringly into those dark eyes and half-smile.

"Nicci," she sighed, smiling softly. "Oh my God. Nicholas. I'm so sorry." Francesca jumped out of bed. Memories of the night and that horrible dream came flooding back. Instinctively she put her hand up to cover her mouth before she said something stupid.

"Good morning my love." His slow pleasurable smile gave way to a soft chuckle. "You had a terrible dream."

Francesca nodded silently.

"You remember." He smiled a tease and his eyes captured and held hers. He came to her, and she was trapped by the intensity of his gaze. "Don't be alarmed little one. It was my pleasure, believe me, to lie next to you all night. Again."

His eyes darkened and his face, his beautiful face, showed an expression of blatant need. Francesca blushed. She couldn't speak. Nic chuckled again.

"I see now that you are recovered and I'll meet you on the veranda for breakfast in a little while. Until then."

He stepped away and bowed slightly. Wearing only black silk boxers, Francesca was mesmerized by that muscular back sauntering out of her room. As the door softly closed, she dropped on the bed holding his pillow to her. She lay on the warm sheets and pondered her next move.

Returning to Sydney was surely running away. And like an Olympic gymnast, Francesca back flipped on her reservations about their future together and strode headlong into a world of new possibilities.

CHAPTER 13

"All is well with your dad?" Nic asked. He was dressed in a tight-fitting green Henley and tailored shorts; his damp, unruly hair misbehaved in a way that made Francesca want to run her fingers through.

"Yes, thank you."

She reached to pour herself a coffee, turning her back from the distraction of his tanned skin stretched over muscular forearms.

"Would you like another?"

"Thank you. Francesca, have you ever seen the Riviera from the water?"

"No." She smiled as he said her name in that particular way.

"Well today you will. A friend is sailing up the coast today and has invited me to tag along. I thought you might like to come too. We're scheduled to stop at Portofino for some shopping and a look around the township. There will be others on board, relatives and a couple of friends. We should be back by four.

"I know you wanted to head to Milan today. Would you be willing to change your plans? I could drive you there tonight or you could leave on the early morning train tomorrow instead?"

"Are you kidding? That sounds amazing. Lead the way."

"Excellent. We'll leave from the dock at 9am."

~

Rounding the last hill overlooking the marina, Francesca stared, gaping at a majestic vessel below.

"There she is." Nic briefly glanced at the boat as he wound the sports car towards the marina. "La Bella Bianca. Quite spectacular isn't she."

Francesca nodded. The impressive white yacht was docked and clearly visible through the sparse tree cover. State of the art and polished to an inch of its life, it gleamed, contrasting with the turquoise waters of the bay. Francesca beamed.

Nic made the introductions once on board.

"Thank you for the invitation today. You're very generous," Francesca greeted her hosts.

"And you, my friend, are very welcome." Lucia Zanda smiled and led her by the arm towards the small gathering on the deck. "I know your father very well. He's always been a great friend to me. Now, come and meet our friends."

The launch glided from the protected Bay of Tigullio, silently veering to round the Rapallo Gulf. Against the rugged backdrop of the wild hills, the party cruised at a leisurely pace. Soon Portofino was in view and the yacht anchored out of the busy Portofino port. As the crew prepared the small speedboat launch, Nic reached for Francesca's hand.

"Unfortunately a little problem has interrupted my day with you. I have to attend to some family business here, so I hope you don't mind shopping with the ladies. I'm sorry Francesca. I'll make it up to you, I promise." He gave her an apologetic look.

"Of course Nic. I understand. Is everything ok?"

"Yes, but of course. It's nothing, just a little problem. Family businesses hey? Work, work, work!" Nic shrugged, waggling his finger as a parent does to a naughty child.

On shore, Francesca stood alone, captured by the vibrant activity of tourists and stall holders lining the small space which formed the harbour. The small group headed for the designer shops and the coolness of cobbled, shaded lanes. Francesca stepped aside in the bustle, listening to the blend of Spanish, German, French and English. She turned upon hearing the familiarity of an Australian accent, locating the culprits easily.

A man led the charge to a charter boat followed by a straggling group of four children. Backing up the rear was whom she assumed was the mum, loaded with towels, bags and goodness knew what else. Each child balanced an array of snorkelling equipment and flotation devices. But what caught Francesca's eye was the enormous inflatable thong that the smallest child, a boy of no more than five years, held proudly in his grasp. Blazing in a yellow and green Southern Cross, it was his height again. He bumped his way through the crowd, a grin splitting his face like a cracked watermelon. Francesca burst out laughing. She watched them pile on the boat and head out towards the point.

By now Francesca had completely lost sight of her group. She started to make her way to the Santa Martino church, whose spire she'd noticed from their mooring. Skirting the crowded Piazza Martiri del Olivetta, she took a shady lane at the end of the harbour and followed a small street. With hours to fill in, getting lost in the narrow streets was all part of the fun of travelling.

As she reached the top step and walked inside, Francesca welcomed the coolness of the elaborate interior. She sat at the back of the church, visually following the black and white checker board floor to the altar. Embellished in gold and marble, the church was both showy and beautiful. Gorgeous fresco paintings decorated the roof cavity and walls.

"Here you are!" Francesca turned to see Lucia Zanda walk towards her. "I thought I might find you here."

"Lucia. I'm sorry, I didn't mean to cause you distress. I lost you all in the crowd," she said, smiling at the stunningly styled woman.

"Yes, it's very busy this time of year. The others are exploring the boutiques doing some last-minute shopping. Mario is with Nicholas. I thought I would spend the day with you, at least until Nicci returns. I'd hate to think of you wandering the streets by yourself." The older lady smiled warmly at her.

"That's very considerate. How did you know I would be here?" Francesca asked.

"It's a part of who you are Francesca. Your father would always visit the churches first. You're very much like him in so many ways. I just assumed."

She smiled sweetly, placing her hand on Francesca's arm.

"Now," she said before Francesca could ask more questions, "it's almost certainly time for gelato."

Lucia stared into Francesca's eyes. "Francesca let me say this. In Rome they will tell you they serve the best gelato in Italy. It's not true. The best gelato in Italy is in Portofino and I know just where to go."

Francesca laughed at Lucia's serious expression, matching it with her own. "Well then Lucia, I guess we'd better try it. Then I'll tell you what I think!"

The ladies stood and Lucia took Francesca by the arm.

"Now be a dear and help me down these stairs," she said, "but don't you dare tell a soul!"

"Wouldn't dream of it."

Lucia was right. It was in fact the best gelato Francesca had ever tasted. She greedily enjoyed the three-tiered monster cone. Wandering down the shopping strip at Via Roma, a small clothing store caught her eye and she left Lucia with a sales assistant to cross the cobbled path, and enter the cool interior.

As she browsed the Italian fashions, Francesca caught sight of a green Henley shirt across the way, through the shop window. Her heart flipped in excitement. Hidden in the shadows of a small café, Nicholas sat at a table with his back to the street. Francesca turned towards the door and was about to walk up to him when her instincts caught up.

He wasn't happy. His fists were clenched for a fight. Even from the distance she could see his angry posture. Surrounded by three men, they were locked in an earnest discussion. Francesca's mind prickled at the position of the men. In policing terms it was known as the triangle of safety. It was used to protect the good guys when dealing with an unpredictable client. A body each side and one in front. These men with their aggressive poses were making ready for confrontation. The only safety issue as far as she could tell was for Nicholas.

She was momentarily distracted from the café scene when she recognised Nic's cousin, Mario. He shot past her and made his way across the street to Lucia who had just stepped out. He spoke quickly, gesturing wildly and they both looked in Francesca's direction. They entered the store.

"I don't like this. Why are they worried about me?" Francesca mumbled, glancing back to Nicholas who was still deep in discussions. She took her phone, focused in on the little group and snapped a quick picture.

Shoving the phone in her bag, the detective turned from the window, swiftly striding to the back of the store. As she passed the last rack of clothing, Francesca grabbed any item she could and headed for the change room, pulling the curtain closed as Mario and Lucia entered the shop. Leaning against the back wall, she breathed. The whole action had taken three seconds.

After a few moments, she heard Lucia call her name.

"In here Lucia, just trying on a few things. It's a long way to come back for returns! This is a fabulous shop. So much to choose from." Francesca chuckled, keeping her voice calm and controlled. "Did you find something in the other store?"

Lucia breathed out heavily. "Oh yes, thank you I did. Now how are you going dear? Can the assistant get you another size?"

"No, I'm pretty good actually."

Francesca looked for the first time at the item she'd selected from the rack. A blue and white bikini, trimmed with gold baubles that gathered at the hips. It was her size. Hanging in the change room was a matching sarong style wrap and a pair of skimpy, white cotton shorts. She pulled the shorts on under her skirt, giving a rare satisfied smile at their fit. *What luck! I'll take the lot.*

The two women left the store and strolled into the sunshine. With the oversized bag swinging from one arm and the other hooked to Lucia's, Francesca glanced in the direction of Nic but he had disappeared along with the three men and Mario.

"What time is it?" she asked.

"Oh my goodness! It's late. It's after one o'clock. We'd better get back to the boat!"

Nicholas was already on board. He stood from his chair greeting the ladies as they entered the outdoor dining area. His easy manner a contrast to the agitation she'd witnessed in the café.

"Everything alright my beauty?" he said helping her with her bags.

"Sure. Why wouldn't it be?" Francesca turned to him smiling at his handsome face. *In business there are disagreements Francesca,* the detective mentally chided herself.

"You look a little upset. I thought something must have happened ashore."

"No. No. Nothing happened. I made us late, that's all. I feel bad for spoiling our lunch." It was some way to the truth. Her inner cop searched his face but he just shrugged nonchalantly.

"Oh. Don't worry too much. We're working on Italian time. No one eats lunch before 2pm in the holidays." He kissed her gently on the cheek, holding her hand in his.

Francesca pushed the earlier incident from her mind. She was being paranoid. In the company of the guests she let the scenery and conversation work their magic.

After lunch, the men retired inside and the ladies moved to the outer deck for sunshine and coffee. When the conversation turned to children, Francesca excused herself and found a lounge on the top deck to sun-bake. From there she had uninterrupted views of the Italian coastline. The sun was stronger than she'd remembered and her burning skin needed attention.

"Let me help you with that."

Nicholas appeared as if on cue, taking the bottle of after-sun cream from her. He sat on the lounge, straddling the chair to sit behind her.

"Thanks." Francesca could hardly breathe.

"Relax my treasure. I promise it won't hurt. Lean forward at bit."

She let her body relax as he began to massage the cream into her shoulders, making his way down her back to the top of her buttocks. Her body moved in any direction he touched.

"All done," he said as his hands rested at the top of her thighs. He cuddled into her, his head bent towards her, his lips pressing against her ear. "You have beautiful skin, so soft."

"Thank you. And can I say that my skin appreciates your touch," she murmured turning to face him.

"Francesca…"

He kissed her, driven by the need to make her want him more than anything else in her life. All night he'd lied beside her, willing himself not to touch her. Wanting to make her belong to him but not daring to trust himself to walk away from her again. After today's meeting it was necessary.

Her familiarity was a love song to his soul. Reluctantly he raised his head. Francesca held her breath. She was ready for him too. Taking her hand he silently led her back to the group as the boat docked in Rapallo.

~

"Do you feel like that swim?" Nicholas asked stopping at a small stony beach close to the villa.

"You read my mind. Where?"

"I know a little spot just along here. Public beach but only the locals know it."

Well hidden, the unlikely beach afforded yet another spectacular view across a small bay of the opposite coastline. Under the road, connected by a steep, narrow staircase it was framed by decorative columns made from stone blocks. Clear water lapped the pebbles, fragments of marble, coral and granite that made up the 'sand'.

It was as mysterious as it was private.

The late afternoon sun lit the columns like candles on a birthday cake. Each one hid a private 'dressing room' backed by the rock face and two sides made from hand-cut stone. Standing within the alcove the couple were completely concealed from view.

"I choose this one and no peeking," Francesca teased hiding behind a column. Quickly she stripped down to her bikini and waded into the salty water. The stones were uncomfortable underfoot and she dove into the rippling water. She came up gasping. The water was freezing.

A curious rock ledge sat just below the water on the outer edge of the small inlet. Francesca made her way to it. She stretched out feeling the currents of warm and cooler waters around her. The sensation was amazing.

I could be a mermaid sitting on a rock in Norway, she silently mused looking over the water. A siren to the sailors.

"What are you smiling about?" Nicholas queried, effortlessly lifting himself to join her on the rock ledge.

Water droplets shimmered on the colourful Delarno shield on his chest. Francesca imagined licking their salty trail until she reached his perfect mouth.

She caught his expression. There was no mistaking the fire in his eyes. He casually stroked her hair and then, gently brushing it away, his lips nuzzled the back of her neck, making their way to her lobes. His fingers moved to the sensitive areas of her neck. Francesca melted into his body as his hands held her to him.

"I'm … thinking … it's," she couldn't get her words out.

"I'm thinking you need to be kissed … my beautiful Francesca"

Francesca held her breath turning to face him, inches from his lips.

"Please," she whispered.

Nicholas placed his lips over hers and kissed her gently, his fingers entwined with the knotted mess of her windswept hair. He pulled her head back revealing her exposed throat for his lips. Francesca felt a surge of emotion as her body arched to him.

The water lapped at her in its own timeless caress. Her head swam.

His passion was driving her senseless. She returned his kiss with all the yearning of the last ten years.

They needed a more private location. The rock platform was sensual but it was too public. He guided her off the ledge and silently, they slid into the dark water continuing to cling to each other. Francesca wrapped her legs around him pushing her body to be closer to his.

She cuddled into his warmth, her hands teasing and caressing his strong back. Together they moved towards the shore, his soft whisper already making love to her in words. Francesca hung on his every word, her body coming alive with every rocking movement.

When they'd reached the shore, keeping his head close to hers, he placed her atop the natural stone of a bench and started moving practiced hands along the curves of her hips. She was ready.

"Nicholas," she moaned.

"Get up." Roughly he pulled her to her feet, and in one movement pushed her against the stony wall, aggressively setting her legs apart. He held her hands together above her head, his elbow forcing her cheek against the craggy rock face. With her quick submission, he roughly took control.

A shocked plea escaped her, "Nic? What's happening?"

"Bend forward," he commanded in a course voice. She obeyed and immediately felt the force of him as he pushed into her again. The feeling was toxic. And she was pinned between the solid barrier of the stone wall and him.

Francesca's alarmed cry drowned in her throat and she whimpered. Trapped, with her instinct telling her to fight, her police training screamed in protest. She resisted him, pushing her body against his. The movement heightened his desire.

His fingers splayed over her hips, bruising the softness he'd treasured moments ago. She smelt her own fear. Humiliation forced hot tears to slide silently down her face.

This was not making love. It was brutal ownership branding itself in the most primal act. Francesca felt a mixture of shock, shame and embarrassment. Then as an overwhelming release left him breathless, she willed her body to relax a little. It was over. The raw pain of his violation burned and she shifted slightly to try and ease the sting.

He turned her to face him and her body stiffened in the embrace. He buried his head in her hair and she felt him shudder slightly.

He nudged a wet cheek against her temple and his lips pressed against shed tears. He was seeking permission from her again. She remained rigid in his embrace.

"Look at me Francesca," he said. His fingers pressed hard into her damp cheeks as he turned her face.

Francesca raised her eyes filled with hurt. At his churlish expression, she tilted her chin upwards, wordlessly challenging him for an explanation.

He couldn't look at her; the rawness of her emotions was too much. His focus returned to her lips. Gently he brushed aside her tears, whispering "I'm sorry. Forgive me."

Grabbing at the soft towel, he wrapped them together for comfort, cherishing her softness and dispelling her shock and wariness with each gentle touch. He held her close.

Gentle waves rolled onto the stony shore, ebbing quietly as the tide pushed its way towards them. He was different. Holding her in a naked embrace until her desire filled the secret space around them, he took the time she needed. In time he would ask her to take part again.

And here, despite herself, Francesca felt her own desire to grant him forgiveness.

Kissing him deeply, she made love to his mouth. She wanted him to taste her. She wanted to feel his desire rush through her, to hear his need for her as he groaned.

She ran her fingers through his hair leaning back against the rock wall, encouraging him. No one ever made her feel the way he did.

"Francesca," he whispered in her ear grazing his lips against her before lifting her onto the rock ledge. Gently caressing, he watched the release as she gave herself to him. At the end, he held her close to him, burying his head in her hair. Again she felt his tears as he sobbed quietly in her embrace.

~

It had been brutal and she'd complied, Nicholas thought, as they headed back towards the villa. Submission. That should satisfy the sick bastard. His mind worked over the new requests set out in Portofino earlier that day. The Commission had demanded Nicholas put Francesca to the test. The gatekeeper was Carlo Seta, a man almost as cruel as Gino Castello.

Nic had gone too far. And to his disgust, he'd enjoyed the control over her. There was no denying it had spurred him on. Then he'd tasted tears and those magnificent eyes filled with hurt and betrayal challenged his demands. That girl had knocked the arrogance right out of him.

As they reached the villa, his mobile phone buzzed disrupting their quiet solitude.

"Pronto?" he answered. "Un momento."

He turned to Francesca and said, "I'm sure you'd love a shower. You go ahead. I'll see you soon."

He walked towards the gate and quickly put some distance between them.

"Nicholas. Well boy, good effort, but it's not enough. Although I did enjoy the show. Raping that horny wench was a nice touch. And who would have guessed. The slut enjoyed it."

"Seta. You perverted prick. You got your fucking jollies watching us?" Nic hissed.

"Of course I'm watching. I can do whatever I like. You and your father need my support. Your dreams of running the Italian operations rely entirely on me. I'm afraid you'll have to try a little harder if you want me to convince the Commission you have the ability. And that little wench you're so hung up on can't be trusted. So you, Nicholas Delarno, will do as I say. Tonight I've made reservations for you both at Café del Mare Azzuri. You must convince Rapallo that Stefano Salucci's daughter is owned."

The line disconnected.

CHAPTER 14

"Francesca?" The knock on her bedroom door made her jump. Nic didn't wait for a response and immediately opened the door. He stood at the threshold, showered and changed into dinner attire. He glanced at the packed suitcases sitting beside the door. The number for a taxi service was scribbled on a piece of paper and sat on the top.

Francesca paused in the middle of the room, and looked at him defiantly; the towel held tightly around her body for sole protection. Her eyes gleamed bright and fierce.

He stepped towards her. She quivered and backed away. The anger rose in her chest and flashed in her eyes. He stepped back.

"Is there something you need to say to me?" she asked.

He stared at her for a long moment.

"Francesca. What I did to you before was inexcusable. To treat you in such a way and expect you to … well." He looked up meeting her strange expression and turned to leave. "It's too much to ask forgiveness." He paused. "I've intruded on you again. I'm sorry."

"Nicci," she said, and cleared her throat. "Wait."

He stared solemnly at her face and whispered, "I'm so sorry." He glanced at the luggage again. "Please don't go."

Francesca gulped down her pride. "I have every right to feel utterly betrayed by you right now. I've never felt so humiliated by anyone in my entire life. Should I ever believe a single word coming from your mouth again? But the painful truth is we are no stranger to each other's physical desires. I can't blame you for thinking of me as another stupid whore when I have laid myself on a platter to you in the past," she said, blushing.

He had begun to protest, but Francesca continued, "I came to Rapallo to say goodbye. Goodbye to you, to our memories, goodbye to a future that doesn't belong to me. And then you turn up and give me hope. Again. That we can both live the life we desire, with each other. And we arrive at today, what the hell Nicholas?"

"It's like I don't even know you at all. What you could even want from me? I will do anything for you Nic. You just need to ask. My day begins and ends with you and I can't seem to make that stop. Lord knows I've spent the last six years trying. But I can't keep living like this. And I won't."

She glared at him from the middle of the bedroom.

"My flower." He was at her side, drawing her to him. "Forgive me. I have no explanation. Believe me when I say I'm truly sorry. I'd never deliberately hurt you. I only ask this, may we start again?"

She scanned his face, studying his eyes, processing his intent. "I'd like that very much," she said at last.

He gathered her to him and held her for a few long moments. "Again, I have to go," he said apologetically. "I'm supposed to meet a business partner for drinks and dinner."

Francesca nodded.

"I'd rather stay here. We could start again over a meal at the villa?" Nic asked hopeful, lifting her chin so she looked directly at him. "It can be easily rearranged … my meeting. My friend won't mind. Or you can dress and I can show Rapallo how lucky I am to have you by my side."

Francesca patted his chest and smiled in a lopsided way. "You look so handsome … and desolate. How can any girl resist you? But let's stay in," she said.

He held her close. "Eat at eight?"

Francesca nodded and stepped away. She dropped the towel teasingly and headed for the wardrobe.

Nicholas smiled at the full curves of her breasts and shapely arse. "You're so beautiful. I don't deserve you. I absolutely adore you Francesca Salucci."

A little smile curved her lips.

"What to wear?" she muttered as he moved away from the bedroom.

There was only one dress meant for this moment: her pale green Pucci. She put it on. At the sway of her hips, tiny crystals caught the light. She'd bought the dress in Rome with Nicholas Delarno in mind.

The skirt was gathered low at the base of her spine, hugged her hips and fell to the floor. The backless design created the perfect excuse for his touch. The cowl smoothed over her breasts and clasped in a halter with a gold clasp. It was not too revealing but showed her body perfectly. The absolute seduction dress. She pulled her hair into an elegant bun at the nape, and chose two long strands of shimmering diamonds for her ears.

Nic watched her glide into the sitting room. He couldn't help but stare. She was the most stunning creature he'd ever seen.

"Oh my god. You. Look at you," he said, and quietly tried to gather his wits for a moment. Then, taking her hands, he kissed each palm and led her through the open doorway to his private library. In the centre was a small table with an array of hot and cold food.

Fuck Carlo Seta and his detestable ultimatums. Nic was right to mistrust the prick. Seta's push for leadership deserved only contempt. A true leader is not bullied into action. And the Commission needed strong leadership into the future.

The information secreted from Francesca's laptop during their tour to Portofino confirmed Nero's carelessness. As well as the crime boss syndicate's link to The Seta Group. It was only a matter of time before Francesca made firm connections between Nero and Seta. Once the Chi You brief was out of her mind, Nic had no doubt the detective would target Nero.

For her own immediate safety, Francesca should stay close to the estate, he thought. It gave him time to work on a new strategy. A new game that would mean he and his father were back in control.

Francesca picked at the food platter and moved to his side commenting, "I've never been in this room. It's quite magnificent. A very private kind of space."

Taking the glass he offered, she wandered to the floor-to-ceiling book shelves, running her fingers along the leather-bound spines. He was watching her from a large single chesterfield lounge.

She walked back towards him and took the position that was hers on his lap. She let herself curl into his arms and asked, "Please stay with me tonight." It was more a statement than a request.

When he didn't respond she tilted her head to gaze into his eyes. She watched them change a shade deeper than black. His nostrils slightly flared as she moved closer to his lips. She liked flirting with him. Pulling away before gently placing a lingering kiss on his lips. She moved away again as he responded. But her tease didn't last long. He pulled her head to his and kissed her thoroughly.

The chair was too restricting. And so was the dress.

Francesca stood, letting the Pucci fall around her. Slowly releasing the fastenings she felt it slide to the floor in an exotic fabric pool before quietly turning and exiting the door in nothing but her heels. Nicholas watched her go, before catching her at the bedroom door.

~

"Buon giorno signorina .. or should I say buona sera," Nic teased his lover at the late hour, with a cheeky smile. Lazily sat on the deck chair, he folded his newspaper, placing it on the paved ground beside him.

"Good morning Nicci," Francesca answered, noticing how his

robe was casually open to his waist. She suddenly felt very shy in the mid-morning sun.

"Would you like a coffee and pastry? Maria will organize for you."

As though on cue, Maria appeared with the breakfast tray.

"Maria! It's good to see you! How are you?" Francesca greeted her old friend with a kiss on each cheek, taking the tray and placing it on the table.

"Bene signorina Francesca. Va bene?"

"Yes, I'm very well thank you."

Maria returned to the kitchen. She'd seen this scenario numerous times over the years, losing count of the many girls he'd brought to this place. She never thought she would see Francesca Salucci play this part though.

Maria clicked her tongue disapprovingly as she entered the vast kitchen. At the timber work table, her husband sat, his features held in a familiar tightness.

"You object, old woman," Gino Castello spoke in his deep voice, tilting his chin upwards.

"Gino," Maria faced him, his gruffness no longer frightened her. "Tell me. Is this real? Is she the one Nicholas has chosen?"

He nodded, reaching for a whole watermelon sitting at the edge of the table. He stabbed it, his precision with the knife suggesting a practiced hand. The long sharp blade split the ripe fruit in a resounding crack. The red juices spilled onto the bare timber. He angled the knife downwards, the large triangular edge of the blade slicing easily until it stopped abruptly before the table surface. The sound of the split filled the air between them.

"Mama! No!" Maria raised her hands to flushed cheeks. She'd been slapped again by this brutal force. "Francesca? No! " Her voice trailed away, eyes searching Gino for solace; a quest she knew would not be rewarded. "But her father…"

"It is the way, Maria. Now serve Nicholas and his guest." He shoved a piece of the red flesh into his mouth. Cutting away large chunks of the fruit, Gino edged around the white flesh of the rind, creating a small crescent-like shape.

"Of course, my love."

Maria busied herself preparing another tray for Francesca, not looking or speaking to her husband again. Upon the housekeeper's return to the kitchen it was empty, save for the bleeding watermelon. Beside it, in the very centre, the large butchers knife standing upright impaled the small crescent shape into the table. Upturned on the rind, it resembled the hull of a small boat; the triangular knife blade, its sordid, menacing sail. It sat surrounded by the red sticky juice of the fruit.

This was her husband's warning. An ancient symbol his family used to advise family members that interference with Commission business was not to be taken lightly. A symbol the Castello family had used since their forced removal of Calabria to Sicily, years ago. One of compliance and solidarity for the cause. Of agreement and loyalty.

Maria turned away from the chilling reminder and resumed her kitchen duties. A small tear escaped her. Through the open doorway she heard Nicholas laugh, the gentle chuckle of a lover. Francesca's musical tone travelled on the breeze as she pitched her wiles on him. Their moment called for discretion and privacy. Maria gently shut the door to the outside balcony.

The housekeeper knew she must act swiftly. Her message must reach its destination without attracting the attention of the Commission. With so much attention on the couple and the household, the task would be difficult but not impossible. Returning to the sink, she formulated a plan to get an urgent message to Stefano Salucci. Francesca was not safe here.

~

In the terrace garden, Nic patted the seat of the lounge in front of him. "Francesca. Come to me. Sit, my darling. That look … what troubles you?" She did not respond but complied with his request.

"Did you sleep well mia cara?" he asked. He brushed her ponytail aside. "I hope so because I have plans for you today."

"What plans?"

"Well, today I thought you might like to have a look around the centre while I do some work. Then we can meet for a late lunch, a picnic or dine in, whatever makes you happy. Then, my love, we can spend the whole afternoon doing whatever you want."

"Whatever I want? Well let me see. There's a place here I need to get to know better," Francesca leaned in to play with the coils of his hair revealed by the open robe. Her hands pinned his arms to his side as she moved her lips over his chest towards his stomach. Nicholas stopped breathing.

She looked up, searching his dark eyes. "And there is another place here," she said as she moved to his neck, gently tasting, holding his arms to his side. "And another here," she whispered, straddling him. His hands broke free and he pulled her to him, wrapping his arms around her.

"So, we have a deal, then?"

~

Francesca wandered the town centre of Rapallo, browsing the market stalls and boutiques. It was the first time she'd been alone since her arrival in the city and she lost herself in the maze of small shops lining the ancient stone arcades that led to the water front.

In the haze of her happiness she remembered her family and friends and made a few gift purchases. Growing tired of the shops, she turned towards the promenade. The shaded cobble lane opened to the waterfront and the spectacular seafront. As she passed under the Saline Gate, Francesca marvelled at the decorative brickwork and the differences between the medieval centre and the romantic seaside. This gate was the last remnant of the walled city. Rapallo once hosted five such gates.

Taking a seat shaded by a row of swaying palm trees, she waited for her lover. A bag hawker spread his wares on the concrete promenade. From the shady spot, Francesca watched him looking about nervously, as he played cat and mouse with the local police.

As a local patrol car swung by the promenade and exited towards the train station, Francesca thought about work and the impending Chi You hearing next week. Pushing the anxiety of the matter from her mind, she vowed to check her emails upon her return to the villa.

It was difficult to focus on the present when so much about her future was about to change. She pushed the uncertainty aside, hoping that her heart would never again endure the familiar twist and turn that always preceded its breaking. A black Maserati pulled into a car park near the marina. He was early. Francesca smiled to herself. *He must be missing me.* She crowed inwardly.

Standing to wave, Francesca froze immediately at what she saw. Nic was laughing and moving towards the passenger door. An elegant hand attached to the arm of a tall blonde reached out for his hand before Francesca's eyes.

Her smile faded completely. She moved to hide behind the nearby foliage and continued observing the scene. Nic, clearly enjoying the woman's attention, was walking with the blonde towards the marina clubhouse. She had rested her arm possessively on his as he carried a large tote bag for her. They leaned in together, walking slowly along the concrete path, lost in a private conversation. The blonde was working it. Brushing against him and flirting outrageously. Nicholas was having the time of his life in her undivided attention.

The girl tossed her golden hair, stopping halfway between the marina and parkland. The exposed area gave Francesca, and anyone else keen to notice, a clear view of the blonde as she poured over Nic like cheap perfume.

Francesca seethed. Unable to contain herself, she stepped out from her hiding place, and rushed towards the pair.

"Nicholas," the girl purred, "thank you so much for the lift."

"You're welcome Benedetta."

"Oh, another thing," she continued to smile up at his handsome face.

"Anything."

"Carlo asks, does the wench trust you?"

The girl leaned up to Nic and pulling his face towards her, kissed him passionately on the lips.

Francesca had seen enough. Turning sharply she stalked towards the sanctuary of the town's centre. She didn't care if she walked all the way to Rome. The bastard had sent her away so he could have personal time with that slut.

It took a little while for Nicholas to register the girl's words and then the kiss that took him completely by surprise. He pushed her aside, spotted Francesca's stricken face and then her back.

"You fucking whore!" he blasted at the blonde, shoving her away. Benedetta laughed in his face and left them to it. It was time to meet her contact and collect the money she was owed.

"Francesca! Wait, let me explain! Stop! Please! Francesca!" Nic called as he finally caught up to her.

"You fucking arsehole Nicholas" Francesca screamed, suddenly stopping and facing him. "Get away from me you slimy piece of shit. I fucking trusted you. I took your abuse and your fancy words. You fucking take the cake. You send me to the shop so you can fuck a whore whilst I'm gone. I hope she was worth it."

Rage filled her. She sprang into action hurrying towards the taxi stand, unspent tears stinging her eyes. She pushed them aside. You're not going to fucking cry Francesca. Not now.

"Francesca, please. Let me explain. It's not what you think. I helped her out," he started.

"Yeah, I bet you fucking did."

She was at the open door of the waiting taxi.

"I don't even know the wench. Her car was blocking my driveway. She had a break down. I pushed the car out of the way and offered her a lift into town. She had to meet someone at the marina. Francesca. Believe me. It's the truth. I swear."

Tears welled in his eyes. His voice lowered to a solemn pitch.

"My love, please don't leave. I left early because I couldn't work; I kept thinking about you. It's the truth."

Francesca stared at him. Her heart twisted. Plain honesty spread across his face as he waited for her response. He was bare.

"I'm sorry to have wasted your time sir." Francesca gave the cabbie a fiver and shut the passenger door. She'd given in.

"Don't you ever do that to me again, you hear?"

He cuddled her into him and led her along the promenade. "You're very sexy when you're mad. Has anyone ever told you that?" He paused, adding, "You're all hair and arms and the way your hips swing as you stride out. Wow!"

Francesca pushed at him, pulling away from his grasp. He held her closer flirting shamelessly until her laughter returned.

~

They moved towards the coolness of the medieval square with its temporary stands of the fruit market in the centre. Displays of fresh tropical fruits and staple vegetables were arranged in neat rows on angled stands under a colourful canvas canopy. Trestle tables filled with treats enticed a hungry lunch crowd.

"Oh! Fresh figs!" Francesca eyed the plump ripe fruit with delight.

"Try it. You won't taste another like it." Nic picked up a fruit and held it to her mouth.

She bit into the flesh, her tongue quickly licking the stray juice from his fingertips. Her mind had settled, sifted through his story and her trust in him had returned. She was back.

Nic noticed her good temper and sighed, relieved. This was the last time Carlo Seta interfered. At the Commission meeting tomorrow in Genoa, he would call Seta out for the dog he was. He smiled at the thought.

Quickly purchasing the rest of the lunch items, they headed along a narrow street to the foreshore park. Francesca, bemused at his fight for restraint, continued to tease him subtly as they rambled along.

A small hollow from a hidden doorway gave Nic the opportunity he needed. He steered Francesca to the hidden spot pressing her against the closed door with his body. Their hands were laden with bags and his lips became the weapon of choice.

Kissing her senseless he just as quickly stepped away, continuing to walk through the Saline Gate archway as if nothing had happened. Francesca smiled at his strong back. They had all afternoon and night to play this one out.

Setting up a picnic on the grassy area near the Chiosco della Banda Cittadina, they ate and relaxed in each other's arms. The beautiful early twentieth century band shell was famous for its gorgeous frescos that depicted musicians and flamboyant guests painted on the interior ceiling. Small music groups usually performed in the summer. Today it was vacant and private.

CHAPTER 15

Francesca awoke to an unexpected silence within the house and an empty bed. She lay in the cool sheets for a minute, gathering her thoughts before rolling over to hug her lover's pillow.

In his place, a card and tiny cream box, decorated in gold ribbon. Francesca's breath caught and she sat up quickly, letting the sheet fall away.

Her fingers treasured the thick parchment, embossed with the Delarno crest. Holding it to her nose, she breathed the scent of the paper and ink. Carefully, she peeled at the wax seal, her attention focused on preserving as much of the envelope in its perfect state as possible.

Inside, a card in Nicci's beautiful handwriting.

Francesca. My beautiful friend and lover. I love you more with every passing moment. You give me strength I've never known. I hope you can forgive me for not spending this last day with you in Rapallo. Unfortunately I have business in Genoa. Tonight I belong only to you. Save the gift for then, my love. I want to see your face when you pull the ribbon ties and reveal this lifelong bond of our future together. Yours forever, Nicholas. X

Francesca re-read the card another four times, holding the small box reverently in her hands. She fingered at the gold ribbon. The box was the perfect size for an engagement ring. She read the note again. A lifelong bond and a future together. It could only mean marriage.

She flashed a kilowatt smile, her head spinning as she held the box to her heart. She placed the small package at the marbled edge of the bathroom vanity. That way, she could look at it and wonder and daydream whilst showering.

Balancing her bag on a little stool in the bathroom, Francesca packed, searching the room for any last items. There would be no time for such a tedious task when Nicholas returned tonight. She sat at last at the writing table. After all that procrastination it was time to check her emails. She opened her laptop to begin, the card and little package within easy reach.

It was difficult to focus. The device was taking its time to boot up so she pulled open the drawer, finding Delarno's stationery and a pen. Francesca Delarno. She practiced writing her new signature.

After a few more test signatures, the detective absently re-hit the start button on the keyboard.

"Bugger," she mumbled to herself. "Flat as a tack." Popping it on the charger beside her bed, she reached for her phone and made her way to the sun lounge outside her bedroom. As she sat down, it rang. A strange sound. It was the first time she'd heard it in days.

"Pronto, my lover. Are you missing me already?" she answered.

Her head was resting against the floral cushions of a chaise. Stretched in the warm sunshine, her mind wandered on the day ahead and thoughts of Nicholas' return. Her last night with him before the tedious flight to Sydney. Work could wait.

"Francesca? Thank God. Where the hell are you? I've been trying to ring you all day."

Johnno barked at his partner, his relief manifesting in anger. Half a world away, his freckled knuckles clenched the steering wheel of the unmarked sedan. He blasted the horn, jamming at the brakes, and then wove tentatively through the bumper to bumper Sydney traffic. Heavy rain pelted against a greasy windscreen, the intensity of the large drops affording only meters of visibility. White knuckles gripped harder as brakes screeched behind him.

It wasn't Nicholas.

"Johnno!" came the startled reply. Work could apparently *not* wait. "I'm in Rapallo taking a few rest days. I managed to wrap up the business in Rome early. I sent you an email," she added defensively.

She peered out to the bay below, thankful that Johnno did not understand her second language. Calling him her lover would require an explanation she was, at present, unwilling to share.

A small child caught her attention. Tightly holding his mother's hand he paddled on the stony shore of the sheltered beach. His dark head rose up to his mother. Promptly she gathered his little body to hers, showering him in kisses. His laughter tinkled up the hillside. It was a projected image of her future. A future she'd longed for and which was magically developing before her eyes.

Perhaps she could finish this matter of Chi You next week in court, hand it over to her trusted team and then she would be free of her commitments to the cause. Free to be with Nicholas in Italy or wherever.

Francesca smiled and let a sigh of pure bliss escape as Johnno droned on. The subject of Chi You she suddenly realised held little interest.

"There's been a breach of security. Francesca we need you to get home today."

At the complete silence from her end of the phone he yelled in frustration.

"Francesca? Are you listening?" His mood was in tune with the slippery road conditions that made for testy driving. Raking his red hair, he released a frustrated grunt.

"I'm sorry Johnno, I'm distracted. And I need to translate; in Italy, English is the second language, remember." Her sarcastic, pitiful responses incensed his aggravation. "Tell me again. What's new?"

"You tell me. The Italian police are going nuts. They claim there's been a breach of their intelligence systems. Encrypted files were accessed by unauthorized personnel. Francesca, it's pertaining to our matter with Fletcher. Someone else is interested in our case." The windscreen wipers worked double time to keep up with the Sydney winter downpour.

"Who?" Francesca sat up, uncrossing her legs, forcing her mind to focus on work.

"Well if I knew that I wouldn't need you to get home ASAP. You can get around Italy, I mean, unhindered?"

"Of course. But look Johnno, I'm heading to Rome tomorrow morning, then on to Sydney in the afternoon. What's the difference between today and tomorrow if there's already been a breach? Then again, maybe I should stay longer to sort it out over here. I have already made plans for tonight, but tomorrow I can be in Rome by 10am."

Francesca's quick thinking hatched a new plan.

"Francesca! This is not a social call," he spat down the phone. She was actually pouting. "What sort of plans?"

"Plans of a personal nature." It sounded pathetic, but she would not discuss her personal life.

"I see." Johnno skidded sideways into a break down lane. Her involvement and its extent was something he hadn't expected. It could already be too late. Goodwood may have just let the crime gangs' key player slip out of the country and out of reach.

Francesca played an integral part in a highly specialized team, specifically tasked to target organised crime. With Delarno now on their intelligence radar, hooking up with Nicholas was akin to professional and personal suicide. Her credibility in any further investigation was ruined, if she managed to stay out of jail. Then again, she may be unaware of the connection. Particularly if she'd been offline and hadn't read the new data.

"Francesca." He changed his manner to reflect his concerned big brother attitude. Johnno had to assume the girl still trusted his judgement. "How about you tell me anyway. Let's start with your social outing on the water and the new man in your life?"

"What? How do you know about that?" Francesca asked incredulously. She paced the confines of the balcony and headed indoors to the bedroom. "I haven't had a holiday in six years Johnno. I'm entitled to a couple of days off with a friend."

"Someone has been taking photographs Francesca. They are now on my email. Clear images of you and your new friends," he said gently, adding for emphasis. "Nice boat."

"Photographs? What photographs? I don't know anything about that." She recounted details of the cruise. His over-reaction to the 'situation' smacked of the jealousy he'd displayed when she had been asked to travel to Italy in the first instance. If there was a serious problem, the local guys would have called. It was not as if she'd been hiding.

"Francesca, no one is saying you can't have a holiday. You're missing the point. How well do you know Nicholas Delarno?"

"Nicholas Delarno is an old family friend," she lied, squirming.

"And your real relationship with him?"

"Our relationship is complicated," she sighed.

"It doesn't look too complicated to me. You're lovers. So, enlighten me. How well do you know him and his family?" Johnno's voice was taut and tired.

Francesca deflated. "We grew up together. The Delarnos and my father have been friends for over sixty years. When my dad emigrated to Australia, Silvio was his sponsor. He is my Godfather. Nicholas is the eldest son. But what's it to you anyway?"

Shame suddenly replaced happiness as Francesca inwardly cringed. What exactly was the content of these photographs? They hadn't been discrete in their affections. The boys in the squad would have a field day, not to mention the embarrassment to her family and her credibility in the court room next week.

"GET DOWN Johnno!" Francesca suddenly ordered, her shocked scream an instinctive reaction to the sound of rapid machine gun fire. She slammed onto the floor as the windows cracked loudly and shards of glass and timber flew in her direction. Francesca screamed.

"Francesca! What?" The unmistakably terrifying noise reverberated through the phone. "Is that gun shots?"

"Johnno! Help me! I'm under fire." Terror froze her thoughts.

"Stay on the line babe. I'll get you out." Johnno kept his voice calm.

Francesca screamed as another spray of bullets took out the doorway she had left moments before. She crawled under the bed and headed for the open bedroom door that led to the shelter of the hallway. The stone wall would provide protection. From there she could escape. Guessing her plans, the gunman shot another round, shattering the remaining window.

"I'm trapped!" Francesca cried again. "I'm completely surrounded by broken glass. And no shoes!"

"Listen babe. Focus. Look around you. Tell me, where are the possible exits?"

"I can't move further into the house, it's too far and they've shot out the window near the bedroom door. I'm stuck on the third floor. I only have the ensuite and my room. I can try the ensuite. It has a window facing the back garden."

"Good girl. Don't hang up."

He waited what seemed like an eternity, listening intently to the noises as she edged herself to safety.

Francesca yanked her laptop from the bed, along with the blankets and slid them in front of her to clear a hasty path. Ever slowly she commando-crawled towards the ensuite. Almost there. Half crawling, half sliding, she craned her neck to check on progress, all the time listening for any movement outside or inside the house. With every small noise her heart beat quickened and she stopped.

"I'm here," she whispered, squatting under the window. She pulled a fresh towel from the rack to brush away the bits of broken glass clinging to her skin. "I can fit through this window and climb down the veranda trellis." She paused. "Wait, what if there are two gunmen, one at the back and one at the front? I don't have a weapon."

"Is that your only option? Are you sure you can't you go out through the house? If there's a vehicle …"

"Shh. I can hear voices and … sirens. Someone's called the police. I need to leave."

Francesca heard the heavy footsteps under her ensuite window and peered over the windowsill to see two retreating figures running through the olive grove. She grabbed her bags and laptop.

"Johnno. I'm taking a car and heading to Milano Linate airport direct. I'm sure they'll expect me to go to Rome. Linate is the regional airport, a far safer option right now … and closer. I'll call you from there. Get me a ticket back to Sydney would you? Text through the details."

The sirens were getting closer. Shoving on her shoes, she stood, carefully crunching over the glass and ran down the stairs to the garage, dislodging the glass from the soles on the expensive carpets. Throwing the bags across the leather seats, she slid in, working through the gears to wind her way down the steep driveway and onto the road that led out of town.

As she drove past the next-door house, she saw the fleet of police cars speeding up towards the villa. Quickly, she pulled off into a driveway, parking close to an Alfa Romeo and ducked her head. She punched the directions to the airport in the car's GPS. The last vehicle passed. That was it. She relaxed and relishing the response of the sports car, hugged the curvy streets of Rapallo until she reached the motorway.

CHAPTER 16

"I'm here," she texted Johnno, pulling into the airport's long-term car park. It was a few miles from the city centre and the main airport for tourists. Heading straight to the ticket desk, she made herself known to the staff and was ushered to a secure location that'd been organized from Sydney. She glanced at the tickets. It was not the most direct route home, but it was good enough. She would take what she could get at this stage.

While she waited to board her flight, Francesca found herself on shaky, familiar ground. Frantically, she tried to mentally harden herself against the inevitable heartbreak that followed her startling array of bad decisions when it came to Nicholas Delarno. She sighed. It was time to call Johnno.

He picked up straight away. "Francesca, IT has texted you a secure login and password. Have you got it?" he asked. "Good. Let me just say this does not look good for you. When you get back I will get an explanation. Open document one. These are the pictures from the detectives in Rome."

Panic and confusion had systemically destroyed her confidence during the long drive here, the conversation with Johnno replaying a continuous news reel on a manic loop.

She revisited the case in her mind. She'd given nothing away in Rome. There was no way she'd compromised the investigation in word. Her actions in Rapallo were, at a stretch, immoral but certainly not illegal.

She couldn't understand how this current crisis was connected to Nicholas. She'd known the family her entire life. Someone was setting them up. Francesca thought about Cesare Augustus and the Roman detectives. Her stomach lurched. She'd surely been played as they steered her investigation towards all things Nero, the Sicilian mafia family.

In the security of the airline lounge, she downloaded the information Johnno had sent. Her world crashed. The first photograph showed Gino Castello, a known mafia figure meeting with Nicholas Delarno at the family villa in Rapallo. It was dated the day before she arrived.

Francesca scrolled through the pictures of her lover meeting with local crime identities. For all intents and purposes it looked like Nicholas was in the middle of some kind of criminal negotiations.

Then she saw them. The confronting pictures of them on the boat embracing on the top deck. Francesca felt the colour drain from her face. There were photos of them at the beach, the café, my god he was even looking directly at the lens in one taken during their picnic on the foreshore. Her first meeting with Nicholas at the train station had been recorded.

Her heart sat heavy in her chest, pressing the breath from her lungs as she tried to piece together the images confronting her. Someone was trying to manipulate the situation. Someone was hell bent on discrediting her. And now they were trying to kill her.

"Johnno. I can't understand it. Nicci. And I. We've been set up," she stammered. "You must believe me. I don't know what to say. I don't know what this is about. Who would do this? Why?" She paused looking for answers. "Nicci knows a lot of people in Rapallo. Castello could be talking about anything. Those other men? Nicci may not even know they're crims. I mean, his father does most of the negotiations here in Italy. I've known that family my entire life. This doesn't fit. There has to be a mistake."

Francesca hardly believed herself. Gino Castello was inextricably linked to Nero and the Sicilian mob. A visit from him meant business. Her heart shattered into a thousand piercing pieces.

"Are you in love with him?"

"With Nicholas? Yes. Absolutely."

"Does he love you?"

"I think so. Yes." She just had to believe he did. "Yes he does."

"Where is he now?"

"In Genoa for the day. Family business matters. He's due back at the house tonight. That's why I wanted to stay. I … we had plans … for the two of us. It was my last night in Rapallo. We were going to talk about our future. Together," she added for emphasis, blushing again at the revelation to Johnno. She shrugged resignedly and her tone went flat. "Our marriage Johnno. We were going to talk about our marriage. We are committed to each other."

"Mmm. All, in what, three days? Have you discussed the case with him?"

"No! Most definitely not. You question my integrity?" Francesca was indignant.

"Where were you staying? In Rapallo I mean."

"At the Delarno villa."

"Did you organise that?" he asked.

"No, actually my father did. He and Silvio are old friends. Like I said, our families have holidayed together for many years, at each other's homes and around Italy. And the world for that matter," she said, hoping it would reassure Johnno. "There is nothing untoward about the arrangement."

"You told me you wanted to personally shut down Chi You. The hearing date for your matter is next week Francesca, in Brisbane. I understand you're frightened by the possible outcome there and you've been under a lot of pressure. So I'm going to ask again. Have you said or done anything to compromise any of our investigations?

Now is the time to tell me. You can trust me. You just need to tell me the truth."

"No Johnno," she replied with force. "I have not done or said anything to compromise any of our investigations. Not this week, not last week, not at any time in my past or, I swear, in the future."

"But now you're making a commitment to him? A commitment that puts you on the edge of the law. Do you understand what I'm saying Francesca? This Delarno guy is taking part in criminal activities. Your motives don't make sense to me."

Francesca felt her blood rush through her from head to toe, and shifted in the seat.

"Allegedly Johnno. Nothing's been proven. And you have to understand. This is all new information to me. Nicci and I grew up together. When my mother died, his mother Cristiana took care of us. Nicholas has always looked out for me. Once we were very close. I fell in love with him when I was 16 and I've loved him ever since. But I never told him and he was always so out of reach for me. It's frigging embarrassing.

"Lord, I'm almost thirty and I just can't get him out of my heart. This week in Rapallo we've both realised we just want to be together. And now there's a security breach. I don't know what it has to do with the Delarno family but I'm going to prove our innocence. You can be guaranteed of that."

Johnno refocused. "Francesca, the breach of Italian security I was talking about. They believe it's you. Your access codes were used to gain sensitive information from the Italian police database. To make matters worse you have been seen socialising with persons of interest. Whether you knew it or not is irrelevant really."

"What! Why would I compromise an investigation? That's simply ridiculous! There's no way anyone could use my codes. They're not written down. I would assume the Italian cops would have stopped my access the minute I left the building. My laptop is encrypted anyway. There has to be another explanation."

"Well, then if your laptop is so secure, you must have accidently triggered the breach yourself. Look I have to ask, is any of your family involved in the mob or have been threatened by them?"

Francesca jumped. She was angry now. Her words were spoken through gritted teeth, her voice controlled and tight.

"What is it with you? Are you seriously asking me this? No! You know that's bullshit. No one in my family would bring such shame. Not all Italians belong to or rejoice in the mafia, Johnno." Her body shook with anger.

She paced the small airport room. "My specialty is Asian triad. The reason I'm in Italy is because Goodwood sent me. Maybe you should be asking him about this!" she spat unreasonably.

Johnno sighed heavily, dismissing her accusations. He wanted to believe her. He had to see her and ask her again, face to face. At any rate, she needed to come back to Sydney and to the safety of the squad.

"Tell me word for word about the business in Genoa with Nicholas Delarno."

"There was no conversation. Only a note. It said he had to go to Genoa on business and he would be back. Then we'd talk about our future together. You know, our marriage."

Johnno sighed, rubbing his face with his hand. The retelling of the story was for his own peace of mind rather than her benefit.

"You say you haven't discussed the case with him but did he elaborate or confide in you in anyway? Did he say anything? Even the smallest detail would help."

"No. He didn't discuss any work with me. And I certainly did not discuss any of my work with him."

"Francesca, I know you value your private life but you'll have to tell me everything. I have your arse covered on this. For now anyway. The boss is livid. God knows what will be in circulation by the time you land. The last thing we need is for this to be leaked to the media. If that happens, you can kiss your privacy goodbye, Francesca. Be prepared for the worst. I will personally pick you up at the airport and then we can talk."

Francesca felt numb.

"Ok. But I'm telling you I'm not involved in any illegal activity."

Suddenly she remembered the curious meeting in Portofino. She was clutching at straws.

"Johnno. I'm going to send you a picture from my phone. Run it through Interpol for me. It's a long story and I'll tell you when we meet up."

"Sure, no worries. I'll try and have the information by the time you arrive. You think you have a lead?"

"Not sure. Just a gut feeling. May be nothing."

She refused to believe that the only man she'd ever loved would deceive her this way.

"Just so you know, general duties are with your father and he has begun communicating with your sister, Luciana, and her family. Until we know who is behind this, we are putting everyone under dignitary protection."

The Salucci family was actually under criminal surveillance. Johnno hated lying to his partner. But family involvement could be very tricky.

"Thank you."

"Francesca, I have placed an agent close by to ensure your safety. He'll stay with you until you board. When you get on the plane, another undercover operative will be seated close. He is armed, because we know you're not. There'll be someone I trust watching you until you land in Sydney."

Francesca nodded to herself. Taking a deep breath she looked at the air tickets.

"My plane leaves at seven o'clock tonight. I'm not complaining but I'm going to be in transit for almost two days. Johnno, there's a small church just close-by. I have hours to fill in. Would it be ok if I go there? There'll be no harm surely. I need some air and ... I need to pray."

Johnno was shocked by the request. He took a moment to consider. "Yeah babe. Be careful. Straight there, straight back. One hour, Francesca. That's all you have."

"Grazie. Thank you. See you in Sydney."

Here she was, a suspect trapped in a game of love and betrayal.

Could this be happening to her? What would Nic say when he arrived home that evening? Maybe he already knew she wouldn't be there. What if they were wrong and Nic was innocent, who would support him? Would he even make it out of Genoa alive?

She had to warn him. Francesca scribbled a small note, folded it numerous times and labelled it with the Delarno name and address at Rapallo. Shoving it in her pocket out of sight for now, she would find a way to get it to him. There was an explanation and she would find it.

~

Francesca strode the short distance to the Basilica di Sant' Eufemia. It was one of the oldest places of worship in Milan. It had been rebuilt in the 1800s in Romanesque and Gothic Revival styles after an earthquake had destroyed the original church.

She pushed past the iron gate to access the portico. The church's front had a three-arch colonnade with mosaic reproductions. Its exterior was terracotta and cream-coloured. Beautiful indigo and gold tiles lit the curved walls, their smooth surface inviting a weary traveller's touch. She did, searching for peace and courage.

Standing in the entrance the detective let her eyes adjust to the change of light, before proceeding quickly to the altar. To the right, against the wall, she found the wooden prayer table hosting a small brass candelabra and kneeling pad. A rectangular timber money box, the tiny opening just wide enough for some coins, sat beside it.

She searched the area for her new constant companion. He was at the threshold of the outside portico. His eyes would need to adjust to the darkness. Now was her chance. In a quick moment, she slipped the paper into the coin slot along with a couple of coins.

Francesca lit the candle and placed it in the brass holder. Kneeling to pray, she let her thoughts turn to her actions and how they now placed her and her family in danger. She prayed for forgiveness and wisdom in action, clasping her fingers tightly until they were numb.

A group of respectful tourists, with a guide, wandered about quietly admiring the inside paintings. There was a collective gasp at the beautiful sixteenth century wooden panel paintings, a recognised feature of the church. The collection was thought to be painted by pupils of Leonardo's school. The Wedding of Santa Caterina and a painting representing Mother and Child were stand-out favourites. Each one of the tourists stood in stillness in front of them, marvelling and pontificating.

Names and dates swirled around the room as the guide gave a comprehensive talk about the artists and artisans of the church.

"The church is dedicated to Saint Eufemia of Chalcedon who was the beautiful daughter of a merchant of Chalcedon. She was arrested, thrown into prison and tortured after refusing to give up Christianity. Eventually she was thrown into the arena with the lions and died in 304 AD. She was fifteen years of age."

After the tour, the female guide herded the group out into the bright afternoon sunshine shepherding them onto the minibus and the next stop.

Francesca followed at a small distance, before returning to the airport and the security of the lounge as promised. She waited quietly for the plane to board and began the journey home with her mind lost in a thought treadmill. Thirty hours later, the plane prepared to land in Sydney. Francesca braced herself for the onslaught of questions. Her closely guarded private life now under the microscope.

CHAPTER 17

"How was the flight?" It was a moot question, just looking at her broke his heart. Eyes swollen with heavy dark circles accentuated the hollowness of her expression and pallor. It was possibly the first time he'd seen her so fragile and her appearance startled him. A stark contrast to the images he had on his computer of her frolicking about the Riviera with Nicholas Delarno. Another bastard. This chick would never learn.

"Let's get you back to my place. Ruthie has made chicken soup for you. You know it's her old-time cure-all."

Francesca nodded and followed him to the waiting car. Johnno scanned the airport for suspicious travellers, pushing her along as quickly as possible. He texted Goodwood informing him Francesca was in his care. It was time to hear her side of the sorry tale.

Francesca propped herself on the bar stool at the kitchen counter, resting her head in upturned hands. Ruthie's chicken soup simmered away on the stove top. Johnno grabbed some bowls and began to serve.

"Tell me," he instructed as softly as he could.

Francesca revealed her dealings with the Delarno family. A personal history stretching almost thirty years.

Johnno made notes as she spoke. In particular key names, places and dates. After she'd finished he revealed the intelligence he'd gathered in Melbourne.

"Despite the wrap up of your investigation into Chi You, the organised crime detectives in Melbourne took it upon themselves to keep tabs on the gangs interests. In particular, the movements of some of the key personnel their Vanguard liked to use."

"Oh? Did they find anything useful?" Francesca's interest peaked.

"A few months ago, there was a lunchtime meeting at an Italian restaurant in Bourke Street between a representative from the Nero group and a representative from Chi You. A third person was never identified. Meaning he had no criminal connections on record."

"Right."

"Gino Castello was also in the restaurant. Not at that table. He sat alone."

"So, you're telling me that the Sicilian mob is working with Chi You and someone else. And now that Gino has been in touch with Nicholas, you think the Delarno family is also in the frame.

"Yes. That is precisely what I am saying."

"Oh." She stared out the window until the trees became blurry spots of light and shade and rested her head on arms folded across the breakfast bar in front of her.

"I should get you home." Johnno said as the conversation wore off and Francesca looked to be fighting off sleep.

They drove in silence lost in thought about the unfolding drama. As they reached her residence, Johnno opened up conversation again.

"You're a smart girl Francesca. Tell me, what would you do given the evidence."

Francesca conceded. "I suppose I would interview Silvio and Nicholas. It looks like we have no choice."

Her partner nodded. "I agree."

He helped her through the locked entrance gate, taking her bags from weary arms. "We've put you under police protection.

The Commissioner thinks it's best," Johnno said as they entered the building.

He scouted her home, checking doors and windows. Francesca knew it was necessary but the whole thing felt like a dream to her. A general duty cop standing in the small lounge room was given brief instructions by Johnno.

"Ok, all good. Try and get some sleep. I will be back tomorrow morning, about eight. You can face the music from the boss then. Ring me if you need to. Constable Rose will be here if there's anything."

Francesca smiled lamely at the young uniform. "Hi," she said meekly. "Help yourself to whatever you want."

"Thanks Johnno," she added.

Francesca was exhausted. Emotionally spent and physically depleted. She climbed the stairs to her bedroom, and turned halfway up the staircase.

"Thanks mate. Thanks so much." Her eyes filled with tears and she turned away to hide her misery. The air grew heavy between them.

Johnno winked trying unsuccessfully to dispel her sadness.

"No worries, movie star. See you tomorrow."

As the door clicked behind him reassuringly, Francesca lay on her bed, too exhausted to move. Her mind ran the continuous reel that was her life right now. Operation Serpent. My god, more like Operation Francesca Fucks Up. She felt like an utter failure.

CHAPTER 18

Nicholas returned to the villa expecting Francesca to be gone, and he was right. He met with Gino Castello.

"You shoot up my house to get to her! Are you fucking mad? Now we have the cops breathing down our necks," Nicholas spoke forcefully. "I had her where you wanted her. The agreement was backed by the Commission. We're on the same team. Including my father. You tell Seta to back off and let me do my job."

"You think this is over?" Gino scoffed. "You're in no position to make threats. That Salucci slut has done exactly as we knew she would. Under pressure she returns to those pigs," he spat. "She has no loyalty to you."

"You conceited bastard! You can't assume that! Francesca has more loyalty in her little finger than all of you put together."

Nicholas hit the ground in a resounding thud as Gino landed his fist across the younger man's jaw. The consigliore pulled Nic to his feet by his hair, holding the knife blade at his neck. Suddenly he pushed the young man aside, the force sending him scuttling along the stone floor.

"Ha! You're not worth it. Son of Capo or not. Your father will be told of your disrespect in Rapallo and you can answer to him. See how you go defending that slut and her actions then!" With that, the enforcer turned on his heel and left.

The young man's solace: Francesca was safe. They did not have their grubby hands on her. Yet. The thought of them handling her twisted him in angry knots. He would personally track down and take out anyone who touched her.

He sat heavily in the leather chesterfield, releasing an exasperated groan that filled the private library with his frustration.

It surged through him and he impatiently leapt forward. The sudden tormented movement propelling him to the middle of the room. These surroundings suffocated him. This sophisticated room of leather bound books offered no sanctuary for the rage filling him. He pushed at a chair, its dark hues echoing the blackness of his thoughts.

At the corner of his desk a crystal decanter beckoned in the half-light. Nicholas strode over and poured a scotch. He took the liquid in one gulp, its fiery response catching him in the back of his throat. After the second, he lined up a third. Glaring into the crystal glass, his face twisted in temper as he retraced the callous events of the day.

Not more than an hour ago, the Milan police confirmed the recovery of his stolen car, undamaged, and located at the Milano Linate airport. Security pictures showed a woman, fitting Francesca's description, leaving the carpark and tracked her movements throughout the airport, where she was led to a secure location by airline staff. Did he want to prosecute? No.

Certain Francesca had seen the same photographs that'd been given to him today he was not surprised her team had pulled her home to the safety of her squad. Picking through the images, he paused at the one taken during their romantic picnic. Her innocent happiness exploded on the paper. Was that only yesterday? Francesca would be utterly devastated. Her trust in him shattered.

There was no question he would find her in Sydney. When he did, he would convince her to trust him again. He would win her back.

Submission, trust and loyalty. The qualities of every mafia wife.

How dare they impose the same on his relationship with her. Nicholas was dedicated to the code and that should be enough. Submission. Trust. Loyalty. He would find a way to manipulate this old tradition to his advantage.

In the loneliness of his silent home, Nicholas sculled another scotch to ease the ache on his bruised chest and bleeding fists. He knew his obsession with her was as dangerous as it was distracting. Today his impatience and indifference to the outmoded traditions stunned and aggravated the other men.

Seta was quick to pounce on his apparent lack of commitment. Nicholas had worn the consequences of their angry fists. Despite the barrage, he'd fought for her and himself. He knew then his protection of her was more important to him than any new treaty.

He drew a frustrated breath, and threw the empty scotch glass across the room, watching it splinter into shards of shimmering light. He wished he could replay the day. He would have woken her before he left. Taken her to Genoa with him. Seta could do nothing when she wore the protection of Delarno. That particular tradition he would ensure was carried through.

That was loyalty. The kind of loyalty she would give to him freely. And the only kind of loyalty he desired. Loyalty to him.

Tonight, instead of being with her, he sat alone in his beautiful home, wishing and waiting. For Francesca. God, he missed her. His memories crowded with her. The images taunted him. It was no use. His feelings towards her directed him in every way. Nicholas slammed his fist on the table.

"My love," he promised under his breath. "I'm coming for you. Be assured that with me you're always safe and that I love you wholly. One day, my lover, I'll explain about the day you meant more to me than anything else. For now, you just have to trust me."

~

Silently the black SUV slipped between the shadowy spaces and parked in the lot. From here he could see Francesca's apartment, the back garden wall vaguely lit in a yellowish glow. Nicholas checked his ammo and without a second look, slid from the leather seats, a grim expression hiding his wildly beating heart.

This would be the first time he would touch her since Rapallo. It had taken him ten long days to track her and avoid detection. He visualised her beautiful face peaceful in slumber. Shaking the picture from his mind, he strode to the wall and gracefully levered himself atop, quickly checking his balance before landing in the garden with a soft thud. He took cover behind a large magnolia that was flush with bright green leaves. He was surrounded by a walled courtyard, in which the tree took centre stage.

On the upper floor of the Abbotsford terrace, Nicholas braced himself at the threshold of her bedroom. He stopped a minute to watch her sleep. After this moment, everything would change. He wished he could stop time. That he could again lie beside her and hold her in his arms, comfort her, love her, just for one moment. Francesca stirred, forcing him to step back into the shadows.

In the quiet he tucked the revolver into his pocket, leant forward and kissed her lightly one last time.

"Francesca," he whispered, his lips pressing against her forehead. "Francesca."

Francesca was dreaming. Nic was whispering to her and she turned her face to the sound, wanting him to kiss her again. It was a beautiful morning; the sun was shining through those gauzy curtains.

"Nicci," she murmured in sleep.

"Francesca." He pulled her to his arms, muffling her screams with his lips. "Shh! Darling shh!" He held her close. "I'm sorry to frighten you like this but there's no other way."

"Nicholas! What the hell are you doing here?" Her heart was beating loudly. The noise in her eardrums drowned out his hushed whisper.

"I need to talk to you."

"There's nothing you can say to me that I'd want to hear." Raising her hand she sent a stinging slap across his cheek. "You lying bastard."

Springing to her feet, she crossed the bed in two steps and glared at him from the other side. A quick glance confirmed her phone and gun lay on the small table beside him. Her eyes scanned the room for a quick escape or another weapon.

His hushed tones begged. "Please, hear me out. I know you've been hurt. We're both hurting. You've seen the pictures too?"

She nodded.

"Francesca, we've been set up. Both of us. But I have a plan. A plan that will rid us of those men and blow open this whole operation. I'm begging you to walk with me because your life and mine depend on it." He was edging his way around the bed to her, calmly and quietly. "Please say you believe me. Our future together depends on it."

Francesca stood mesmerised by him. He was a snake, charming his way to her side. His held out his hands, she took them and placed them gently against her cheek. She couldn't help herself. She needed to know the truth.

"This is crazy Nic. I can't talk to you. We'll both end up in jail. It's insane," she spoke desperately, her eyes wide.

"I won't let that happen. But we need to work together," he said taking the last step before her.

She looked at his weary face, his eyes blackened from sleepless days and nights and the deep lines etched at the corners. Her hand reached up and gently smoothed the crinkles. He sighed. "God, I've missed you."

His finger traced the outline of her lips. Tilting her chin so he could taste her neck, his lips led a trail to hers, crushing her last resolve. He whispered the words she longed to hear before his mouth returned to hers.

Francesca leaned into him, pressing her body to his. She wanted to feel his desire match hers, to be assured that she could again spark that wave of need in him as she had in Italy. She held his head to her lips. He didn't resist.

Her demands deepened. Restless hands pulled at his shoulders, reached his hips, urging him to make love to her. He buried himself in her passion. Relief came quickly with a fervent kiss. Nicholas was breathless.

He held her to his chest, gathering his thoughts and stilling her for the instructions. "I have one more thing to do tonight. So tomorrow morning, follow the usual route on your morning run. But this time stop by the old broken pier. You know the one, about halfway along. There's a park bench close by and I want you to stall, perhaps fake a cramp. Stretch it out at that spot. We can talk from a distance. I'll be disguised as a fisherman, but you'll know it's me. By then I'll have everything you need to close this investigation. Names, dates and evidence. Francesca will you do this? For us."

Nicholas watched her nod in agreement and added, "It's really important you do exactly as I say. Do you understand?" He spoke close to her ear and finished with a kiss.

The detective nodded again.

"You're truly mine," he whispered, relieved. "Say it to me Francesca. Tell me how much you love me." He stepped back slightly, looking sternly into her face.

"Nicholas Delarno, with all my heart I belong to you. I always have. There has never been another who's made me feel as you."

She pledged her loyalty to him. Nicholas hugged her tightly to him for a brief moment and stepped back.

She stood naked before him, not attempting to cover herself. The combination of vulnerability, passion and honesty in her never ceased to astound him. She looked particularly beautiful in that instant, her lips reddened from his, that hair tousled by their passion. This was how he loved her the most.

He laid her to bed and pulled the cover over her. He smoothed her hair gently from her forehead. A kiss to the cheek and he stood to dress, watching her watch him, still and quiet.

"Use this later if you need. It's my new room number and the code for the lock. If something goes wrong, I'll come back for you there. The room is safe and secure. Only you and I know about this."

She took the motel business card, and asked, "Nicci, after tomorrow, we'll be together again, won't we?" She turned worried eyes to him.

"The pictures. Those men. It's circumstantial, right? You do have the evidence? And I will get it in the morning?"

He knelt beside her and kissed the top of her head holding her face gently in his cupped palms.

"My beautiful flower, I love you and when this investigation is over, I promise you'll have all the answers to your questions and we'll return to Rapallo to begin our new life together." He paused for added emphasis. "Francesca. Tomorrow ... absolutely no cops."

She nodded.

He glanced at his wristwatch. "I have to get going. I'll see you in the morning." He paused again. "No cops Francesca, not even McCrae." He kissed her one last time, and went out the way he'd arrived, leaving Francesca to wonder and worry in the dark.

Even with protection Nic had found his way into her house. Her bedroom. It frightened her. She had to assume she was no longer safe. Calling Johnno would only complicate it more. Nic had explicitly requested no police. Besides, Johnno would never let her go through with the meeting.

Francesca found the cleaning kit on the floor of her walk-in robe. By the ensuite light she sat in the small walk-through, laying a towel on the bare boards in front of her. Piece by piece she pulled apart her pistol, cleaned it and checked it over. The systematic approach of the action calmed her. She'd practiced it many times on the night before a sting. Francesca aimed the pistol at a point above her window and another halfway along her wall. The detective had specifically placed the marks there for this purpose.

Satisfied, she returned to bed and shoved the pistol under her pillow. With any luck she would be back in her apartment by the scheduled 9am pickup and have the missing information they desperately needed. It was a chance to rebuild her tattered credibility after the Italian debacle. Then, she would be free to make plans to return to Italy. With Nicholas. She smiled to herself, tasting him on her lips.

CHAPTER 19

At 5.30am, on schedule, a lone figure exited the terrace apartment and slowly made her way to the running track along the Parramatta River. A nervous shiver ran through her and she mentally checked the contents of her small pocket sewn into the waistband of her fitted running pants. House key. Mobile phone securely attached to the exterior.

Concealed in the purpose-built singlet, her pistol sat neatly under her arm, resting in the secret pouch against her ribs.

Francesca tried to relax and keep her focus as she did every morning, following the same path, doing the same stretches to warm up. She hoped she was convincing because she could feel eyes watching her, imaginary or not.

About halfway along, the bush track cleared to a cycle way that followed the river. Still protected by the cover of trees Francesca surveyed the scene in front of her. A small jetty and park bench were in view. She pressed record on her phone, drew a breath and began to emerge from her cover. At this point she was still reasonably protected by the scattering of trees. A person sitting on a fold-out chair had dropped a fishing line into the river inlet.

She slowed her pace as if beginning to cramp. The track was deserted except for the lone fisherman. The meeting location was within range of a good rifleman. It was too exposed. Francesca felt the hairs at the nape of her neck prickle and casually looked over the bay inlet. A small number of boats were secured at their moorings.

As she rounded the last corner before reaching the open parkland, a previously hidden, smaller and obviously quicker craft came into view. Something about it wasn't right. Anchored up, it sought protection from a bigger catamaran close-by. And was positioned for a quick getaway.

Francesca clutched at her side in fake cramp and limped slowly to the bench. She glanced at the fisherman who was taking pains to avoid looking in her direction, and examined the figure.

He was bigger than Nic and his movements did not reflect his mannerisms. She felt a moment of confusion before she realised that it was, in fact, not Nicholas. The bastard had set her up again! This time she was too exposed.

Immediately, she sprang to action, racing for the closest protection, the treed parkway ahead of her.

How fast do you have to run to beat a bullet? Her mind questioned. In the distance she heard Nic scream out, "Run! Francesca Run! Get out!" before a sickening thud of fist hitting skin and then silence.

The figure jumped up shrugging off his jacket. He reached into his pocket. Francesca could hear him swearing in a combination of English and Italian. Stumbling the first few crucial steps as he negotiated the fishing gear gave Francesca the precious moments she needed.

He took aim. Francesca screamed as the bullet grazed her arm. The next group of trees was tantalisingly close. With lungs exploding, her legs pumping hard, she tried to pretend her arm wasn't burning like fire. Behind, the man continued to follow her, his thumping footsteps fast closing the distance between them.

As her footing lost itself, Francesca fell behind the massive buttress root of a Moreton bay fig. Crashing headlong into the leaves and debris, the girl crawled into a hole carved in the trunk. She waited. The steps were getting closer. The path ahead curved sharply before opening onto the road.

Francesca hoped that he would follow the path, thinking she would head for the safety of a busy road and apartment buildings. She held her breath, fingering the pistol in her pouch. The detective dare not make a noise. The footsteps were getting closer. Francesca made herself smaller, sucking in silent shallow breaths. The footsteps stopped, shuffled and then followed the direction of the path.

She waited, her ears straining. Everything was quiet. She had to try and get a closer look at the boat. Looking up, she realised she could climb the tree that had afforded her so much protection and still be safe.

Quickly shimmying up the trunk, she took refuge against the massive branches and sparse foliage. As she reached her new hideout position she heard voices approaching.

Francesca held her breath, drawing her pistol. A burst of laughter and she realised that the area was becoming more populated; a trio of women were power walking together into the open sunlight. Another was jogging towards her.

He would have reached the road by now and Francesca wondered if a car was waiting. Still she did not move. Her vision to the bay only confirmed that she could no longer see the speedboat. Perhaps it had already left.

Reasonably assured of her safety for the moment, Francesca reached for her phone.

"Hey babe. How're they hanging?" Johnno's greeting would normally be met with a smart response. He waited. "What? I can't hear you. Why are you whispering?"

"Johnno. I need you. Come and get me. Bring backup. I'm in trouble."

"Sure babe. Where are you?" He strained to hear her.

"Follow my running track, past the clearing and jetty to the next set of trees. Be careful. Shit, someone's coming." Francesca killed the phone and waited for silence.

"Fuck! Francesca! Francesca! Are you still there? Fucking Hell!" Johnno pulled on his jeans racing out the door yelling. "Ruthie, call the cops. Tell them to meet me at Francesca's apartment."

Francesca dialled again. "I've been shot. Nothing serious. Perp wearing dark beanie, grey flanno and jeans. Medium set frame. Maybe 6ft. Hurry Johnno. I'm bleeding."

"Copy. Stay out of sight."

When the sirens announced Johnno's arrival, Francesca heard the outboard motor of a speedboat. They'd been waiting for her to emerge from the trees. Her arm ached terribly, the blood staining her skin and little drips splashing onto the branches below. She stripped off her running jacket and tried to wrap it tightly around the wound.

She watched Johnno stepping cautiously into the scrub. He surveyed the area and continued on towards the road. Presently he turned back and stopped near her tree, scratching at his red head.

"Up here, you big oaf." She released a nervous laugh.

He looked up in amazement. "Never knew you had monkey in ya! You can come down now, it's safe. We've checked it all out."

"I know, I watched." She jumped the last few metres, landing heavily. With Johnno there, she felt safe again. It also helped that the area was crawling with cops.

"Let's take a look at that," Johnno noticed the blood stained jacket wrapped around her arm.

"The bullet grazed my arm. I think it landed in that tree." She said pointing to the tree that saved her life. "I also have some footage on my phone. Not sure how good it is but …"

Astonishment showed across Johnno's features. He strode over to look at the tree and called to a general duty officer.

"Come on let's get you to the doctor," he said, gently guiding Francesca to the car. "You can tell me all about your early morning adventure."

He glanced at the purpose built singlet. "Often go jogging with your piece? This is going to be quite a story."

CHAPTER 20

Nicholas set a determined jaw and refused to acknowledge the knifing pain of broken ribs and deep muscle bruising in his back and stomach. Bound to the chair in the centre of the room, he faced the armed men opposite and looked squarely into the faces from his youth.

Don Giovanni Nero. Gino Castello. Nicholas paused at the rigid expression of his father, Capo Silvio Delarno. Seated beside him the strangers newly welcomed into the fold. Robbie L, President of the Ares Outlaw Motor Cycle Gang and Ri Lee Wong, Vanguard of the Chi You triad gang. The son's gaze returned to his father and his eyes narrowed as the commander of the bike gang spoke.

"You see Silvio. At your request, your son is still in one piece. In our club, he would be dead for less, family or not."

Silvio raised his right hand to silence the biker.

"Nicholas, you disrespect me," he started. "You disrespect our code. You failed to bring closure in Rapallo. Today you warned her to run. I think you value your lover more than your honour to our family." Silvio's eyes turned downwards. "It saddens me very much, my son, that a Salucci has turned you against me."

"That's not true. My loyalty is to our code and my family," Nicholas ground out. "Seta is working against us. He's the one driving the wedge between our friendships. Disrupting old loyalties and putting us in a very vulnerable position. His actions have brought the unwelcome attention we currently receive."

"Can you prove it?" Don Nero enquired.

Nicholas turned towards the traitor. "Not yet. But I will. And I'll get evidence of anyone else working with him to destabilise our group."

"Wild accusations!" scoffed Nero theatrically. "And I suppose you think a Salucci is going to help you. You are loco." He twirled his fingers to his head in emphasis.

"I know Francesca will comply," Nicholas retorted.

"Ha! That girl again!" Silvio slammed his fist on the table. "It's not enough that she's a Salucci. You insult us all with her at your side. I warned you last time to stay away from that cop wench."

"Or what? You'll take her out? Beat me to my death? Even for you, father, that is rash. It'll bring more attention. Francesca knows nothing of our operation. And I intend to keep it that way. She trusts me. She's pledged her loyalty to me."

The son challenged with venomous rebellion.

Silvio continued unfazed. His mind was made up.

"This time, there's no debate Nicholas. You took the oath. Your hands will take her life and then you'll take your own. As is the way with traitors within our code."

Nic snapped his head back to his father. "And if I refuse."

"You can watch me do it," Robbie L taunted menacingly. "It won't be an easy time for your slut. That cop will pay for your stupidity. And you can watch."

Nic lurched forward in the chair and sprang back as the ropes burned, catching his wrists and ankles. "You filthy piece of shit. How dare you! You're not part of us and you never will be. You disrespect our honour as men! You know nothing of our traditions!"

"And neither do you, sunshine, by the sound of it. Rule number one. Never protect a cop," Robbie L goaded. He looked at Silvio. "Let's just say, in this new team, some of your outdated traditions will make way for new customs. Starting with you and your cop slut."

"Enough!" Silvio shouted. "Untie my son." The old man turned menacingly to Robbie L. "Disrespect any member of my family again and *I* will kill you."

Nicholas watched the tinderbox of heated emotions exchange between the pair. If only he had a knife, he would kill the fucker right there on the spot. They didn't need Ares. He glared at Ri Lee Wong. Or Chi You.

Silvio turned to his son. "You have three days."

CHAPTER 21

Alone in the quiet sanctity of the doctor's room, Francesca did her best to explain the last six hours as Johnno listened and took notes. Exasperation gave way to forward planning. Francesca's desperate attempt to clear her name and get the investigation back on track was wrapped in that tidy bundle known as Nicholas Delarno. Again, it came back to the two of them and Johnno knew he would have to isolate Nic.

His phone buzzed. "Jonathan McCrae."

"Sergeant, it's Constable Rose from Five Dock. We have had report of break and enter at a listed address in Abbotsford. It's Detective Sergeant Salucci's house. Thought you should know."

"Thanks mate. We'll be right there."

Johnno looked at Francesca.

"What?" Francesca was looking considerably uncomfortable after the tetanus shot and her solemn face was highlighted by questioning, glassy eyes. There was not much the doctor could do for a bullet graze. Ointment, bandage and rest. He handed her a script for some strong pain relief and the antibiotic ointment.

"They've been through your house."

Francesca paled and burst into tears. "My house? What do they want?"

~

Young constables always attract attention. Today was no different. A small group of teenage girls stood close to the Police bull-wagon, flirting and giggling as they waited at the nearby bus stop.

"Uniforms," Francesca mumbled indicating the scene to Johnno, who nodded and shrugged. Guiding her elbow, he helped her through the front gate towards the small apartment. Francesca braced herself.

Surprisingly everything seemed in order on the lower floor. A trio of framed JH Lynch prints caught Johnno's eye, as it did every time he entered the small terrace. He loved gawking at those beautiful, tantalising women naked except for their suggestive expressions.

A quick check of the dining area and kitchen also showed no sign of disturbance. Van Gogh replicas hanging along the back wall brought their usual vibrancy to the small, simply furnished space. The coffee machine hummed in the corner, ready for breakfast activity. Everything in place, tidy and clean.

The detective climbed the wrought iron stairs that led to the mezzanine bedroom. From halfway he could see the mess, framed by the papered wall behind her sleek leather bed. The wall paper print of dramatically oversized charcoal etchings from a pale canvas depicted a botanical theme. The white linen bed cover was pulled from the bed, shoved to one side. A haphazard pile of pillows and cushions decorated the floor.

Francesca froze nearing the top of the stairs. Her bedroom had turned to chaos. Clothing and drawers spilled out onto the floor. The laptop sat in the middle of her bed, open and blinking an unfamiliar screen saver.

Francesca made her way to the bed, raising her hand to her mouth in astonishment, as Johnno came to stand beside her. The identical image of the holy card they had seen at Lightning Ridge, complete with a bloody finger print and the word TRAITOR ran in a loop.

Francesca moved closer to Johnno for protection and looked around, feeling faint. "Johnno," she whispered. "Lo non sono un traditore. I am not a traitor. I don't live by the code of the Mafia." Her eyes rolled backwards as the room was sucked of its air and started swimming.

Francesca felt the hardness of the timber floor rise up to meet her cheekbone, splitting the delicate skin above her eyebrow.

"Francesca! Francesca! Come on Movie Star. Wake up." The detective heard a distant sound and rallied herself towards it. "Oh dear, look at you. No good for your looks babe."

Johnno checked the oozing split and wondered what the doctor would say when he turned up for the second time that morning, this time needing stitches. Locating his hankie he applied pressure, propping her against the end of the bed.

Someone had inserted a golf ball under her skin above the right eye. The same bullet-grazed shoulder had hit the floor unchecked, and in the intense pain she squinted. Francesca tasted blood and felt her swollen top lip as it puckered under her nose.

Her sorry face searched Johnno's expression bewilderingly. She could hardly see and although her mouth opened and closed, no words would come out.

"Shh babe. Take it easy. You just fainted and hit your head. Looks like you split your lip and we need to get you back to the doc for some stitches. You're in the wars today babe huh?"

A General Duty cop appeared at the top of the stairs. "Everything all right?"

"Yeah, she just fainted. It's been a big morning. Get me a drink of water would you please for Detective Salucci. And a box of tissues." Johnno continued to apply pressure to her head that was bleeding profusely.

"Let's take a look at this." The blood was slowly thickening and a horrendous bruise was forming. Checking for concussion he asked, "How many fingers Francesca?"

"Three," she mumbled. It hurt to raise her eyes.

"Good. What day is it?"

"Tuesday."

"Excellent. Am I the most handsome man you have ever seen?"

Francesca gave a wry smile and tried to nod. "Yes." Pain shot through her skull and she paled.

"Correct."

He waited on the floor with her a few more minutes. When her colour returned he helped her stand.

"I'm ok. I need to use the bathroom. Might have a shower."

"Not likely young lady. But you can freshen up before I take you back to the surgery. That head is going to need stitches. I'm leaving the door open, just in case."

Francesca showered quickly anyway; the warm water providing an antidote for her morning's misadventures. It gently streamed down her back and she swayed slightly. A combination of pills and delayed shock, her body started to shut down for a drowsy sleep.

"Everything all right in there?" Johnno stepped into the open doorway, averting his eyes.

"Si." Came the quiet response as she stepped out of the small enclosure.

Francesca watched in a trance as a small piece of paper floated to the ground. After reaching for her towel it had appeared, reminding her of a falling autumn leaf. She bent to pick it up, calling to Johnno who entered the small room like a shot, helping her upright before she fainted again.

"This fell out of my towel." Together they examined the note that was written in a lover's hand. It read: "No time. Be safe love. Will find you when safe for both of us. Yours, N."

The detectives looked at each other in amazement.

Francesca flipped the page over. The back was the treasured old photograph of them both. He'd been through her mother's jewellery box. The sickening swelled in her stomach and her feelings of violation spewed into the toilet beside her. Francesca burst into angry tears. Nothing was sacred. She wiped her face on the towel and held it to her eye. Her head wound started pounding again.

"That's Nic's writing," she said quietly. "He must have come after the boat thing. He was here with them. He used my picture."

"Get dressed. Put some clothes in a bag. You can't stay here. You're out until this is sorted. I'll call the boss. This is an entirely new situation," Johnno directed.

"I also have this," she said. Having placed it in the back of the bathroom drawer for safekeeping, Francesca handed him the motel card. Johnno was speechless.

He immediately deployed a crew to the address.

~

"Gav's away. You can stay in here." Johnno opened the office door. "I'll find a pillow and blanket and you can rest on the lounge here until we sort out what to do with you."

Francesca was too tired to argue. He shut the blind and after a short hunt, located the remote for the small television concealed in the cupboard. He disappeared, returning with some bedding and a cup of steaming hot chocolate.

"Thanks Johnno." Francesca looked up at her friend and colleague gratefully.

"Come here you." Johnno's gravelly voice strained as he gathered her into his arms. She looked an absolute shocker. A nice shade of purple around her right eye was beginning to spread below the golf ball swelling on her forehead. A nasty bloody line cut her bottom lip where her teeth had pierced.

"You are safe here and now. No one can get you in police headquarters. You need to rest. The pills will help. Then we can talk about where you can go to lay low for a few weeks."

He carefully placed her on the lounge and covered her with the blanket. Gently shutting the door behind him, he dialled Ruthie from the situation room.

"Ruthie, Francesca's hurt. She'll be ok but I need to clear her out of Sydney. Would you try and get a hold of Sinclair for me? He's on leave, up in Queensland somewhere. Ask him to call me please. Not sure what time I'll get home tonight. Love you too. Hey babe. Thanks."

Johnno looked at a recent photo of his partner and Nicholas in Italy. It was a postcard for Valentine's Day. Two lovers in each other's arms framed by an ancient structure and abundant garden. Surely now she would see sense. Bastard.

He threw the photo on the pile of papers in disgust, and focused on the investigation. Before long, a knock at the door interrupted his thoughts.

"Johnno, we found the boat. Also, fingerprints have gone into overdrive to confirm a person of interest in Francesca's flat. Looks like one set of prints belongs to Gino Castello. Still searching the databases for the second set but wanted you to know."

"Yeah, well we can certainly make an educated guess there," he growled. "Come on, I'll drive. You fill me in on the way."

He strode the corridor to the lift, pausing at the secretary's desk.

"Susie, would you pop your head in on Francesca for me please before you head off this arvo? Going out for a while. On my mobile. Just tell Francesca that I'll be back with something for her to eat a bit later. There's a TV in her room to keep her company. I doubt she'll stir though, she's pretty whacked."

Water police had secured the boat. By the time he arrived there was quite a crowd. Forensics as well as the coroner waited by the dock and as a news truck pulled up, Johnno strode over to the young reporter.

"Mate, you might think this is a great story but let me ask you to choose your words wisely because your actions from now on will have a huge impact on our investigations. How did you come to know about this so soon anyway?"

"G'day Johnno. Anonymous tip off, you know we can't reveal the source." He glanced at the boat, noticing the two bodies slumped in the seats. Dead bodies turned his gut. "Looks gruesome. What do you know?"

"Nothing. Just arrived. Boat was found drifting in the river and causing minor problems for ferry services."

"Is it linked to the recent OMCG shootings in Sydney and Melbourne? I mean, Ares are responsible for that shooting in North Sydney last week. Could be a Warlords retaliation," the reporter speculated, craning his neck to try and get a good look around the bulky detective.

"Does it look like a motorbike to you? I don't think the OMCG gangs are using boats."

Johnno wanted to steer him off that train of thought. The last thing they needed was a rogue reporter running around fabricating stories promoting more fear and panic so he took another tack.

"Look mate, I know you have a job to do, so let me say as soon as we can, we will feed you information that will help you present the story of your life. You might be able to help us. An opportunity to bring viewers on board."

The journo puffed his chest, instantly handing Johnno his contact details. "Sure Johnno, that sounds great. Here's my mobile number. Cheers."

"How's Joanna Stevens these days? Is she still in senior management?"

"Joanna? Yes. Yes she is." The young gun wondered how the detective knew his boss.

"Tell her Jonathan McCrae said don't be a stranger."

"Yeah? I'll be sure to pass that on."

Johnno returned to the boat. Two male occupants deceased. Of Mediterranean appearance. Neither resembled Nicholas Delarno. The bright yellow and black combination fitted the description given by Francesca.

He stood on the edge of the jetty, using his phone to take a picture of the deceased. Perhaps Francesca had seen the men before and could help with the identification and context.

Using the zoom, Johnno zeroed in on the bodies, looking for any identification markings. A professional hit, as he would have expected from someone like Gino Castello, would leave no traces of identification, but Johnno looked anyway.

"What's that?" Johnno asked the forensic police who by now had boarded the vessel.

"What?"

"That! Wedged in the seat near the controls."

The senior photographed the evidence in situ and with gloved hands pulled the item from the seat. He beamed at Johnno.

"Well! Well! Looks like a mobile phone to me! The gods are smiling on you detective."

Johnno beamed. "Sweet! Let me know when you're done."

Leaving his partner to co-ordinate the crime scene, Johnno headed back to the office, via the pub to pick up some dinner for Francesca and give Ruthie a squeeze. When this was over they were going on a holiday, he would make sure of it.

At the office he found Francesca awake and watching the nightly news broadcast. The breaking story featured the runaway boat on the harbour and the disruption it had caused to the ferry services. No mention of the bodies, thank goodness. He had won that round. Johnno sent a quick text of gratitude to the journo.

"One chicken schnitzel and chips and gravy, madam! Plus a side salad and for sweets, sticky date pudding complete with an extra dose of butterscotch sauce and vanilla ice cream."

"Thanks." She cast an eye over the food wishing she had the appetite to eat.

"They found the boat then," Francesca said. "What can you tell me…?"

"Two deceased males on board. My gut says they are representatives from the Nero group. Professional hit. I took some photographs. When you're up to it, I thought you might like to take a look."

"Do you think Nicholas is still alive?" she asked hopefully.

"Don't know," Johnno replied absently, thinking he'd like to string the guy up by the nuts.

"Do you think he killed them to get away?"

"Was he on the boat with them this morning?" Johnno couldn't believe she still cared whether the bastard was alive or dead.

"I don't know. I can't be sure. I thought I heard him yell out to run, and then a fight. But I couldn't see, I was more looking out for myself at that stage," she said, her tone doing nothing to ease the pressure mounting between them.

"Finger prints have identified that Gino Castello was in your home today," he continued. "The second set of prints is still in the process. The blood drip found on the note hasn't been traced yet."

She nodded, concentrating.

"We are assuming it belongs to Nicholas Delarno because of the photograph and you have identified his writing, but it may well be one of these guys. We found a mobile phone Francesca. At the scene this afternoon. Hidden near the controls. As soon as it arrives downstairs I'll order a data dump from the provider. Hopefully it will give us something more or at least confirm our suspicions," he said, matter-of-factly.

"Why would Nic call me a traitor and write a note to say I was in danger? It doesn't make sense." Francesca asked.

She was back on Delarno again. Johnno wondered if she'd even heard him. In astonishment he looked directly at her. "He's reaching out to you Francesca. He wants you exposed so that you will turn to him. Why? I don't know."

Johnno faced her fully. He couldn't hide the exasperation in his voice.

"But when I find the bastard, be assured I'll be asking."

She was too tired to argue with his grumbling. "I've been thinking. I know where I can go and be safe."

"Yeah?" At last a sentence that didn't feature that bastard Delarno.

"We have a river house in Queensland. Our old family farm that my sister, Luciana and I bought off dad so he could move into town. I can be safe there. It's secluded and there's one small community around it. Any stranger will stand out like dogs' balls. I haven't been back in years. I think it's time. It will help with my recovery and I can think clearly there. We have satellite access so I'll still be in touch."

"I don't like the thought of you out there exposed."

"Well I can't very well stay in Gav's office until this is over. I tell you, the community is tight. Any stranger within a ten mile radius and I will know."

Her sudden irritability surprised Johnno. It was no use arguing with her when her mind was made up. Besides, he couldn't think of another suitable solution.

"Where exactly is this place?"

"It's called Wild Dog Creek."

CHAPTER 22

Two elderly Italian gentlemen sat at the usual table outside the café, sipping a morning cappuccino and discussing the day's events. At a glance, two old friends, enjoying each other's company in the spring sunshine.

"This is ridiculous. How can she just disappear? Find her father, he'll tell you." In a low voice, Silvio spoke in rapid Italian dialect.

Gino nodded and Silvio continued. "The Chinese are furious she escaped. We look foolish. I will not put up with another ultimatum from Lee Wong about her involvement. Whilst ever she's alive and close to this operation, he thinks she's a risk to our success. I know he's right to be wary of her. I know that girl like my own daughter."

Gino nodded in agreement. "I'll make enquiries. The family's in hiding too. But not to worry, I'll get her."

Curiously Silvio turned to Gino. "I took a call this morning. From my cousin in Rapallo. He was full of praise. Congratulated me on turning a Salucci. He said that the Commissions were impressed with my son. Particularly with the way Nicholas handled her. She was completely compliant."

Silvio's eyes narrowed, noticing Gino's wary eyes and his hand resting gently on a hidden blade.

"You were in Rapallo Gino. What were your observations of them?"

"I noticed some obedience. Let's just say she is no Cristiana. Surely you are not weakening to her too?" Gino asked.

"Of course not! But I'm thinking of my son. Perhaps Nicholas was right. The dissatisfaction within the Commission is limited to Seta and Nero and the few who follow them. That small group has always been trouble. Perhaps it's time to eliminate those risks as well. Teach their families a lesson. My son may be many things but he's no liar." Silvio glanced over Gino's manner and looked out towards the shore break. "You mean to slit my throat old friend? You too have turned to Seta?"

"No Capo. Of course not. I serve you as my father served yours," Gino responded in compliance. He was not stupid enough to remove his hand straight away, instead letting the arm relax in the pose.

"Then get rid of her, once and for all. We will find another one to take over the case and put Chi You out of the picture when the time is right. Always, new opportunities arise. Spare Nicholas. I want to see what more he can do for our group when he has added responsibilities. And no Salucci to distract him."

Gino nodded again. "As you wish."

Silvio continued wistfully, remembering the plans he had masterminded since his children's youth.

"Francesca has not turned out as we were hoping. Cristiana would have shaped her, had we pressured Stefano more during the girl's teenage years. She's been strengthened by police training and grown much like her father. Maybe we should have targeted her sister instead." Silvio shrugged, adding thoughtfully, "But then, Francesca was always her father's favourite. It was more prudent I chose her."

The two men sat back in their chairs, watching the surf break over the sand. At last, Silvio stood. Turning his proud head to Gino, he said, "my son will get over her soon enough."

CHAPTER 23

Francesca leant forward, resting her head against the seat in front, feebly trying to ease the piercing pain that threatened to blow her head off her shoulders. Her eardrums screamed an agonised protest. Desperately she stuck at them with her fingers, trying to ease the building pressure.

Squeezing her eyes shut momentarily, she pushed sweaty palms along her skimpy shorts. The white loose tunic stuck to her back as anxiety antagonised nervous energy.

The small aircraft suddenly dipped as it hit another air pocket. Francesca turned to face the tiny window. Treetops seemed tantalisingly close to the lowered wheels. Peering through the porthole, she could easily make out the rocky terrain beneath the tree canopy. They dropped altitude again as a clearing with a short runway spread out around them.

Still travelling at speed, the aircraft shifted, audibly protesting as the wheels landed heavily on the tarmac, jolting passengers roughly in their seats. The cabin was quiet. The aircraft twisted again, groaning in an attempt to brake hard. Surrounding them, the deafening roar of the propellers, its horrendous noise vibrating through the seats.

They were catapulting to the end now. The momentum pushing them forward at breakneck speed. They would never stop in time. The trees they'd almost skimmed from the air surrounded the short runway. A tiny mistake could have them careering into thick bush land at the end of the single bitumen strip. Every fibre within Francesca pressed on an imaginary brake at her feet bidding the plane to halt as it skidded, broadsiding in an effort to slow.

Abruptly, the plane stopped. Francesca headed face first into the seat in front, the seatbelt catching her across the hips. Momentum threw her backwards and she winced in pain as her arm and elbow slammed into the window casing.

In slow motion they turned sharply towards the small terminal, making the short distance at a snail's pace. The contrast was not lost on Francesca's fragile state. Relief almost made her burst into hysterical laughter. The whole scenario made her think of the cops loading an offender into the back of the truck after a robust confrontation …

"Now watch your head."

When they finally came to a standstill, a collective sigh escaped the cabin. Silently, the small group of passengers exited the open doorway, curtly nodding to the air hostess whose fake smile remained etched from years of practice.

Francesca stood briefly at the top of the stairs, regaining balance and composure. The pain within her ears had been replaced by a fiery burn in her jaw. She pulled the cap down onto her head, tucking her pony tail to the side. Dark glasses covered the bruising to her eyes and face. Instinctively she grabbed at her throbbing arm to check for seepage from the hidden bandage. Her skin was wet. The wound had started bleeding again thanks to the bumpy landing.

Heat rising from the tarmac blasted Francesca's face. It burnt her nostrils with each breathy intake. She inhaled it deeply, a great gulp of the warm humid air. Her throat caught it and tasted familiar molasses. Ripe sugar cane. It was good to be home. Francesca walked quickly to catch the tail end of the passengers, stepping in pace to blend with the crowd of tourists.

A quick glance for security purposes and she gathered her bags from the trolley. She was alone. In the makeshift car park, as instructed, her old land cruiser beckoned from the back corner. Reaching behind the bullbar, she located the keys. Francesca slid into the familiarity of the worn seat and took in the smell of grease and dust. She smiled to herself, a release of joy and freedom. She was home ... almost. With another cursory glance for unwelcome company, she turned towards the highway heading north. Ahead a long, lonely drive. Destination, Wild Dog Creek.

Familiar surrounds brought comfort to her weariness, easing the tensions of the journey, as each sugar cane plantation rolled into the next. The rhythm of tyres on bitumen, combined with the isolated silence of hours on the road, urged her rambling thoughts to remember and process. This ten-year crusade was done.

At the last town Francesca stocked up with long-life stores, fresh ingredients and fuel. Emergency supplies could be bought at the corner store at Wild Dog Creek, if she couldn't get back to town. On a whim she bought some potted herbs and vegetable seedlings. As a kid she'd hung about in the vegetable patch with her father. The satisfaction of growing fresh produce would ease the boredom of endless days of isolation.

Her nerves had calmed considerably since the flight from hell, softened by childhood familiarity and solitude. She texted Johnno to assure him she was safe and continued on, checking the rear view mirror again. No followers. It was comforting.

One hour later a discreet right-hand turn from the highway led to a bush track marking the entrance to the property. Pulling up at the locked gate, Francesca looked about relieved to be home at last.

"Honey I'm home," she said to the gentle breeze picking up the smells of salt spray and lemon-scented gum trees. She breathed it deeply, smiling about nothing in particular. This was her magical healing place. A haven that had given her freedom to cry her eyes out and whoop with joy. Through the towering eucalypts she could just make out the wide verandas of the low built Queenslander homestead, freshly painted and gleaming in the afternoon sun.

No one lived in the house full-time these days; it was more a holiday shack for the family, offering privacy and activities amongst which horse riding, fishing, crabbing, exploring and swimming. In the evenings, old-fashioned fun centred on board games, cards or an eclectic array of well-read books. A radio picked up the local station and the occasional two-way from cruising fishing trawlers. A long stretch of sandy beach was about two miles east and reached by a dirt track that meandered through a tea tree scrabble of bushland.

Francesca's nieces had modernised the old home, insisting on an iPod docking station and a game console hooked up to an enormous television in the living room. An array of antennae and satellite dishes on the roof helped with internet coverage and television reception.

She unlatched the gate, startling a family of kangaroos grazing peacefully on the vast lawn stretching before the house. They raised proud heads but made no attempts to flee. Behind them, the wide creek ebbed its way inland, gently passing the mangroves.

As the salty air filled her lungs, Francesca stretched her arms above her head and flexed, releasing some of the tension of the last few weeks. She rubbed around her aching right arm, seeking refuge under the huge frangipani close to the side steps.

During the summer months, the glorious heady scent of the flowers filled the night air. As an encore, towards the end of the season, a carpet of flowers would lazily form, laid at the feet of the thick branches and trunk.

The whole scene was quintessentially Queensland. She wondered what Nicholas would think. It certainly wasn't as grand as his Rapallo digs. But where this place lacked finesse, this one had spades of freedom, friendship and warmth. Would he lay her on a bed of flowers under her favourite tree and make love to her? Was he even thinking about her now? She shook her mind to the present. Thinking like that about Nic was not going to help her.

The front lattice door squeaked in protest, as usual, when she latched it back. She stepped onto the veranda and made way to her sleep-out bedroom. With windows along both sides, a small hanging cupboard and chest of drawers, it was simple but perfect.

Francesca looked towards the river and opened the windows wide. From her room she could see straight up the river, towards the beach, for about a half a mile before it bent in a casual way. She ran her fingers along the faded pink, chenille bedspread and put her luggage on the bare timber floorboards. Tomorrow morning her room would be the first to greet the sun.

She wandered through the old house, checking the rooms and picking up the occasional item, remembering its place in her heart. Her nieces must have visited with her father. The dates on the works of art stuck on their bedroom walls indicated the last school holidays. Francesca found herself in the kitchen and filled the old-fashioned kettle, setting the gas alight to prepare water for a cup of tea. She headed out to the truck to begin unloading.

The process was demanding on her aching body and fragile mind. As much as she tried to focus on the task at hand, she couldn't help but feel a creeping desolation. It was akin to wading through a muddy memory and this time she did not have her work or team to pull her out. Francesca was completely alone.

The kettle whistled impatiently as the girl hauled the last box up the stairs. A case of red wine was left on the veranda to stow later.

"Alright! Alright!" she muttered before pouring the steamy liquid into the china pot. She filled the pale green and white cupboards with supplies. The décor belonged to another era, as did the rose-patterned curtains, faded and thin, edging the white, painted windows.

A red laminex table with silver edging and ten vinyl chairs of varying colours and styles dominated the centre of the large space. A crazy arrangement of tea sets and trinkets decorated the hutch along one wall. Mostly in a floral theme. They reminded her of an abundant spring garden.

Flicking on the radio to ward off late afternoon loneliness, Francesca headed to the outside room, hot tea in hand. She missed her family and her friends. More to the point, she missed that she could not just pick up the phone for a chat.

On the road today she was focused on what she needed to do, where she needed to be and arriving at the river home before nightfall. Now, with all that behind her, what? How long would she be in this solitude?

Her family was safe. It was a huge relief, but it meant radio silence with them. Johnno refused to discuss the case with her. The sounds of the fist fight on the boat haunted her but not as much as Nicci's last words, "Run! Francesca, run!"

A light breeze lifted off the river and brushed Francesca's cheek and the sensitive spot above her eye. She checked around her eye socket, now a mottled blend of greens and yellows. The stitches could come out in two days. Her arm needed attention. Francesca popped another two painkillers and placed her hand gingerly over the bandage. How many pills was that now? Who cares, she thought irritably.

Francesca's thoughts came back to Nic. She'd spent the last few days crying her eyes out over him. She held her teacup close, wrapping long fingers around the pink rosebud design. In the heat and humidity of the late afternoon, she sought comfort in her mother's pretty cup.

It was time. Confronted by her anxiety and the solitary confinement, it was time to deal with the emotional black pit that was Nicholas Delarno. It was the only way she could move forward. Using the isolation to sort through her emotions was her only chance to be of any use to Johnno and her family.

She'd given Nicholas everything in Rapallo. Blindly believing the pretty words of fate and destiny he'd so freely shared with her. He'd used the knowledge of her love to manipulate her actions. To compromise her integrity amongst her friends and piers.

The Prosecution had adjourned the Chi You matter in the hope of getting clear air. Who would believe her evidence now anyway? Francesca felt the intense pressure squeeze her chest. She'd played the unwitting pawn in a game without rules. A game she'd not even realised she was playing until now.

Tea was not enough. The first bottle was a pinot. She breathed the complex top notes, filling the tea cup to the brim. She took a long sip. She swirled the ruby liquid around the cup, watching it rise up to the rim and then subside. She sculled the contents and poured another.

"How can I still love you?" she asked herself quietly in the late afternoon. "In fact, why do I even care about you at all? You've treated me with contempt my whole adult life."

Yet she wanted his arms around her, needed his comfort. It made absolutely no sense. Francesca simply could not understand the hold he had on her. An invisible binding that held her to him. A dependence.

She looked beyond the veranda to the white-barked trees glowing like candles in the afternoon sun and breathed out his name.

"Nicholas," she said. "My safety net when things get tough. Or when I'm lonely. I use your memory to give me strength. To help me feel alive when I can't feel anything at all."

Just to look at him dissolved any rational thinking. When he touched her, her body reacted on its own volition. Should he ask, she would comply. Attraction and obligation fuelled by her upbringing with the family and the statements of her father blended together with her own stupid daydreams.

All those lovers and none made her feel the way he did when he simply noticed her. It was nonsensical.

And she was daydreaming about him now. Remembering Rapallo. How easy it was to love him, even after so much time apart. How he'd picked up where they'd left off years before. And this time he didn't hide their affair. It was like their love for each other transcended time and space. A storybook romance come to life. Francesca paled. Perhaps he had no choice but to seduce her.

"Oh my God," she suddenly thought, sitting upright. "How could I be so stupid?"

Mortified, she covered her mouth with her hands. She knew exactly what it was all about now. She knew the protocol. Mafia instruction. There were three tests. Submission. Trust. Loyalty. Traditional guarantees belonging to an organised crime network. She'd been put on show for the benefit of the Italian Commissions. At the hand of Nicholas Delarno.

Three tests. Rape. Infidelity. Threats to life.

Francesca screamed into the silence, hurling the tea cup into the darkness. Her shoulders shook with anger and she sprang to her feet, pacing the deck like a demented warrior.

Finally she collapsed to the floor, pushing her head against the timber panelling. She let the edge of the tongue and groove lining slide up under her skull and found the pressure points. It hurt like hell. She persisted until the pain subsided.

Staring into the darkness she waited. The empty wine bottle and the full crate beside it got her attention. Oblivion. It sounded like a nice place to hide.

Upon the night air, the tempo of her mind dulled and Francesca found a murky clarity. She pulled a folded piece of paper from her pocket. The list she had compiled in the airport lounge.

It was headed: 'Francesca's Checklist for Wild Dog Creek.'

- Find a way to get over Nicholas
- Let Johnno do his job
- Be safe and recover
- Track the investigation and try to help where you can
- Set a new life plan

"Number one. Tick," she said and contemplated the rest.

"Oblivion." She re-read the list. "You know what. Oblivion, you're not on my list. How could I forget you? Such a lovely place to be."

She paused, staring for a long time into the darkness as her mind tossed the notion around. At last she focused on number five. Set a new life plan.

Into the night she called, "My name is Francesca Salucci and I am an ... I'm strong. I'm wilful and I refuse to give in."

And Nicholas? What about him.

"Well, Nich-o-las De-larno. You're fucked. And I'm done. I'm done with you."

For too long she had planned her life around that man. Here was her chance. A chance to live a life without him. And by God she was going to take it.

She had the strength to walk that path. She'd done it before. And now she would do it again. She thought about Chi You and the little boy who'd died for their cause. She'd managed to put aside her personal horror to bring closure to that group. Court case or not, that group was significantly weakened by her determination and persistence.

The only way to deal with Nicholas was detachment. To free herself of the emotional bindings once and for all. It was time to take the first step. She could be a victim or she could fight. She made a new list.

- Recovery.
- Detachment.
- Dissect the Delarno involvement with this case.
- Remove him from my life.
- Fight. Her family and her freedom relied upon it.

"I choose to fight!" Francesca called to the night, clenching her fists in the air. In that instant Francesca felt a release of emotion within her. She breathed a little more deeply, staggered to the bedroom and promptly passed out.

CHAPTER 24

She is safe. All good. Sinclair McCrae returned from his makeshift post and checked in with a text. The river passed between him and the homestead. He'd been told it could be accessed by a small footbridge. He returned to his camp further back behind the ridge and stoked the hot coals surrounding the camp oven.

He was a few miles from her by foot. It was not an ideal arrangement, but it was the best he could do in such a short time period. He'd driven all night and most of the day to get there. Come morning he would seek a more suitable location.

The late afternoon circus of parrots darted amongst the leaves chattering about the new arrivals to their home. Below, the deep, dark river calmly reflected the last rays of sunshine.

"Won't be long now mate," he said to his friend lying on the ground after the long hike. "Then I might join you in the sleep stakes old mate."

His mate groaned and stretched but remained prone.

"Great company you are," Sinclair grumbled good-naturedly.

Sinclair searched the heavens for the first star, the same ritual since childhood almost every night. It was a race between him and his brother to find it and make a wish. Even in the most dangerous places he'd sought the star. Keep us safe he had prayed every night on his overseas deployments.

Here in the safety of the Australian bush he prayed again to the star … keep us safe. He did not know what the future held for him and the girl.

Only when the damper was done and an enamel plate swollen with stew, did his mate sit up and look interested. Hopeful brown eyes, adjusting from the slumber, looked up to his master, golden eyebrows twitching as he glanced from the laden plate to Sinclair. A heavy tail thumped on the leafy ground.

"Here you go, I didn't forget you."

Sinclair placed the bowl of food near his foot and sat down on the tree stump, patting the kelpie pup's head. Huge gum trees, their strong arms reaching towards a dusky sky, pressed themselves to the moon and stars. By day, their long branches stroked the sunshine and their ruby leaves almost sparkled. He breathed their smell deeply, listened and watched.

When the darkness befell the silent camp, he moved back to the vantage point to watch her. After she moved to what he assumed was the bedroom, he returned to his camp and checked the remnants of the fire. Tomorrow morning he would take a look at that footbridge across the river for himself. Judging the amount of wine and pills she had consumed tonight, that girl would be lucky to be up by lunchtime.

Exhausted from the long drive and the humid hike up the small hill to make camp, the soldier rolled out a double swag and drifted into a dreamless sleep, leaving Chief on guard for any unwelcome company.

~

Francesca awoke to the warbling magpie sounds and morning sunshine streaming through her windows. She rubbed her temple and the dull headache that was quickly emerging. An insistent growl in her hollow stomach reminded her that food was the number one priority.

It was then she noticed it. Over coffee and breakfast, the relief. A weight had lifted from her shoulders. Somehow she felt stronger this morning. Her body itched for activity. Last night's revelation and twelve hours solid sleep had done wonders. An amazingly calm feeling surrounded her and the stresses of the real world seemed a million miles away.

"I'm going to make the most of it," she thought. "Before sadness wraps its bony fingers around my heart again."

Strolling along the veranda she paused to look at the protective hill on the neighbouring farm. Just inside the boundary of the two properties a small swimming hole was fed by a freshwater stream and pooled in a rock basin. In the dry season the stream trickled in and the basin became rank. This year the area had received plenty of rain and that little stream would have filled the basin with cool, fresh water. In fact it could still be running.

When Francesca was young, she and her sister would build small cubby houses on the ridge from broken branches. Spending hours spying on the house and the comings and goings of visitors. Sometimes making up stories to entertain their dolls. From the peak, on a clear day you could almost see the ocean. Well, at least as a kid, you said you could.

She bent to pick up the list from the floor and glanced at the hill again. Some old-fashioned rock pool swimming and exploring was the best start for her recovery.

From the farmhouse it was a five-mile hike to the highest point of the hill and about two miles to the water hole. She crossed the small tidal footbridge that marked the end of their property. In high tide, the bridge was under water. One had to keep track of time. Up ahead, the familiar, well-marked route gave way to a motorbike track leading to the top of the first small ridge.

Francesca marched through the invisible Salucci - Westaway property boundaries. Bev Westacott, a silver-haired lady of the land whom she deeply admired, managed the massive holdings with the help of a few seasonal workers and a foreman.

It was about the time of year that Bev would have extras on board and Francesca wondered if she might help, once her arm was fully healed. It would certainly fill in the lonely days ahead. Tonight she would make a phone call and ask.

At a small clearing Francesca stopped to rest. There was no rush and her energy levels were probably not up to her enthusiasm quite yet. Humidity amongst the undergrowth was heavy. Her head ached from the hangover and the tightness of the cap around her skull.

Pulling at the water bottle from her backpack, she drank greedily leaning against a large rock boulder. The sounds of the bush surrounded her, bringing comfort; the call of the storm bird echoed around the hills.

Today Francesca felt newfound clarity. It was as though she could finally observe and understand herself. Like an outsider looking in. Her mind travelled from loss and despair to a vision of life without Nicholas in a strange combination of fragility and determination. She supposed she was grieving.

Francesca could feel eyes watching her. Perhaps it was the wildlife. She hoped it wasn't a snake. She felt the same way about snakes as she did dead bodies. She shuddered.

Standing, she turned in the direction of the basin and saw, crouching in the undergrowth, the tan and black of a kelpie pup. It was in good shape. Probably belonged to Bev or one of her workers. They must be heading her way checking for strays. Perfect. A chance for her to ask if they needed a hand over at Westaway.

"Hello there fella. Pleased to meet you. My name is Francesca."

She bent low to draw him out, noticing the light tan markings above his eyes moving in a quizzical greeting. In the distance she heard someone whistling. She froze. What if it wasn't Bev? The tail on the dog started thumping wildly and she knew whoever was coming through the bush must be his owner.

She decided to meet this arrival head on and walked towards the noise. She pulled the backpack in close and chose a sturdy stick to help her along the track.

"Shit! You frightened the hell out of me. What are you doing up here?" Sinclair's startled greeting was not how he had anticipated his initial meeting with the girl.

"I could ask you the same question. This is private property. I trust this is your friend?" She pointed to the kelpie sitting happily beside her.

"Chief! Come here boy." The dog moved quietly to his side and sat.

"Looking for something?" Francesca asked, wanting to establish how he had found himself in this isolated area. Chief was an unusual name for a working dog.

"Ah, yeah!" Sinclair tried to gather his thoughts, frustrated to be discovered on the very first day.

"Well there are no strays towards the river if you come from that way," she said, pointing at the track she had just crossed.

"No strays?" Sinclair wondered what the hell she was talking about.

"You know, stray calves," she insisted. "That's what you're looking for, isn't it?" She pressed her hand against the pistol hidden in her backpack.

"Oh! Yeah, right."

This conversation was going nowhere. He had to get out of there. Fast.

Francesca looked at the giant in front of her, dressed in fatigues and a camouflage T-shirt. Reddish blonde hair stuck out under his cap. He carried a backpack over one shoulder, which looked more like a small handbag next to his large frame. He was in good shape. His bicep curled as he pulled his cap off his head and ran a huge hand through spiky hair.

His face was open and friendly. Eyes of dark chocolate were fringed with chunky brown lashes under which a random splattering of freckles spilled across his nose. His strong chin and jaw protruded from a thickish neck. A rugby neck.

His perfectly formed lips had just the right amount of fullness; a sign of a giving nature, she thought. Even so, he looked like he would be more at home carrying an AK47 than locating lost calves. And yet Francesca felt the safest she'd ever felt. An instant connection. He looked at her, a little bemused.

"Francesca." She held out her hand. No need for surnames. She was, after all, trying to lay low. Besides, if she was going to have to work with him at Bev's, she'd better show some courtesy.

The dark sunglasses hid the bruising and stitches above her eye, but as he took her hand, she could not hide the wince that came over her, as renewed pain shot through her arm.

"Sinclair. Pleased to meet you Francesca." He took a gamble. "Look Francesca, I'm not working for Bev. I'm on leave. Up here for a bit, camping out. Taking a holiday away from it all."

He changed the subject. "It's a beautiful spot. So quiet."

Francesca smiled. "Well I must say you don't look like much of a ringer, not the types I've met anyway. Have you been here long?"

Leave, she thought, the language of cops.

"We arrived yesterday."

"We?" Francesca asked, masking the caution in her question. She was not too happy about having two men camping so close to her hideout.

"Yes. Chief and myself," he replied, and saw her relax a little.

"Oh. Well it's nice to meet you Sinclair. Enjoy your holiday."

She attempted to step around him.

"I'm on my way to the basin," she blurted, wondering what possessed her to reveal her destination.

"The basin! Fitting name. It's quite a place! Chief and I had a swim this morning, didn't we mate."

He bent down to ruffle the dog's head who looked upwards at the mention of his name. He was relieved she believed his story.

"I haven't been there for years. So it's full of freshwater then. Great," she chatted on. "Do you want to come along? I mean if you want company. You don't have to." The invitation was out her mouth before she could shove it back down her throat. Francesca mentally kicked herself in the shins.

"Sure! Would love to! It would be nice to have someone to talk to," he said, chuckling. "I mean, someone I can talk to and who can reply."

Such an instant ease between them. She mentally kicked herself again. She should've gone to the beach.

CHAPTER 25

Together they walked along the track; Francesca took the lead when it narrowed. Sinclair noticed she was travelling well despite her recent ordeal. Her favoured right arm was giving her discomfort and she clenched and released her fingers regularly.

He had sensed her intelligence from the start, but there was a kind of naivety about her he would never have imagined; an honest vulnerability that made him instantly protective regardless of his task ahead. He shrugged his shoulders to shake off the feeling. He was just there to babysit for a few weeks.

At last the tree cover opened up to reveal a hollowed-out rock pool, etched into the side of the mountain. Chief ran ahead and splashed into the pool, biting at unattainable dragonflies.

"He'd do that for hours," Sinclair said sheepishly as Francesca watched the pup in amusement.

They stood together on the threshold of the pool, Francesca impatient to strip off to her bikini. She was hot and the sweat that dripped between her breasts irritated her. She stalled for time, suddenly feeling self-conscious. The t-shirt covered the waterproof bandage on her arm. She could keep her cap and glasses on but to explain the bullet wound would be very awkward.

"How deep is it?" she asked, thinking she could quickly dive in and keep that part of her anatomy hidden under water.

"Not enough that you can dive… about up to your elbows I expect. You going in?"

"Might just sit on the edge for a bit."

She peeled off her shorts, socks and boots and hoisted her t-shirt to a knot above the navel. She was wearing the bikini she had bought in Portofino; its gold trim and beading glinting in the morning sun. She sat on the edge of the basin with her legs, still tanned from the Italian sun, stretched out in front of her.

"Thought you said this was your favourite swimming hole," Sinclair goaded.

He was hot from the humidity, something he still needed to get used to after weeks of dry desert heat. Stripping off his shirt, he quickly lost his pants and boots, revealing swim shorts. She failed to keep her eyes off his muscular body.

He looked like a rugby flanker. She'd always thought they had the best physiques on the field. His height and build would warrant such a position. He waded in to his waist. Duck diving, he turned to face her, brushing the water from his eyes in one sweep of his huge hands. From the short distance she saw the twinkle of mischief in his eyes, and his lips twisted in an attempt to hide a threatening smile.

"Don't you splash me! I know that look."

"C'mon Francesca. Would I do that? I'm a gentleman you know… not." He flicked the water towards her, dousing her head to toe.

"Right! You're on, mister."

She stripped off her shirt and ploughed through the water, her arms pushing hard to create waves. Sinclair dived and ducked out of their way, his agility out-manoeuvring her feeble attempts. Francesca laughed.

"That's not fair. You're twice my size," she protested after he soaked her with a single-arm move, thwarting her attack.

"That's not my problem lady. You started it."

"I did not!" She looked at Chief. "Your Honour. If it pleases the court ..." she started her defence to which she received a face full of water that made her splutter.

"Nothing noteworthy to say Counsellor? Don't try and influence this judge. He's on my payroll."

Chief barked and continued to chase dragonflies, his tail wagging in enjoyment.

"Wait! I have to stop. My arm hurts. I need to sit down."

She waded to the edge and sat with her waist and legs submerged, holding her arm close to her chest. Rocking back and forth slightly, the pain numbed her brain.

"Ha! Go the sympathy vote," he scoffed.

Her face had lost colour.

"Francesca are you all right?"

She could feel her face going numb and her head beginning to spin. Any minute now she would pass out.

"There are painkillers in my bag. Would you get them for me please?"

"Sure thing babe." Sinclair immediately strode to the small backpack before sitting beside her on the water's edge. "Here."

Francesca smiled and said wryly, "Thanks. Damaged goods."

She took the pills as he propped her against his warm chest until the pain subsided. "War wound. Comes with the territory."

"Tell me about it," he replied and turned to show her a scar that grazed his hip. The exit wound had made a mess behind it across his lower back. "How is the nerve pain?"

"Bad."

"Hmm. It gets better or you just get used to it ... I haven't figured it out yet. We'll just sit here for a while and enjoy the sun."

She nodded. Obviously her brain was more ready to move on than her body. She sat leaning against him in the shallow water. Finches and blue wrens darted to the pool taking little sips of water.

He remained silent, letting her recover in her own time. After a while, the grip on her damaged arm relaxed. Colour returned to her face.

"Can you stand?" he asked. "There, I'll help you."

"Thanks."

"You'd better eat something with those," he said, referring to the pills she'd swallowed. "Or we won't get you back down the mountain."

"I have some food in my backpack," she said, her voice regaining its strength.

He noticed her slight accent for the first time.

"I have a better idea. Come to my camp and we can have damper and golden syrup. It's not far. By the time you finish that apple we'll be there." He handed her the pink lady and whistled Chief. "Time to go mate."

Sinclair took the lead, periodically turning to check on the girl's progress. Chief trotted along beside her, keeping pace and looking up to her when Sinclair turned around. If she hadn't been in so much pain, Francesca would have burst into laughter at the sight of owner and dog checking on this stranger's welfare.

~

"Take a seat," he said pointing to a nearby stump in the shade at the tidy campsite.

"Thanks. Sorry to be such a downer. It's been a rough couple of weeks." She removed her cap and glasses fearing her head would split in two; the headache that was developing could take no restrictions. She took another long drink of water, hoping her injuries were not too obvious.

Next she pulled out the ponytail and let the weight of her hair collapse on her shoulders. She ruffled out the tangled mess of curls down her back. At least she could have brushed it this morning.

Sinclair tried to hide his shock at the stitches and yellow skin around her eye. He squatted in front of her makeshift chair, his expression barely concealing his concern.

"Those stitches look like they are about ready to come out. Are you right with them?"

"Yes. Time's up tomorrow." It had been the longest week of Francesca's life.

"Ok. Let me know if I can help."

"Thanks. You're very kind." She smiled weakly, paling again under the grips of the headache and nausea.

"I hope you're hungry."

He stood, taking the camp oven from the coals and resting it on a flat rock beside the fireplace. The leftover damper smelt divine. A great lump was placed on an enamel plate with lashings of butter and syrup and handed to Francesca.

"I have coffee," Francesca said, remembering the thermos in her backpack. "Do you have another cup?"

She poured the steaming liquid into two cups. They drank it black with sugar. Sinclair settled on the ground opposite her.

"Thank you Sinclair," she said after a while.

Chief breathed out in a small growl and flopped himself amongst the leaf litter behind Sinclair. Rolling his damp body in the dirt he then rested on his back, all four legs in the air. It was time for a nap.

Francesca laughed at the curious sight, she'd never seen a dog sleep that way before. She cleared the empty plates and cups, washing them in a small bucket of sudsy water that was the kettle come cooking pot.

"Well, I'd better get going," she announced reluctantly. "I've taken enough time out of your day. Thanks for the swim and the morning tea." Her loneliness was not his problem.

"Don't rush on my account."

He looked disappointed that she was taking leave.

"I have to get back."

"Oh?"

"You know make a few calls. Do a few jobs. Things like that." She was rambling. Must be the drugs. "How long have you and Chief been on holidays?"

"Over a month now."

"On your own?" she asked, surprised. "Christ you must be lonely."

He looked sheepish. "What else did you have planned for the rest of the day? After you've finished your jobs." he asked.

"Nothing really," she said. "What about you? Where were you headed when we met on the track?"

Sinclair blushed. He was looking to find a better scout point to watch over her, but he was not about to tell her that. "Just going for a walk, you know, to see where the track ended up."

"It ends at the river."

"Oh! Well where did you come from?" Sinclair asked. "Don't tell me you can walk on water too!"

She laughed. "No. There's a tidal footbridge made from a pile of rocks. It's exposed at low tide. My place's quite a way along the track, in the township down the road," she lied.

"Yesterday I noticed a little cottage across the creek. Is it far from here?" he asked.

She glanced at the spot and paled. "Not really. Why?"

"Thought I might pop in and let them know I'm in the area. You know, in case they see smoke from the campfire. So they don't get worried."

"Oh. I don't think anyone is there at the moment. The owners don't live there full time." She paused assessing him. "When we were kids, my sister and I used to build cubby houses here and spy on that house. Funny you should be here in this exact spot too."

Francesca avoided his eyes, she was a terrible liar. She hoped he hadn't seen her unload the truck yesterday. Thankfully, he seemed pretty happy settling further against the tree stump seat.

"Really? Yeah, funny that. Did you and your sister ever discover anything interesting?"

"No. Not really." She stared at the space behind him. He would be able to see straight through to her bedroom from that location, if he had binoculars, that is. She was being paranoid. He would have harmed her by now if that was his intent.

"We arrived last night so I haven't really had a good look around yet," he said. "I just caught a glimpse of the lights when I was gathering a bit of firewood.".

"Do you know where the other walking track leads to? The one beyond the basin?" He squatted and made himself busy checking the fireplace. He wanted to get her moving, distracted from the train of thought she was on. Too many questions.

"Yes actually, I do. It leads to some caves where the bushrangers used to hide. Years ago my sister Luciana found rock paintings on the walls left by the Aboriginals. I think that's what inspired her to become an archaeologist. It's an easy walk. Would you like to visit it Sinclair?"

"Paintings in caves? Absolutely. Lead the way m'lady."

~

The views around the small ridge were like a familiar song to Francesca. Stopping at vantage points to rest and enjoy a distant ocean view, the conversation resumed, flowing easily between them.

After a makeshift picnic at the caves' entrance, Sinclair went in search of the paintings while she napped in the shade, at last succumbing to rest.

When Francesca woke, the shadows were already too long and she knew it was well past the time to begin the long trek home. The tide had already blocked her way; she didn't fancy a swim in the darkness as well. She called to Sinclair who was milling in the caves' entrance and bent down to pat Chief on the head.

"Thanks for the great day," she said. "I'd better get going. Might see you around the traps if you come to town." She put her hand out to shake his. It was a formal gesture but a hug seemed just as inappropriate.

"A pleasure," he said, distractedly taking her proffered hand. "I'll walk you back to my camp." His desire to get to know her better hindered his judgement and now it was almost impossible for her to get home. He silently berated his lack of forethought. He should have insisted they start moving sooner. Not only had he compromised his task, but it was creating a curious friendship and feelings towards her he would do well to ignore. Now, they would have to spend the night together at his camp. As they reached the small makeshift set up he stalled. "Wait. Francesca, it's getting late. I think you need to make a decision."

I know, Francesca thought. She had to make a lot of decisions.

"You can stay here at the camp," he said, holding his hands up, palms out as a sign of reassurance. "I promise to be a gentleman. Or I can walk you down the track and help you across the river. Make sure you get home safe. Now, it's almost dark and I think we'll be halfway down the hill before we run out of light. Which is ok, I have a head lamp. So the darkness is not really an issue."

Christ, Sinclair thought, I*'m talking round in circles. I'm not even making sense to myself*. He continued none the less, "But here's the thing. I'm not keen on you getting home in the dark. And I'm worried about the height of that tide. We can take you home first thing in the morning if you decide to stay. You're a big girl. It's your decision. What would you like to do?"

Francesca thought about his unexpected offer. "How about I go home and you stay here."

"No," he said, shaking his head. "I don't think that's a good idea."

"Well, I don't want to put you out and both options you have presented do exactly that. I've been foolish. I know the tides. That path across the river is tricky at the best of times."

Francesca looked at his stony expression. She was not going to win this argument. She needed to make a decision.

"I guess I'll stay." She outwardly winced. "That way at least you're dry! And we're both inconvenienced."

And I'm armed. The thought of the pistol stowed in her backpack gave her comfort should her instincts prove wrong.

"Deal. Let's get organised then before we truly run out of light. Can you stoke up that fire for me please? There's a little pile of kindling over near that tree."

Sinclair worked quickly and before long they were hungrily enjoying tinned lamb and vegetable soup with leftover damper and billy tea. Francesca took on the clean-up duties again as Sinclair settled the campfire.

Soon, there was nothing left to do. It was too early to call it a day and both were still happy to chat about the events of the afternoon and their unlikely encounter. They lay on their backs, gazing at the stars in the clear night sky.

"I can see Orion... and the Southern Cross. Francesca can you see that satellite?" he asked tracking it across the sky with his finger.

"There's the Saucepan!" Francesca chimed in. She was a hopeless astronomer. "It's so beautiful, isn't it? Millions of light pinpricks in that milky haze."

"Sinclair! Shooting star ... quick make a wish!" She sat upright in the swag and turned to face the soldier.

"You know I've always wanted to learn a foreign language," he said. "Want to teach me some Italian?" It was the first thing he could think of. He sucked at learning languages but this way, he would have an excuse to keep a close eye on her and not rouse her suspicion.

"Sure. But you're not supposed to say the wish out loud." Francesca laughed and propped herself on her left elbow contemplating Sinclair sprawled out on a tarp beside her. It was unlikely he was comfortable, yet he didn't complain.

She lay back down, wriggled about, rolled to face him and finally lay on her back again. It wouldn't do and she could think of no other way to approach the subject than straight out asking.

"Sinclair?"

"Hmm?"

"Would you think I was forward if I insisted on you sharing this swag with me? I mean I am a gentlewoman."

Francesca's face reddened at the thought of how she must sound and she quickly blurted, "I just can't bear the thought of you lying on that tarp all night. I'm the intruder here. In the very least, let me sleep on the tarp."

"That's very kind of you Francesca. Thank you. But I can sleep anywhere." His eyes were already closed as he drifted.

"Please," she insisted with childlike innocence.

Sinclair turned to look at her forlorn face, inches from him and said, "Move over."

His exasperated response brought a radiant smile. He squashed in beside her. Francesca moved to the edge of the swag to give the giant as much room as she could.

He looked at her squashed against the side and laughed. "Surely that's not comfortable."

"I'm fine," she replied defiantly, thinking she would move to the tarp at the first opportunity.

"I hardly think so. This was your invitation. If either of us is going to get any sleep, you'd better move a bit closer honey. Promise I won't bite."

Francesca snuggled into him and rested her head against his shoulder. He wondered how long it had been since he'd felt the warmth of someone beside him. Too long obviously, as he realised she fitted perfectly into his shape.

"How's your arm?"

"Good," she lied. It was actually throbbing so much she thought she would pass out, but she didn't want the fuss. "Are you comfy?"

"Sure."

He placed a heavy arm firmly across the middle of her back, pressing her into him, his hand draped across her elbow to support her injury. She felt the relief almost immediately. His fingers wrapped around her small frame. She stilled close to him.

"Good night Sinclair." She planted an involuntary kiss of gratitude on his chest.

"Good night Francesca." He returned the favour on the top of her head.

CHAPTER 26

Francesca knocked on the bathroom door. "One egg or two?"

"Three, please!"

"Mushrooms?"

"Yes please."

She returned to the kitchen. Fresh from the shower and changed into a pretty summer dress, her damp hair was caught in a loose knot at the base of her neck. Tiny Venetian crystal drops hung from her earlobes catching the morning sun. She pottered around the kitchen, humming to the radio.

Happy to be heading home after the impromptu overnight camp, she'd made another risky decision: to tell the truth about the cottage across from the soldier's campsite. She was a terrible liar. The confession was softened with an invitation of a cooked breakfast and hot shower by way of apology. The soldier had promptly accepted. Francesca reasoned she had no reason to distrust him now.

"Perfect timing." Sinclair emerged from the shower, shaved and looking ready for action.

She felt her heart skip a beat at the sight of him dressed in fatigues.

A tight-fitting tee stretched across his massive chest. The sleeves bunched carelessly at his biceps.

She placed the laden plate in front of him, poured the tea and took the seat beside him.

"Thanks babe," he said, at once devouring the meal. He looked up guiltily as he popped the last bit of bread in his mouth. "Sorry, I was famished. That was delicious by the way."

Francesca watched in amazement and good humour as he stood to put four slices of bread in the toaster, before heading to the fridge and picking up the jam. She had never seen anyone eat so much in such a short space of time. The familiarity of the scene was not lost on her. Yesterday they'd been perfect strangers and today, well, they could almost pass for lovers.

Mutual attraction was obvious and uncomfortable after the intimacy of a shared swag. It was almost impossible to spend all night in someone's arms and not feel even the slightest desire in the morning.

Francesca shied away as much as she could. She didn't want another relationship. She had work to do and then there was Delarno. Nevertheless, she couldn't help but wonder at the depth of feeling a man like Sinclair might possess. It made her curious. He was a man of great integrity she was certain, which made Francesca feel suddenly ashamed of her own pettiness; embarrassed by the way she wasted her life over Nicholas and the mindless love affairs of her past.

Curious also about the man: his inner strength and confidence. There was a certain quality about him, humbleness in his manner. And then there were the stories he told from his deployments as an army medic. Stories of human tragedy and hope for a future.

"Are you going to let me get those stitches out today? Good girl." He didn't even wait for an answer and continued to speak. "Thought I might do a beach run and swim this morning, before it gets too hot."

Francesca nodded. Total relaxation was not her strength either. After all, she had spent her whole life shoving activity in the gaps when she didn't want to think.

"Then, it's up to you? What would you like to do today?" he asked.

The toast popped up. After a liberal buttering and loading with jam, he handed one to Francesca. She watched his every move.

"I'm not sure." She was absolutely captivated by him.

"Here, eat this babe. It will give you extra strength."

Was it her imagination or was this the most delicious buttered toast she had ever tasted? Steady on there girl. Maybe she should send him on his way.

He waited for her to finish then went to grab the medical kit on the bathroom shelf. Guiding her to the sunlit veranda, he pointed to a cushioned chair, and dragged a low stool in front of her.

"Doctor Sinclair will now see you," he said with a smile. "What have we got here?" His tone showed gentle professionalism and assurance.

He removed the silk threads with ease, tilted her head gently to check the eye socket, pressing here and there and asking a few questions. After removing the gauze, he checked her arm and nodded in confirmation, "It's healing well."

He covered the wound with ointment and secured a new dressing. When it was all done, he looked at her expectant expression and mumbled, "All good. You have great healing skin."

The girl was attractive, there was no argument there, but there was more to her than just looks. His curiosity fed upon itself. The more he knew about her, the more he wanted to know. Exploring his intuition had motivated him yesterday and he couldn't let it rest until it was fully satisfied. He had known from the start that getting to know her was a risk. Who would have guessed he would turn out to be such a hopeless romantic.

This morning he wanted more. He rested his gaze on her lips, only inches from him, and the urge to taste them was strong. It was dangerous territory. His behaviour had already compromised them both and he wouldn't risk crossing that protection line. Another time. Another place.

But those lips.

Francesca watched the range of expressions that crossed his face, guessing the turmoil of his thoughts. She held her breath.

Aware of his struggle, she pressed her face to his, her lips grazing his cheek with a kiss, the traditional way and said, "Grazie. Thank you. Your first Italian word and custom for the day," her voice filled with emotion. She sat back and smiled at his troubled expression.

He took another risk. Holding her chin he kissed her tentatively. He opened her mouth and his hands slipped under her hair gently cradling her jaw. She responded fanning his desire with her own.

"Francesca. I'm sorry." Sinclair pulled away.

What the hell was he thinking? This was not his style. He'd never taken advantage of a person in his care yet. And he was not about to start now. Besides, she needed the opportunity to get over that Delarno prick first. Sinclair was not the sort of man who worked the rebound. Knowing what Nicholas had done, he would be a bastard to use it to gain advantage. Francesca would never trust them again.

"Darlin' I'm sorry. That was unfair," he said and absently played with an auburn curl, wrapping it around his fingers. What the hell was wrong with him? He just had to touch her.

"I'm sorry too," she replied, with a quick shake of the head as if to erase the moment. "Old habits die hard."

She buried her head in her hands to hide the embarrassment. Adding to her mortification, unstoppable tears of frustration slid through her fingers.

"Hey, Francesca, don't be sad," he said. "Please don't cry. I think you're an incredible person. But you've had a rough time. Yesterday, you wandered into my life when I least expected it. And I'm really glad you did."

He took her face gently between his huge hands and raised it towards his.

"If it makes you feel better, I can hang around a bit? You can get to know me and I can get to know you. No pressure."

Francesca smiled weakly. She felt pathetic. "Sure," she responded, gulping a deep breath to steady herself. She looked at the floor wishing it would swallow her whole. She would do better to ask him to leave. She was in no position for any type of friendship. She opened her mouth to speak.

Sinclair looked at her, and then swore under his breath. He wasn't going to play this game with her.

"I can't lie to you Francesca. My brother will kill me, but you need to know the truth. There's already been too many lies." At her surprised look, he continued, "Johnno sent me here to look after you. He was worried about your safety. Please don't be mad."

"Wait. What? Johnno? Johnno McCrae put you up to this?"

She sat back in the chair; she needed to put air and space between them. She thought of the team in Sydney laughing their heads off at her expense as Johnno's brother fucked with her.

"So this is all just another lie? You. This whole scenario. I'm being set up again?"

"No. Well, not really. Everything I told you yesterday is true. I'm on leave. I'm a medic with the Australian Army. My name is Sinclair, Sinclair McCrae. I left out the part about Johnno, that's all. He was worried if you knew I was here to protect you, you would not react well," he explained calmly, as he would give a patient bad news.

"You're bloody well right about that. I can't believe it. I can't believe you. You string me along all day and night. Have I got bloody useless wench stamped on my forehead? Ten years I've spent building my credibility. Ten long fucking years. I don't need protection. I can look after myself. Tell me, did he tell you why I'm here?"

"Yes, he did."

"Everything?"

"Yes. I know all about you, Nicholas and the case you are working on with Johnno."

"Great! So what, now you feel pity for me? For a good time call Francesca? Is that what this is all about?"

"What? No. No way. Francesca come on. Give me some credit."

Francesca thought about Sinclair's camp. "You said you arrived two days ago. Did you watch me unpack?"

"Yes."

"Did you watch me on the veranda that first night?"

"Yes, I saw you. I saw what you were doing to yourself. I also heard you …"

"Well that's just fucking great isn't it," she cut him off mid sentence. "I thought I could trust you. I thought I could trust Johnno."

Francesca ran a hand through her hair irritably. "Excuse me, I need some air." She pushed past him and ran down the steps, heading towards the river.

Sinclair rubbed his hand along the back of his neck, and absently scratched the top of his head. "That went better than expected," he muttered to Chief as they watched her climb into the moored boat, cast off and gun it towards the ocean. At the first inlet, she guided the dinghy to take the right-hand bend heading deeper into the river system.

Sinclair grabbed his kit, running towards the creek crossing. Carefully navigating the slippery stones, he jogged the path that led to his camp.

Yesterday, as she'd slept, the soldier had tracked his way around that low ridge and back towards the property boundary where it connected with the creek inlet. He'd memorised the layout of the river system. The inlet Francesca had chosen formed a large oblong circle that eventually led back to the main river system and her home. Cutting through Westaway's bottom paddock would put him more or less within range.

From the high vantage at the edge of the paddock, he paused. Taking the binoculars, he scanned the area ahead along the river bank. Then he saw it. Bev's herd of Brahman cattle were camped in the shady stand of eucalypts. All except one, who seemed to be bellowing near the edge of a small ravine. Something was upsetting her. She stopped and looked around at the herd who remained settled in the cool shade.

Sinclair checked the co-ordinates on his compass.

Heading in that north west direction would put him close to the place he'd heard the outboard motor stop. The soldier took the punt and climbed down the last rocky edges of the ridge to reach the flat paddock below. Crossing a fresh running stream, he checked his co-ordinates again, adjusting his path as to skirt the herd and end up near the distressed cow.

"Easy," Sinclair instructed Chief as they neared the massive breeder, her udders filled with milk. Sinclair moved closer to the edge of the ravine. It was a sand bank that had been carved out by a small inlet of the creek. The area had slipped away and fallen trees crossed the deep creek, blocking access.

Here, as a spring shower began to fall, he found Francesca. The boat was pushed on the upturned roots of a fallen tree. Halfway up the sandbank, huddled in her arms was a small Brahman calf, barely a day old. She looked up at him, her tear-stained features covered in sand and mud.

"He's slipped down the bank. I've tried to help him up but my arm won't let me. I felt something tear."

Sinclair's attention moved to her arm which was seeping blood through the exposed bandage.

"I'm coming down. Chief. In the boat."

He slid down the bank as calmly as he could, easing himself beside her on the small sand ledge. The calf, too weak to struggle, looked at him with large mournful eyes and bellowed softly.

"Let me see," he said, gently holding her arm. Sinclair brushed her sodden hair from her eyes as the rain continued its steady beat. "Wriggle your fingers for me. Can you move your arm at all?"

"Yes, but it hurts. Like it's splitting open."

"Ok. I think it's the healed tissue that's rupturing. Here's what we're going to do. I want you to climb up there with the mother. I'm going to try and lift, walk, slide whatever works, this baby up the ravine. I want you to use your good arm to pull him towards you and keep it steady. Let me do the lifting. You just guide me and try to hold on as I get my footing. Are you up for it?"

"Yes."

"We don't have much time. Goodness knows how long the poor thing has been down here."

Francesca climbed the steep bank, lying on her stomach to get maximum reach over the bank. Sinclair helped the calf to its wobbly feet. It moaned in protest and so responded the mother.

"Are you ready Francesca?"

"Whenever you are. Mum is quiet as. I think she knows we're here to help."

Sinclair grunted pushing the calf towards the Francesca. "Come on mate, help me out."

The calf's head popped over the sand bank and as it came within reach Francesca grabbed at the skin folds around his neck. "I've got him!" she yelled. "I've got him. Come on little mate!" She pulled at his shoulder.

"Great! I'm going to try and get him to walk up the wall. I'm pushing from his butt."

"I've got his front legs." Francesca screamed excitedly, ignoring the ripping pain in her arm and grabbing on with both hands. One foot, then another. "One more push Sinclair."

Sinclair grunted loudly again climbing the sand cliff with arms raised above his head. The baby pushed upwards along the bank. Then a sudden release as Francesca miraculously hauled him towards her. Sinclair tasted the sand as he fell face first into the bank. Brushing it away, he climbed up, sticking his head over the grassy edge to see Francesca lying flat on her back, her arms spread out beside her.

The calf was on his feet, drinking thirstily from his mother, who sniffed him loudly. She looked towards Sinclair and Francesca.

"I swear she is saying thanks to us," Francesca said, looking at the scene from upside down. She turned to head towards Sinclair and burst out laughing. All she could see was a neck and head covered in sand.

"Thanks," he said. "Take a look at yourself."

Francesca climbed down the small embankment to the boat. They sat quietly on the water's edge resting from the ordeal.

"Why did you come looking for me?" Francesca asked eventually.

"Because I wanted to."

"Not because you promised Johnno to look after me?"

"No. But he would have my nuts if I lost you. I came to you because I wanted to find you. I needed to find you." He shifted in the sand to face her. "Francesca you don't need protection. You can look after yourself."

"I know."

"You need a friend. Someone you can trust. Someone you can talk to. Someone who understands where you are physically and emotionally. Someone who won't judge you. I want to be your friend. I'm not asking for you to give me any more than a chance to be the friend you need."

"Why do you so desperately want to be my friend? Don't you have any of your own?"

"I have many. Until yesterday, I didn't think I needed another. But for some strange reason, now I think I do. I want you to be a part of my life and I'd love to be a part of yours." And that was the truth about it. He couldn't put it any more plainly than that.

He added quietly, "Everybody makes mistakes Francesca. The past is the past. You can't change what's happened, but you can change how you look at your future. It's how you move forward from here that counts."

Francesca felt a shadow of self-forgiveness briefly cross her heart and head.

"Tell me Sinclair, did you kiss me because you think I'm easy?"

"No. I kissed you because I couldn't help myself. I'm sorry. It won't happen again." He blushed.

"No need to apologise. It was a nice kiss." She smiled at him, her hair plastered to her face as the rain started to fall faster.

"Francesca, your lips are turning blue. Are you ready to go home now?"

"Yes, I think so. Thank you Sinclair."

CHAPTER 27

Johnno looked with dubious satisfaction beyond the blinking computer screen. Data covered three walls of the situation room he shared with the Outlaw Motor Cycle Gang detectives. Photographs of various criminals, victims and organisational trees created a mind map of a complex crime organisation. A recent history of illegal activities linked by individuals and common relationships.

One wall was dedicated to OMCG's recent activity, specifically the escalating conflict between the Ares and Warlords. Another sported a map of Australia. Known drug transport links and points of interest were highlighted and colour-coded.

Alongside, a world map was in the process of being marked with shipping routes from Genoa to Australia. A valuable and particularly thorough contact in customs, had been feeding the investigative team with shipping data pertaining to vessels using the Italian port, as part of their regular travel route to Australia. The information included shipping companies, routes, ports visited as well as each ship's cargo manifest. With farming enterprises that stretched from Townsville to Kununurra and ranged from citrus to livestock, the Delarno family entity not only crossed an enormous area geographically, it was a massive farming enterprise that grossed millions of dollars annually.

Forensic accountants continued their covert work with the Tax Office, examining returns and statements of the Delarno Family Trust. It would take months to get a result. Months. Time that Johnno didn't have.

The detective's key informant was missing in action. A swing by the regular meeting places might prove fruitful. He decided to take a punt and changed into a pair of old tracksuit pants and a hoodie.

Arriving at the Birkenhead Point wharf, Johnno sat at the usual table and waited. The shopping centre was crowded and after a short while, the detective strolled along the wharf towards the Iron Cove Bridge. Johnno sensed he was being watched and stopped near a wire fence and low hedge. He smelt Jacko before he saw him.

"Holy hell! You need a shower man. You fucking stink," the detective gasped at the intoxicating array of smells emanating from the man's filthy body and clothes. "Did you shit yourself?"

"You'd stink too if you'd been living like me for the last month. It's not safe. I need to get out of Sydney," the addict grumbled.

"How much do you need?"

"$1000 cash."

"Yeah right so you can shoot it up your arm. Fuck off. Your information will want to be good for that."

"How about $500 then? I can go up the coast and hide out." He screwed up his face and pouted.

"What have you got for me?"

"Melbourne. Nero, not happy. Too many cops."

"Really? I already knew that. What else you got?"

"Warlords and Ares, one of them is working with Triads. Offer a deal: protection and distribution."

"I would've thought they could manage that on their own. Why do they need triads?"

"Cause triads have something they want."

"Oh yeah? What would that be?"

"Access." The addict screwed his nose up and sniffed.

"Access?"

"Yeah, ac-cess," he replied importantly, dragging out the two words and swaying slightly.

"Give me some names Jacko. First, the Chinese."

"Sunny Day Cleaning."

"From Brisbane?" Johnno questioned. Francesca's nemesis. Ri Lee Wong, the owner and Vanguard of Chi You.

"And Perth. And Melbourne. 'It's a sunny day,'" the addict sang the jingle and waved his hands in front like a rainbow. "Yeah ... Sunny Day." He held out his hand for the money.

"Fuck off. Which bike gang is working with the Chinese?"

"Hmm. That would be Ares. Yep. Pretty sure that's what I heard."

"What's this access all about?" Johnno asked.

The addict put his finger to his chin in a theatrical gesture. "Oh. Yeah. There's a cop. A real beauty. Got photos and everythin'. Doing the old ..." he whistled and made a crude gesture. "She's gonna help 'em."

Jacko continued, remembering, "Yeah and anyway they've fucken lost the girl! Can't find her. Vanished mate! Poof!"

He made a starburst with his hands and smiled. "Chinese have gone nuts. When they find her ... she's ..." Jacko slid his hand across his neck for effect in a slicing motion and stuck out his filthy tongue. "The boyfriend got close but ... It's fucking crazy man."

"Tell me about Nero. What's his relationship with the Chinese?"

"No idea."

"What do you know about the Ares murder?"

"Nothin'."

Johnno knew he was lying and waved a $50 in front of his face. "C'mon Jacko, spill your guts."

Jacko looked longingly at the money. "He was a cop with the Feds. For another $50, I'll tell you something else." He looked hopefully at the detective.

"Yeah? Will want to be good."

"Shh! It's a secret. A Warlord was torched and dumped in the bush!"

Johnno held onto the money. Everyone knew that.

"What do you know about the Delarno family?"

"Not much. Only that Nero hates them. And he hates bikers. Kills them too." Jacko's eyes focused on the notes in the detective's hands.

Johnno pressed further. "So the access, it's the cop? That's what they're fighting about?"

Jacko gave an exasperated sigh. "No." The informant looked at the detective like he was a half-wit.

"What then?"

"Man!" Jacko whined realising he'd said too much. "I only know rumours."

Johnno waited quietly.

"The new supply is better." He held his arms to protest. "I haven't tried it. Honest. That's what they are saying."

"Right. Better in what way. Supply? Quality?"

"Both. Try it once, you won't go back."

"And it's coming from Queensland or Victoria."

Jacko lowered his head. "If you say so boss."

"No peanut. You tell me. Is it coming from Chi You or Delarno or Nero?"

"Well." The informant visibly squirmed. "Both."

"Both. What do you mean both? Are they working together?"

Jacko nodded. "There are three. Another from the seas."

"Do you have a name?"

"I need more cash." Jacko looked behind his shoulder. His paranoia took hold. "Have to leave town; been here too long. I'm a fucking dead man," he whined. "Give me the cash."

Johnno agreed. They had been there too long.

"Here, $600 … take that. Stay close, I'm not done with you yet." Johnno handed him the money.

The addict shoved it in his pocket. He was not stupid enough to count it in front of the cop. "I'll find out more and get a message to you."

"Yeah, No worries. You've got my number, fucking use it next time. Don't make me chase you. Got it?"

"Yes sir!" Jacko gave a mock salute before disappearing along the Bay Run.

Johnno stepped into the sunshine, casually strolled along the wharf and disappeared into the crowded lunch area. His stomach churned at the thought of Francesca and the role she had unwittingly found herself in. It was only a matter of time before they found her.

It was time he made his own social call. A trip to Queensland and a meet and greet with the Delarno family was well and truly overdue. There was another reason Johnno wanted to be there. He would need to move quickly with Francesca. He phoned Sinclair.

"Mate thanks for the messages. There has been a development. I'm heading to Queensland for a bit."

"Want to meet up?"

"No. It's too risky. Look mate, she's a target. I'm going to send some support up around the area. This is big mate. Do you want to stay on?"

"I've never backed down from a fight before, what makes you think I will now?"

"Well you're doing it as a favour, not serving your country. And your kin, I don't want to see you get hurt. These guys, they're bastards. Desperate and they fight dirty."

"Look Johnno, my eyes are wide open. Combat is no stranger to me. Anyone I should be looking out for in particular or is everyone suspect?"

"Yeah … try Italian mafia, Chinese triad and bike gangs."

He whistled low and long. "Well, she doesn't do anything half-arsed does she? Copy. Take care mate. Over and out."

"Over and out buddy."

CHAPTER 28

"Do you know where I was 35 days ago today?" Francesca asked as she set the crab pots amongst the mangroves. With one almighty heave she cast the steel cages the way her father had taught her many years before. Holding gently yet firmly, her hands slid along the last of the thick ropes until they reached the colourful ice-cream lids. Markers that indicated their placement amongst the glossy leaves.

Feeling playful, Francesca's mood tempted her for a good stir. Edgy and full of mischief, she breathed a sigh of sheer release. Thankful her back was turned from Sinclair's broody stare, she allowed a quick smile to escape. In the glorious afternoon sunshine the detective composed herself.

He had paced the floor again last night. She'd heard him stop at her door and wait. In the darkness, she could almost feel his hand poised to knock, before turning and walking away silently. His vast levels of self control straining in the isolation of Wild Dog Creek.

Their sexual tension needed a release and Francesca was curious just how far she could push this disciplined giant. For almost two weeks now she'd sidestepped around his attraction towards her. Something was different this morning. The strength of him pulled her towards him. And Francesca accepted it.

As the small dinghy motored to the middle of the creek, Francesca baited and dropped two fishing lines into the turning tide, hopeful of catching dinner. Around her the thick stench of bait and raw fish blended with the salty air. Continuing to speak, she busily washed her sticky fingers in the cool water lapping at the shallow hulled boat.

"On my last day in Rome I bought a Pucci dress. Oh how I loved that dress. That dress was going to get me places, make things happen for me. And it did, but not in the way I expected. Feels like another life now. I mean the whole thing seems so trivial here in the middle of Wild Dog Creek. Do you get me?"

"Yep." Sinclair lazily toyed with the fishing line running taut in the current. "Spoken like a true addict. Going cold turkey from the shops will do that every time."

"You dag! I'm serious!" Francesca threw a half-frozen prawn in his direction.

"Don't start something you can't finish Francesca." His relaxed pose beside the small outboard motor belied a warning glance in her direction.

Francesca knew him well enough now not to be fooled by any small changes in his demeanour. She recognised the slight bunching of his bicep, despite his outward tranquil manner. She continued nonetheless, desperately wanting to play.

"What I'm trying to say is that at last I feel secure in myself. Stronger. Like I can make decisions with a clear head, without first looking to the past. I know where I want to go."

She turned her head so he couldn't see the mischief tugging at her lips. Despite the monkey of torment sitting on her shoulder, goading her on, the small boat in the middle of the creek made for an uneasy arrangement.

"And where do you want to go?" he probed cautiously. Sinclair couldn't prevent her from leaving if she felt ready to reveal herself.

"I want to settle. Live a simpler life. Might even try a real relationship." Under the rim of her cap she watched his face constrict slightly. Beneath his cool exterior, the nerves twitched in the side of his neck as he struggled to retain his composure.

Ooh, she just loved poking this tiger. And she couldn't help herself. Come on, she thought. Give it up Sinclair.

"I see. Do you have anyone in mind for your real relationship?" Sinclair was almost too afraid to ask, steeling himself against the crushing devastation if she chose Delarno. He held his breath.

"Perhaps." Francesca smiled bewitchingly, tilting her head to fully face him at last, her eyes sparkling in mischief. "Perhaps I do."

Her hand quietly slid over the side of the boat and with an almighty effort she splashed the water in Sinclair's direction.

"I warned you," he laughed, releasing the coiled tension within him as he lunged for her, making the boat rock wildly.

"Don't! Sinclair! You'll tip us in! Stop!" Francesca screamed in genuine fright as she felt the boat tilt on its side. It rocked back with an almighty splash and steadied with a couple of aftershocks. Francesca's white knuckles gripped the aluminium edges each side of her. Her game was over.

"Alright! All right! You're quite safe. But we'll have to move now. You've scared all the fish with that yelling and wild behaviour."

With that Sinclair pulled up the anchor and steered the small boat to another location. After they settled, his mood subdued. He wanted to know more about the Delarno family and the extent of her feelings towards them. Did she still love Nicholas after all he'd done to her?

The soldier almost whispered, "Francesca, tell me about the loss of your mother. You never talk about her. What was your mother's name?"

The question startled Francesca. She sat back, leaning against the bow of the boat. Serves her right. She faced her comeuppance bravely. The naughty monkey that'd been egging her on suddenly disappeared.

She glanced at his pained expression and felt a wave of compassion towards him. Head bowed whilst he silently berated himself for bringing her here. She reached out to touch his arm reassuringly. It was difficult to speak of that part of her childhood. Francesca owed this much to him at least.

"Arabella," she said. "Arabella was her name. My father was devastated. I was eight and my sister Luciana, six. My dad was lost. So lost and so very sad. For a long time it was like he didn't have the will to live. They were absolutely devoted to each other. Her death was a great shock to everybody." She paused momentarily.

"Their happiness was evident to everyone who met them. Dad has some footage of us on 16mm home movie reels. My parents were both so handsome. Dressed up and going to dances. Everyone says my mum was beautiful. Luciana inherited her goodness and gentle manners."

She smiled. "I remember when she heard my dad come through the front gate at the end of each day, she'd send us to have a bath. I would get Luciana started and sneak back down the hall to secretly watch them.

"He always greeted her with a kiss, taking her apron from her. Then he would hold her close. Even when he was dirty and dusty from the farm. My mum would scold him but she was never serious. Sometimes they would dance around the small kitchen. He would gently cup her face and rub her cheeks with his rough fingers. It was a very intimate scene between a husband and wife. It was almost like he knew their time together was short and he wanted to make the most of every day with her."

Francesca laughed. "Then, he would come stomping down the hallway pretending to be a fiery dragon, making Luciana squeal."

Francesca smiled again, her eyes distant in the memory.

"How did she pass away, your mum?" Sinclair spoke gently.

"She died when my brother was born"

"You have a brother? You never mention him?" Sinclair's surprised response brought her focus towards him.

"He died as a baby too. My dad named him Ari Bello Stefano Salucci. He is buried in town. Signora Delarno, Cristiana, became a second mother to us. The Delarno family lived in our town then, on the next farm. They didn't move up north until I was about 11, I guess, but we still holidayed with them until I was 16 or so." Francesca shifted uncomfortably, averting her eyes, but continued.

"I missed my mum so much. That ache, you know, it never goes away. It lessens, but it never fully goes. My dad never re-married. He's a very handsome man but no one was like his Arabella. He worked so hard. Even harder when mum died.

"You know, he's still great friends with Silvio Delarno. I don't understand it. I guess he feels indebted for their kindness. They are a powerful family in farming and international business. A family unlike ours in many ways. As kids, Luciana and I often holidayed with them. Each time it was another exotic place full of beautiful people.

"I remember, from a young age, despite their kindness always feeling out of place. That sounds ungrateful but it's not. Signora Delarno is a most sincere and loving person. We just lived in different worlds. I remember Silvio often asking my father to invest with him and my father always politely refusing. When money was tight I would always think, why not Papa? It would make your life so much easier." Francesca shrugged involuntarily.

"I think my father secretly hoped that one day, one of us would marry into that family," Francesca chuckled awkwardly as she realised where her ramblings had taken her.

"Oh?" Sinclair mentally braced himself for what she would say next.

"He often calls to give me news from the Delarno family. As Luciana is already married, quite happily, that leaves me! I used to think, until quite recently, that it was my destiny, my fate, to be linked that way to them. Now, I'm not so sure."

Francesca masked her discomfort with another nervous laugh. Despite everything, the pull of family loyalty remained strong. And yet, sitting here with Sinclair, the detective found herself confessing things she had told no one, not even herself. As her secrets unravelled before her, an amazing sense of relief filled the space.

She had pushed Sinclair and he'd pushed back, gently and respectfully, knowing she'd needed to break down her grief to the source and understand how it had influenced her decisions.

The man before her would be gone soon, back in Afghanistan and in control of his medical team. Soon she would face off the Delarno family. That was coming. She could sense it. It was time for a fresh start. Time to close the chapter for good. Her desire to do it all at once, in a sweeping gesture of defiance and strength was palpable. Sinclair knew she needed clarity. And more time.

The knowledge of it made Francesca like him more. *Really* like him. There, she had admitted that to herself too. And she found she couldn't tip toe around it anymore. Her heart filled with hope.

"I don't want to marry out of obligation," she added quietly, wanting to finish the conversation she'd carelessly begun.

"What would make you marry, Francesca?" Sinclair needed to know. He looked down into the boat, avoiding her eyes in the close proximity and drawing himself inwards in self-protection.

"Love, of course! I am Italian after all!" She said lightly and sounding more like the biggest flake on earth. Shifting in the small boat, she added earnestly, "It has to be a special kind of love. When hearts are safe and filled with wonder. A gentle passionate love nurturing over time and distance. A respectful bond that allows freedom and yet captivates at the same time. I will marry that man, Sinclair."

She looked fleetingly at the medic, suddenly shy in front of him. She had not meant to speak so openly. Francesca turned her head quickly, before she could read his expression as Sinclair raised his head to her. His eyes would not leave her beautiful, tragic face. He willed her to look at him, for he couldn't speak. It was the love he felt for her.

Francesca gazed unseeing over the shimmering water. Her mind was racing back to her childhood, feeling the invisible comfort of her mother's arms around her, as her loneliness and grief coursed down her cheeks.

CHAPTER 29

In the small interview office within the Gold Coast police command, Detective Jonathan McCrae couldn't hide his feelings for the man sitting opposite him. Frustration clouded his thought process and Johnno knew he'd let Francesca down. He handed Nicholas Delarno a transcript of the interview they'd just completed.

"Read this and sign the bottom if it is correct," the detective instructed abruptly, wanting to punch the smugness out of Nicholas Delarno's expression.

DET SGT MCRAE: I want you to explain why you were in Italy in August this year.

NICHOLAS DELARNO: My father had a business problem and he was unable to attend, so I went in his place.

DET SGT MCCRAE: What was the nature of the business problem?

NICHOLAS DELARNO: I don't think that has anything to do with you, detective.

DET SGT MCRAE: It interests me when the people you were consorting with are persons of interest to the police. So I'm asking again. What was the nature of the problem?

NICHOLAS DELARNO: There was a difference of opinion on a contractual arrangement.

DET SGT MCRAE: What type of contractual arrangement?

NICHOLAS DELARNO: A transport issue. Surely we are not here to discuss the ins and outs of our business dealings, detective. Because I'm afraid it's really none of your business.

DET SGT MCRAE: I want to talk about a meeting that took place at a restaurant in Melbourne on the 28th of May of this year. In attendance was Gino Castello as well as two well-known crime identities and a third person. The next day, Gino Castello was recorded visiting a Gold Coast address. The business occupying that address is listed as a subsidiary of Genoa Holdings. You were also present.

NICHOLAS DELARNO: Well I would have to check my diary. Who can remember what they did on what day. That was months ago.

DET SGT MCRAE: I know you were there. I have evidence that you were on site during his visit.

No answer recorded.

DET SGT MCRAE: Two weeks later, you met with Gino Castello again. This time at a café located at Broadbeach and as well at a charity fundraiser that night.

NICHOLAS DELARNO: Am I not allowed to talk with business associates? Is that against the law now, detective.

DET SGT MCRAE: I find it interesting that you meet with a known criminal three times in one week and then miraculously almost six weeks later you find yourself in the same small town of Rapallo, Italy, where you meet again.

NICHOLAS DELARNO: I don't find it interesting at all.

DET SGT MCRAE: Tell me about Detective Francesca Salucci.

NICHOLAS DELARNO: What about her?

DET SGT MCRAE: Did you know she would be in Rapallo?

NICHOLAS DELARNO: No.

DET SGT MCRAE: Yet you met her at the train station and arrangements were made for her to stay at your home.

NICHOLAS DELARNO: Yes.

DET SGT MCRAE: Explain.

NICHOLAS DELARNO: My father called to say that Francesca would be visiting.

DET SGT MCRAE: And when was that?

NICHOLAS DELARNO: The day before she arrived.

DET SGT MCRAE: The same day you met with Gino Castello. What was his interest in seeing you?

NICHOLAS DELARNO: He wanted to talk.

DET SGT MCRAE: About?

NICHOLAS DELARNO: The weather.

DET SGT MCRAE: The weather?

NICHOLAS DELARNO: Yes.

DET SGT MCRAE: And you discussed the weather for twenty minutes.

NICHOLAS DELARNO: Yes. Pretty much. The weather in Rapallo is so beautiful that time of year.

DET SGT MCRAE: You see, Mr Delarno, I think he was there to talk about a business arrangement between your family and others. I believe there was another meeting between you and Carlo Seta at a small café in Portofino. It occurred the day after you collected Detective Salucci from the train. I believe you sailed there on the yacht known as La Bianca Bella.

No answer recorded.

DET SGT MCRAE: I think the meeting was to negotiate a new deal with these crime families.

NICHOLAS DELARNO: You can think what you like. I don't have time, detective, to sit here and listen to your accusations. I'm a very busy man, as I'm sure you can appreciate. So if there is nothing further, I'm done here.

DET SGT MCRAE: I'm assuming this is the way it works within your organisation. That you have seen these photographs as well. You see here, Mr Delarno, you're meeting with Gino Castello. And then with Carlo Seta. Let the record show that I am showing Mr Nicholas Delarno photographs of the meeting in question.

NICHOLAS DELARNO: Traditori.

DET SGT MCRAE: Perhaps Mr Delarno. For the purpose of the recording Mr Delarno said traitors in the Italian language. Is that correct Mr Delarno?

NICHOLAS DELARNO: Yes.

DET SGT MCRAE: For the purpose of the recording please refrain from speaking in any language other than English. English is your first language, is that correct Mr Delarno?

NICHOLAS DELARNO: Yes.

DET SGT MCRAE: So getting back to the meetings with Gino Castello and Carlo Seta. What were they about?

NICHOLAS DELARNO: Like I said, we spoke about the weather and then I had a business meeting with Carlo Seta. I was in Italy to do that. To discuss a misunderstanding in a contract.

DET SGT MCRAE: What contract?

NICHOLAS DELARNO: Transport. We use the Seta Group to transport our freight throughout Europe. Disputes happen in business, detective McCrae.

DET SGT MCRAE: Did you resolve it?

NICHOLAS DELARNO: Not to my satisfaction.

DET SGT MCRAE: And you didn't stay in Rapallo to finish the conversation. You left after your house was attacked. After Detective Salucci left.

NICHOLAS DELARNO: Yes. I felt it best to return to Australia.

DET SGT MCRAE: Because?

NICHOLAS DELARNO: Because I wanted to check on my friend and there was no point continuing the conversation with Seta. The matter had been passed over to my lawyers.

DET SGT MCRAE: How well do you know Gino Castello?

NICHOLAS DELARNO: He's a man who does business with our company in Italy. We've met occasionally at social events.

DET SGT MCRAE: I want to return to an earlier comment you made. The one where you called the people in the photographs traitors. Could you please explain why you said that.

No audible response.

DET SGT MCRAE: You will have to speak up Mr Delarno. For the recording.

NICHOLAS DELARNO: (Audible sigh recorded) I called them traitors because they have not fulfilled a transport contract and it has cost my company a lot of money. As I said, it is a dispute that has been handed over to my lawyers.

DET SGT MCRAE: I will need verification from your lawyers to confirm your claim.

NICHOLAS DELARNO: As you wish. I hope you like to read. It is a very complex matter.

DET SGT MCRAE: I want to go back to Francesca Salucci.

NICHOLAS DELARNO: Why?

DET SGT MCRAE: Because she seems very important to you.

NICHOLAS DELARNO: And that's a criminal offense?

DET SGT MCRAE: Depends on whose opinion you seek. You had quite a thing going on over there. How long have you known her?

NICHOLAS DELARNO: Since we were kids. Seriously. My personal life is really none of your business. I'm done here. Are you going to arrest me? No? Then I really must be going.

DET SGT MCRAE: When did you last speak to Detective Francesca Salucci?

NICHOLAS DELARNO: I'm not sure. A week maybe two after I came home.

DET SGT MCRAE: And where was that conversation?

NICHOLAS DELARNO: In Sydney. I was there for a meeting and then we caught up.

DET SGT MCRAE: Right. Did you go out for dinner or something?

NICHOLAS DELARNO: What?

DET SGT MCRAE: Was it a social or business call Mr Delarno?

NICHOLAS DELARNO: What does it matter? We met and we talked!

DET SGT MCRAE: Where?

NICHOLAS DELARNO: At her home.

DET SGT MCRAE: So she just invited you to her home after fleeing for her life in Rapallo?

NICHOLAS DELARNO: Detective, we're old friends. Our families have known each other since childhood. Francesca was a guest in my home in Rapallo. And then she left unexpectedly. I wanted to make sure she was okay.

DET SGT MCRAE: Right. And how did that go?

NICHOLAS DELARNO: Pretty good actually.

DET SGT MCRAE: Oh?

NICHOLAS DELARNO: Do you want to know word for word what happened between us? I kissed her. She kissed me. We had sex. Then I left. I haven't seen or heard from her since. Now that is not unusual. We have a very casual relationship. Happy?

No audible answer recorded.

NICHOLAS DELARNO: I think we are done. You have my number.

CHAPTER 30

Francesca paced the room, walked to the window, looked out at the easing rain and returned to the lounge. She plopped on the cushions. Stood and began the process again. Cabin fever. If she didn't get out soon she would explode.

"Sinclair, would you like to go to the Harvest Festival on Friday night?" If he agreed, it would be the first time she'd left the property.

"Do you want to go?" Sinclair asked, watching the caged lioness.

"It's a gamble, I know," she said, "but I think it's time for a new focus." Francesca was keen to flex her emotional muscle but there were considerations. Her family. And Sinclair.

He looked unconvinced.

"Sinclair, this is a calculated risk." To her way of thinking it was a matter of fact statement, backed by practical assessment. If a social outing triggered action, she was prepared to take the consequences. "I need to get back into the investigation and I want to do it on my terms. Besides, Johnno needs a new strategy."

Last night she'd caught herself up on the investigation. Logging into the police network, she was relieved Johnno had copied her in on every update. She couldn't deny it the police interview with Nic was embarrassing and it hurt.

"So, now you're willing to set yourself up as bait? You know once this happens there's no going back. Francesca these guys you're playing with. They won't miss next time."

"Yes. I'm aware of that." She looked earnestly at him. "I have to do something Sinclair. I'm tired of hiding out. I want my life back. These people have influenced my life for 20 years. I'm over it and I'm over them. I'm ready to make this happen. My only sadness is that you'll probably leave."

"What makes you say that?" he asked.

"Well, I just thought you probably would. I mean you and Johnno had an agreement. With me back on the case you could continue on with your holiday before you head back to Afghanistan." Francesca stumbled through the conversation. She walked up and down the room again.

"Do you want me to leave?"

"No. What I'm trying to say is that your obligation to me would be finished." Francesca looked into her wringing hands, her back to him as she faced the window.

"So that's what you're thinking."

"Well Sinclair, that's the reality of our situation." She faced him. "How do I know what I … " she blushed and turned away. The rain had stopped. A distant low rumble of thunder rolled across the evening sky. After a moment Francesca returned to the safe topic of the investigation.

"I'm the lynch pin. My family are safe and with you and Johnno aware of my intentions, I think it's a good opportunity to move the investigation forward."

Sinclair cocked his head to one side. "Are you asking me on a date to the Harvest Festival?"

Francesca looked at him squarely. "Yes," she said shyly despite her determined face.

"Well then, Miss Francesca Salucci. I'd love to go. With you." Sinclair's eyes twinkled, he crossed the floor to her and wrapped his arms around her waist. The detective gazed up at him and he couldn't resist the invitation. Sinclair tweaked her upturned nose gently between his thumb and finger.

"You'll love it." She suddenly smiled a radiant, kilowatt grin with her soft eyes beaming at him. "It's quite small. Mainly for our local community and the contractors to celebrate the end of harvest. I remember going as a child … at night after bedtime, which was a huge deal, and dad buying us fairy floss and toffee apples! We stayed until the fireworks finished and walked back home along the bush track."

"Can you still get to the siding that way? Along the track?" Sinclair asked.

"I'm not sure? Might check that out tomorrow."

~

Francesca stared at her reflection. After weeks of holiday fishing outfits, she felt like a princess. The simply styled summer dress, a birthday present from her sister, had never been worn. Made up of numerous tightly crocheted floral tiles, it possessed a music festival vibe. Its colour reminded Francesca of the beach. She beamed at the relaxed face staring back at her in the mirror.

A final spritz of perfume and she wandered onto the creaky veranda to see Sinclair dressed in casual long pants and shirt, its collar raised and sleeves rolled halfway up his forearm emphasising his physical strength. Trepidation showed on his face and despite his training, a certain vulnerability could be seen in his chocolate eyes.

Her knees buckled. At the sight of her, his shocked gaze slowly moved from her hair to her toes and back again. Francesca felt the warmth rise to her flushed cheeks.

"Ahh," he stumbled. Striding towards her, he closed the gap between them in two long steps, gathered her in his arms and kissed her. Slowly.

Francesca's immediate response surprised him. Her lips opened as weeks of self-control unhinged, igniting a liquid fire within them. The kiss deepened. Francesca's body shivered in anticipation.

His lips left hers. Francesca opened her eyes to see his face close to hers. His eyes of molten chocolate searching for permission.

"Again?" she whispered. "Kiss me again Sinclair." Parting her lips slightly in a shy smile.

His gentle hand toyed with her hair and he wrapped the lengths around his fingers. Brushing her face with his fingers, he placed a gentle thumb on her lips. So soft. He breathed her perfume deeply; the musky floral scent taunted him.

His love-filled gaze stole several beats from her heart before she was able to calm herself. She waited, thinking she might faint from the intensity of the moment.

He whispered close to her ear, "Take me to your festival and when we return…" He let his voice trail away.

Finally, he had the courage to reveal his love. Tonight he would knock on her door and she would know exactly what she meant to him. Tonight he would show his commitment to her before he had no choice but to leave. The notification had come through. Deployment in ten days.

For now, he held her hand as they drove along the bush track to the highway. Every now and then, he would raise her fingers to his mouth, pressing them against his lips.

Jiggling about beside him, Francesca couldn't sit still. That kiss and the excitement of a social outing had her stomach doing butterfly rolls. She shivered, thinking about his incomplete offer, her brain on a one-way track to Pleasureville.

After about twenty minutes they arrived at the old railway siding. "It takes longer to drive than to walk!" Francesca laughed as they found a park close to the entrance.

Music and laughter erupted from a large tent that served as a bar and dancing area. A number of smaller stalls stood in a colourful circle around the outer perimeter. A large group of people were already enjoying the festivities. Old fashioned music from a small merry-go-round echoed around the fair.

Sinclair held Francesca close and canvassed the area. His eyes worked the crowd. He moved her to the security of the sugar cane display that showed a number of prize-winning entries. Holding hands, they leant close together.

"My dad used to win every year you know," Francesca said with a hint of nostalgia.

"Really? And how do you judge a good stalk of sugar cane Francesca?"

"Well," she started, "it has to be straight, tall, and thick with even diameter, nicely rounded with evenly spaced ratoons," she said with a sweet smile.

"You cheeky brat! You're just making that up!" He loved that side of her, the sassy bullshit she spun when she had no clue.

"Yeah I am," she laughed. "I've no idea. Hey, check out the street performer!" Quickly a circle formed around him, drawn in by the juggling and gregarious nature of the artisan.

"Hello everyone! My name is Ernesto! I will be performing for you today at your harvest festival." His accent was a mix of European and American and the whole time he spoke a continuous twirling and juggling took place.

"I am going to perform a number of tricks for you today…" He threw the balls high into the air. "Some which will be quite dangerous, some will require help from the audience, but all will entertain and mesmerise." He finished juggling and bowed to the audience applause.

Sinclair stood behind Francesca maintaining a clear view over her head. The crowd grew steadily. Francesca seemed lost in the performance, but he remained alert and kept moving further back for uninterrupted views of their surroundings.

Most were under the spell of the entertainer. The youngest of children sat within an inner circle with adults standing behind them.

Sinclair felt the presence behind him the second before he saw it. The movement saved his life. He felt the sting as the blade sliced his upper arm. In the next second, a swift hand movement had the soldier on the ground. Francesca was grabbed from behind and stumbled backwards. Sinclair turned towards her as he hit the ground, watching her struggle, her face frozen in terror.

Simultaneously, Chief who had been sitting at Francesca's feet let out a small warning growl.

"Scream! Francesca, somebody help!" he was trying to say but the words could not come out. It was too late. He blacked out as the two men pulled her away from the crowd. Chief stood growling, guarding the soldier's prone body.

A fit of ferocious barking to protect his master drew the attention of the crowd. The dog's eyes darted to Francesca. He knew something was wrong. He didn't know who to protect but chose his master and let the girl go.

Francesca twisted her arms furiously in an attempt to break the firm hold. It happened so quickly. One in front and one behind, they forced her forward. She propped and jolted. A knife blade was pushed against her back and she froze as sheer terror took hold.

They were nearing a car, its engine running and spewing foul fumes into the air. The two men argued as they struggled with her. She tried to remember their words.

Everything happened in slow motion before her. She tried to scream, her mouth opened but no sound escaped. They were pulling her, twisting her, pushing her. Francesca's mind raced.

If they get me into that car I'll never escape. Her body stiffened. Her mind focused. Suddenly ducking forward, she forced the man behind her to stumble. She bent low and twisted. As he slid off her back, her elbow connected with his sternum, winding him. A swift side kick to the knee and he grunted falling to the floor. His shirt had ripped in the struggle, flagging about his heavily scarred torso. Chi You initiation scars. There was no mistake.

With the distraction, the second offender turned to face her. He went to grab her at the waist but she was faster. Her hands pulled the bridge of his face onto her raised knee and with the momentum, she pushed him directly into the spewing exhaust.

Francesca bolted. Hurtling around the crowd towards the track she had walked that very morning. This was her turf. She knew this place better than anyone. She searched for Sinclair amongst the people. There was no screaming. No gunshots. Following her every move around the fair ground, a growing sinister silence and Chief's angry growling.

There wasn't much time. She darted behind the tents for protection as the obscure pathway appeared before her, and she paused. She had to make a choice. Never leave a man behind.

Circling the tents, she caught a glimpse of Sinclair lying on the ground. Chief was standing above him as the crowd dispersed in a wide circle. She watched him command the dog to heel. He raised his hand to rub the back of his neck and head checking the injury.

The two men had split up and were making their way through the crowd. With furious faces they quickly moved towards Sinclair, who by now was getting to his feet. Francesca reacted instinctively.

"Leave him," she called. "I'm here."

All three turned in her direction. Francesca glanced briefly at Sinclair and then with a nod of challenge, faced the two men before launching her escape. She darted behind the tents again and increasing her steady pace, negotiated the overgrown path back to the homestead.

They followed a short distance, doubled back to the waiting vehicle and exited in the direction of the highway.

Sinclair reached for his phone. "Johnno, we need back up. They're here. Francesca is heading to the homestead. On foot. They've taken the bait and are following by car. We worked on an exit strategy should this happen. She should be on her way to safety by the time they get there."

The crowd gathered around Sinclair encircling him. Blood seeped through his shirt sleeve.

"Someone get a doctor. This man is injured."

Sinclair glanced at the injury. He was lucky this time. "It's ok," he said. "I'm a doctor. I have a medical kit in the car. Thanks." With that he strode away from the group and followed Francesca's path to the homestead. His phone rang. It was Johnno.

"Where are you?"

"On my way to the farm. I'm taking the bush track. I'm about two minutes behind Francesca." Sinclair let Chief take the lead.

"Call me when you've finished the recon. The support team is less than ten minutes away," Johnno replied. "I'm going to make a house call. If we're wrong and they do find her, I know exactly where she'll be taken."

~

Tea tree branches tugged as Francesca sped along the dirt track. The men would try and head her off at the farm. At last the tight space opened onto the back of the sheds and the farmhouse beyond.

Quickly checking the surrounds, she bolted to her rusty Land Cruiser ute. Inside the cab, an overnight bag had been pre-packed with essentials and an emergency kit.

Francesca wheeled around behind the shed. Behind the protective cover of the outbuildings, she took the forestry track leading to the beach. It was also a back road to the highway. The main driveway wasn't safe. It was the first place they would wait.

"Delarno," she said out loud as she checked the rear vision again, "this is ending right now."

Seconds later, Sinclair arrived at the house. Through the trees he saw the high gable roofline and moved off the path to silently track behind the shed. Quickly collecting the hand gun he'd hidden in the rotary hoe, he whispered, "You want to play like thugs." The magazine slid into place and he felt the click. "No problem."

Motioning Chief to sit and stay, he moved silently towards the veranda that led to Francesca's bedroom.

A small reflection caught his attention and Sinclair stepped behind the water tank and waited. The pistol rested neatly in his palm. His finger eased onto the trigger.

The boards on the front veranda steps creaked softly under the strangers' weight.

As they took another step it resounded again and Sinclair resisted the urge to move. If Francesca hadn't managed to get away and was hiding inside the house, he would need to act fast.

The screen door squeaked, as always, and then silence. Sinclair waited.

A black SUV pulled into the driveway and stopped near the front steps. The footsteps from the veranda thundered down towards it. Sinclair moved to gain a better position and view. Two men yelled at each other. In their flailing arms each now carried a semi-automatic weapon. Amateurs. Sinclair thought. Dangerous.

He studied the third amongst the group. Sinclair was not deceived by the flecked grey in his hair and craggy face. Every movement suggested a man used to killing and holding a position of power. He backhanded the closest man in one swift movement and sent him sprawling into the dusty driveway. The other turned to run and he dropped him on the spot with a bullet in his back. The grey-haired man turned back to the one on the ground, facing him.

Sinclair was affronted by his gall. He eased his sights on the older man who suddenly looked up. Sirens. The older man pushed the other towards the car, took the driver's seat and made a hasty retreat towards the highway. After a few moments Sinclair moved from his location, approaching the prone body and protecting himself should another shooter be about. The medic quickly checked for a pulse before running up the steps calling to Francesca. He phoned Johnno.

"We have a dead body and she's not here. I'll give you a statement. But first we need to locate Francesca."

He was moving towards the open shed. "She's gone. She got away." Relief tasted in the back of his throat. Sinclair sat on the dirt floor and leaned against the pole, his emotions threatening.

"I know you may have worked on a plan together but you realise at this moment I can almost guarantee she's on her way to the same place I'm heading now. My team will be with you any minute. Sinclair, I need you to stay there, but I need you to be safe. If there is another shooter, I don't want to risk you getting hurt. I'm going to try and intercept Francesca before she does something stupid."

Sinclair found cover wedged between the tractor's steel back rims.

From here he had a good vision of the house but enough cover for combat if necessary, as well as an escape route. The men wouldn't be back, he knew, but like Johnno, he wouldn't take the chance on another hiding in the scrub around the house.

Sinclair eyed Chief who was now crouched behind him, silent. They'd practiced this drill many times. Sinclair patted the dog's head in appreciation. "Thanks mate. Not long now," he whispered as the dog's tail lifted and thumped once on the dirt floor.

CHAPTER 31

Francesca hit the highway at speed. As the wheels met the black tar, she jammed the ute into fifth gear and broadsided out of a plume of dust. Destination Sunshine Coast.

Her worried thoughts turned to Sinclair. Chief's warning growl and frightened barks echoed through her mind. The phone buzzed beside her.

"Salucci," she answered briskly.

"It's Johnno. Where are you?"

"On the road. Sinclair. I need to know. Is he ok? Have you spoken to him?"

"Yes. He's fine. Worried about you."

Francesca let out the breath she'd been holding since Wild Dog Creek.

"Where are you now?"

"On the road," she repeated.

"Francesca, I'm calling you in. We need to meet. Get you safe."

"I'm safe Johnno. That's all you need to know," she disconnected, returning her focus to the road. She felt her lips tremble in relief and clenched the wheel more tightly.

"Nicholas. It's time you and I had a chat old friend," she said. "But first I want to know what else you've been up to. I need to find a place. Somewhere safe. Somewhere I can hide in plain sight. Somewhere away from the cops."

Francesca checked the rear view mirror for company. She was clear. Hours later she turned off the Bruce Highway onto the tourist route of the Sunshine Coast strip.

Her mind returned to Nicholas. The past was the past. She couldn't change it. But she could certainly change her future. And she would use her intimate knowledge of the family to do exactly that. Find the link between the attempts on her life, the investigation of a biker's death and the Italian mafia.

She settled on a small resort on the outskirts of Coolum. In a short time the detective located her room, grabbed some takeaway and once secure, fired up the laptop. She checked the windows one more time, drew the curtains and prepared for a long night ahead, beginning with Johnno's emails. Francesca took a moment to digest the information and the date she knew like the back of her own hand.

Two years ago, whilst her team had been focused on the biggest drug haul in Far North Queensland, another scenario was unravelling in Fremantle, Western Australia. Whilst they'd been parading around high-fiving and back-slapping, a more sinister kind of shipment was being unloaded.

Johnno's team had uncovered a covert stream of imported cargo, smaller somewhat regular amounts of chemical and legal pharmaceutical drugs that would eventually build drug manufacturing to an extent that this country had never seen. A delivery pattern and amount that didn't set off alarm bells in customs. The Seta Group were the international couriers.

Francesca read her partner's dogged research into the Delarno family's interests. Their business model changed dramatically about twelve months before the Chi You bust in Townsville. Genoa Holdings broke long-held shipping contracts to focus only on smaller, less lucrative ones. The Seta Group, based in Genoa, bought most, including the Australian opportunities.

Europe was in economic turmoil and had been since the financial crisis in 2007. The family would have no doubt been affected. But at the cost of breaking contracts?

At the same time, the illicit drug industry was growing significantly within Australia where demand exceeded supply. Johnno based his analysis on medical and police data. Federal Police and customs suspected another delivery very soon. Francesca checked the date on her watch. The latest container to arrive under the same M.O. was delivered … yesterday.

Francesca drew a mental picture of Australia. A week or two going through customs, then the transport to the new location. It could be up to three weeks or more before they had some closure. Anything could happen in that time.

Sighing loudly the detective sat back and pressed her head against the wall. It was getting late, her eyes were burning. She headed to the bathroom and let the tepid pressure relieve her aching shoulders and back. She shut her eyes, took a deep breath and sprayed her face with the water one last time before wrapping herself in the soft robe.

Chewing on a slice of cold pizza she stood facing the bed. She thought about Johnno and his obsession with the Delarno family's relationship with the Seta Group and Gino Castello. He was a dog with a bone for the family. Francesca had always trusted his instinct. She was compelled to explore his fixation despite feeling like she was ratting out her own family. Well, Almost.

What to do next? A light glint caught her attention from the edge of the laptop case. The gold packaging of the boxed engagement ring winked in the bedroom light. Funny it chose to reveal itself now and not during one of the many times she had rifled through the case at Wild Dog Creek.

She took the packaging and the envelope and read his words. Carefully she pulled at the ribbon. What type of engagement ring would Nicholas have chosen for her?

"Are you ready for this?" she heard herself ask in the still air.

Opening the box slowly, Francesca held her breath. Her wildly beating heart threatened to push through her chest. Startled, she stared for a long moment at the contents. Finally, she slowly lifted what was not a ring but a medallion, holding it to the light as the chain dripped through her fingers.

The Delarno crest. A heraldic shield shaped emblem set in a combination of Venetian glass, diamonds, precious stones and inlaid into a solid gold border. As the lamp light shone behind the glass, the pendant gleamed in stained glass translucency.

The craftsmanship was extraordinary. It was the most stunning piece of jewellery she'd ever seen contained to about the size of a fifty cent coin. Nicholas wanted her to have it on their last night in Rapallo. To place it around her neck and speak to her about their life together. The first memento for the love they'd shared.

Francesca held it to her chest, looping the length of chain overhead. The medallion sat above her breasts and close to her heart. She studied it closely, her fingers respectfully tracing the elements of the design.

A red cross emblazoned in the middle was set against the white background. The cross of St George was the centre-piece.

The detective looked at it for a long moment. Perhaps, there was another way to go about this.

~

Family crests were symbolic of allegiance. Decoding the crest might just provide the answers she sought. Italy was made up of patriotic regions that existed for centuries in isolated segments. Each region identified with its own heraldic images, more significant to them than a state flag.

Nicholas came from the Genoa region. A red cross on a white background was the mark of St George, the patron saint of the region. It held prominence within the family shield, at the centre, a location of absolute importance.

She began to unravel the meanings of the different symbols. Nic had mentioned Venice and Florence in his family history lesson. The medallion had a golden-winged lion sitting atop the shield. This symbol was a tribute to the family connection to Venice. It was holding Florence's symbolic Fleur de Lys in its paw. As she discovered the red cross of St George also swore allegiance to the Crown, the House of Savoy.

"My family were great friends of the royal families of Europe..." Nic had said. She knew she was on the right track.

She noted the colours of the three regions were also replicated. On a notepad the detective drew a rough sketch of the shield. Beside the drawing she connected the colours and symbols by region in a detailed plan.

Turning her attention to the shapes on the shield, she discovered that the top border resembled a castle. The bottom pattern, a chevron, often referred to water. More references to Rapallo, she thought. It was the dominant theme. The most powerful of the alliances.

Johnno believed there was a strong connection between the Seta Group and Delarno. Both families held significant business interests in the Genoa region. Francesca had been privy to the history lesson of the Delarno family in Rapallo. She knew the family had held shipping interests for centuries. The water symbolism was significant in that way as well. She laughed at herself ... she'd need more conclusive evidence to draw that long bow.

Colours had meanings also, aside from the regional connotations. The deep purple of the castle stood for justice and the turquoise glass was almost identical to the Rapallo Bay waters. It was the most enchanting colour and the shade varied as she rotated the medal in the lamplight. She allowed herself to be lost in the beauty of that water for a minute.

At the base of the delicate shield, a black, swirling pattern offered a protective embrace. It looked ominous, almost sinister, against the brighter colours of the plate. It was too heavy in colour and design, embracing the whole shield to eventually create a rectangular box surrounding the Venetian lion.

Perhaps the lion was trapped? The Venetians were trapped? The swirl pattern reminded Francesca of stylized smoke, similar to a Disney drawing of the unsealing of a genie bottle. It was flecked with red and gold. The design was precise, symmetrical. The more she looked, the more it resembled pincers or intertwining of limbs. Dismembered contorted limbs? Francesca shuddered.

A smaller medallion, about 5mm in diameter, was suspended at the bottom middle point, inlaid with a three-pronged design that looked like bent legs extending from a central point. It featured diamonds set in black onyx. This was the seventh symbol. Francesca had seen it before in the photographs of the Sicilian mob during her trip to Rome. The men had it tattooed on their bodies.

That connection could not be disputed. The three-legged creature in the bottom medallion was the Trinacria. Nero and Delarno were working together.

Perhaps it wasn't a trapped lion as she first thought. Perhaps the cage symbolized protection for the lion. Nero provided the protection, the arms. He carried out the demands of the Genoese mob. A mob made up of Castello, Seta and Delarno.

Francesca nodded then thought, "No." Giovanni Nero was too egotistical to be a mere servant. Too prominent. He wasn't merely the arm of the operation. He must have some influence within the organisation. Nero must head a Commission. With Silvio Delarno and Giovanni Nero working together, the shield could represent a symbolic meshing of the two groups.

Two Commissions co-operating. Plus Castello. Seta perhaps. So who was the Capo? Francesca wrote the four names in the notebook, drawing a circle around each. Under Silvio, she wrote Nicholas.

She looked at the colours again. More specifically the turquoise. A significant colour without an obvious meaning, perhaps even another family. Turquoise. Green. Verdi? Francesca was stumped.

Perhaps turquoise did just indicate the beautiful waters of the Gulf of Tigullio after all. The family had been in a love affair with the area for centuries.

So, where did the Seta Group fit into the equation? What was their representation within the family crest? She found the group's website and read the proud and detailed account of its business.

The Seta Group is based in Milan, Italy and was established in 1975 as a road transport company throughout Italy and Europe. Offering a range of services, its primary economic activity is specialised overland freight distribution and logistical freight movement. It has depots scattered throughout Italy and turned over 120 million Euros last year. With 850 employees, and a specialist IT department, the Seta Group owns its own fleet of vessels and is proudly partnered with, amongst others, Genoa Holdings.

"Well," Francesca told herself. "Let's take a look at Genoa Holdings then."

She clicked on the link, amazed at the detail in the website.

Established in 1850 by Giovanni Nicholas Delarno who won the business in a game of chess. He named the business Giovanni Nicholas. Back then it consisted of a small fleet of fishing vessels. With the help of his children and grandchildren, Giovanni Nicholas Delarno grew the business to include general cargo and eventually state-of-the-art container ships.

In 1978, when Silvio Delarno overtook the management and ownership, he changed the name of the business to Genoa Holdings. Today it turns over 275 million Euros, has over 1200 employees, a dedicated IT department, and offers specialist Maritime law services. Genoa Holdings owns a fleet of vessels and has dedicated partners who reflect the same high standard of customer service and dedication to the industry as Genoa Holdings.

Francesca raised her eyebrow questioningly. "Hmm. What else have you got Genoa?"

Partners included the Seta Group, no surprise there, and a number of other shipping companies as well as CMA UK, a crew management agency based in London and Indonesia. It was underwritten by ADC Maritime Insurances.

She followed the link to ADC.

ADC Maritime Insurances was established in 1986 by Alessandro Delarno in Milan. Compliant with government regulatory agencies all around the world, ADC has 25, 000 employees worldwide and an income in 2010 of 800 million euro.

Francesca blinked at the figures.

Last year customs officials had tracked a container vessel leaving Genoa bound for Fremantle, Western Australia via Egypt. They had found out thanks to an intelligence report stating the vessel had vacated the Egyptian port of Damietta. Customs officials had secured a job number for the suspicious cargo, tracked its movements using satellite technology and when the vessel arrived in Fremantle, a search of the containers in question had brought about a dead end. The container ship, believed to be carrying illicit drugs and cash, was clean.

Eighteen months later, a similar job number had triggered an alert. This time customs officers tracked the containers in question beyond Fremantle. Five separate containers, with similar numbering systems were distributed by road transport to various addresses around Australia. Two were filled with innocuous cargo.

One container was offloaded in Fremantle and taken to a storage yard. Undercover agents searched it and discovered a large amount of cash hidden in bags of green coffee. They resealed the container and waited. And so did the contents of the container. The funds and goods were never claimed.

The last two containers were sent to separate addresses in Victoria. The property owners were known to the police. The goods seized from those two containers contained illegal fire arms, ammunition and large amounts of cash. It wasn't too difficult to track the load to associates of the Nero family. The Australian Federal Police arrested and charged two men and one woman.

Francesca shook her head. "Nero is not that dumb. Surely. Sending the gear to himself. No way."

She pondered. "Johnno has this information. If there was a trail to Delarno here, he would have found it. All the evidence is pointing to Giovanni Nero. Maybe it's personal."

CHAPTER 32

The Delarnos were all about family. Logging into the International Births, Deaths and Marriages database was a long shot, but arranged marriages formed alliances too.

Silvio Delarno married Cristiana Zanda in Genoa. Four children included Nicholas, Sophia, Paul and Chiara who died at birth. Cristiana was born in Milan.

Francesca looked up the father. Antonio Delarno married Giuliana Verdi in Genoa. Two children included Silvio and Alessandro. Giuliana originated from a little town in the south.

Verdi! The last colour in the symbol. The Verdis were from a small town in Calabria, the region that formed the 'toes' of the Italian boot. There had to be some sort of alliance. It was the way of this family.

Francesca researched the history of the little town, looking for founding family names. And there it was. Historical records of Calabrian society told a story of two powerful families.

The Verdi and Nero clans were mortal enemies. During a land grab in the early 1800s, the Verdis took control of the Nero family's fertile lands, forcing them to settle in Sicily. Sicily at the time was in the grips of its own war. A mafia war that had begun to emerge in the late 1500s as a result of a new feudal system. It had gained momentum and having been unchecked for hundreds of years, the problems were now generational; woven into the very fabric of Sicilian society. The Nero clan who had been respected landholders in Calabria were suddenly outcasts in the mafia-controlled middle class.

Francesca imagined their new life. Living in poverty, no connections and unable to earn a decent living. The family would have been desperate. She noted a sudden change in their fortunes, two years after fleeing Calabria. Here was the catalyst.

Aldo Nero, the head of the family, was murdered whilst protecting an innocent child, unwittingly caught in a bloody street battle. The girl, unknown to Aldo, was the favoured and youngest daughter of the most powerful Mafioso leader in Sicily, Don Bandoni.

The Bandoni clan immediately extended their gratitude to the Nero family by aiding their assimilation into the Sicilian society. Supported by and bound to the Bandoni family, Nero sought a bloody revenge against the Verdi clan.

As the power of the Sicilian mob grew over the late nineteenth century into the early 1900s, the Verdi family paid the price with many lives. So much so that the war between the clans was attracting attention in Rome. Their unaccountable brutality threatened to stall the political and economic progress of a united Italy. Controlling Sicily played an integral part in gaining respect in the Mediterranean. Enter Antonio Delarno, young, ambitious and connected in the North, who, with the benefit of Mussolini, silenced the warring families.

Now all Francesca needed was a name, a Nero name to confirm her theory. An event or a family link that would silence the Sicilians. Something so powerful it would cause them to stop and take notice. The social media networks gave Francesca a detailed insight into the Nero family tree. Pages of social events, elaborate weddings, baptisms, holidays and family trivia showed a varied range of business associates and friendships.

As an interesting adjunct, the detective noticed every family with a female child shared a similar name. A tradition that began in the late 1930s. The girls were called Marinella or variations thereof. A family tribute to a beloved lost matriarch?

Francesca looked at the family tree. Marinella Nero. Deceased at 17 years in 1938. No descendants. So it must have been a significant event, a tragic death.

Hidden in the Facebook links the detective found a shrine to Marinella Nero.

"Ha! I've found you at last! Hiding there, you would be easy to miss. A name. A lonely name amongst the thousands. Tell me your story, beautiful. Antonio Delarno's mistress."

Antonio Delarno. That was Nic's grand-father.

"Oh God, you poor darling," Francesca muttered to herself as she delved further into the family tree.

Marinella Nero died of haemorrhage during labour and her child, Sophia Antonio Nero, was stillborn. All of that happened in Rapallo. Marinella was described as flamboyant and charismatic as well as being the older sister of Giovanni Nero. After a quick calculation Francesca realised Giovanni would have been 6 years old when his sister was taken to be Antonio's lover.

Outside of wedlock, the shame of a mistress, her family would have been incensed. At 17, Marinella was but a child herself. The Nero family dominated in the south, but by then Antonio Delarno was well connected and more powerful.

And then, twelve months after he takes her to Rapallo the poor darling dies in childbirth. Alone. And away from her beloved family. To add insult to injury, he married Giuliana Verdi, sworn enemy of the Nero clan. Any boy would have grown up hating that family.

What sort of man takes a young lover the same year he is married? Francesca felt infuriated by his arrogance.

Written in a combination of Latin and Sicilian dialect, a series of posts sparked Francesca's curiosity. Francesca pieced together fragments of the language as she worked through the dozens of personal messages.

However, the 90th post, written by Don Giovanni Nero himself, needed little interpretation. It was a call to arms.

Marinella. In Memoriam. 90 years. In God you rest beautiful sister. We honour you. We honour your sacrifices. Genoa will feel our pain. My family, Honour Rewards the Brave. With Justice Comes Peace. It is time.

Giovanni Nero was issuing a challenge on Delarno. A revenge to honour his sister. Francesca wondered why, at 84 years, Giovanni would suddenly decide this was the time to settle a score. Unless someone was pushing him along. Someone younger. Someone wanting Nero's influence within the group. A newcomer perhaps?

Was this the link to the Seta Group Johnno had been looking for? Francesca remembered the heated meeting in Portofino between Nicholas and representatives of the Seta family. Nicholas hadn't lied in the interview with Johnno. She smiled. It was indeed a contractual disagreement ... between organised crime syndicates.

A disagreement of leadership and membership of the clans. She and Johnno had joked about Chi You, Ares and Nero sitting at the table together. Regardless of those arrangements, if they did in fact exist, she was on the verge of unravelling one of the biggest Italian crime rings in the country.

Francesca paused briefly contemplating the information she had just discovered.

Could it be so simple? He's such an egotistical bastard, she suddenly thought, returning to the family tree.

Triumphantly she cross-referenced the ship's manifest. There was no vessel name to link the families together, as she had once thought, but there was a voyage code.

A booking number for the two vessels eventually bound for Western Australia were listed under the voyage code 39MN, followed by a series of numbers akin to a product barcode. She recognised the significance of the number sequence that had triggered the initial customs alert. Following on from here, each special container bound on this particular voyage was then allocated a different code depending on its end destination and cargo. And each of these special containers began with the reference GDA.

Francesca smiled to herself. She was in Silvio's head. How do you find a number of special containers in the hundreds of thousands being shipped around the globe? When you are as egotistical as Silvio Delarno, you give each a personal meaning.

Johnno knew the containers with the code GDA were the starting point for the illegal cargo, but he didn't realise that the numbers following bore instructions for the team in Australia. Police had recovered two containers because each was sent to a destination of interest.

Francesca worked the new number system. She tapped out Johnno's drum beat on her notebook with the pencil.

Those containers bound for Australia were organised by Genoa Holdings, a company owned solely by Silvio Delarno. G the code for Genoa and DA for Delarno.

39MN. 1939. The year of Silvio's birth.

MN. Marinella Nero.

The number sequence of the voyage code started with the birth date of Marinella Nero. But what about the other numbers? She studied them. What if …? Years ago there had been a store in her town. Its name corresponded with the latitude of the town. Francesca had always thought it a pretty cool name for an outdoor adventure store. She wondered. To test her theory she plotted the numbers of the voyage code of the container that was seized in Melbourne on a map. Longitude. Latitude. Bingo! She tested her theory on the second and smiled. Each number marked the co-ordinates for the end destination of the containers and now she knew exactly where the container delivery was headed.

Silvio was luring the breakaway Nero clan with flattery towards the Don's dead sister. To try and placate the family for his father's abhorrent behaviour towards the mistress before things flew out of control.

To undermine Nero's desire for revenge, Silvio orchestrated the illegal containers to be delivered to specific localities held by Nero. He'd set him up. Shut up or face the consequences. In the meantime Silvio Delarno secured his place at the head of the family crime tree.

~

Thwack! Francesca threw her shoe at the wall in frustration. She could scream.

Nicholas had said that Silvio ran the Italian interests of the Delarno holdings and would not give it up despite ill health and old age. Nero paraded as the head of an untouchable organised crime family.

Two families filled with hatred for each other bound by a code. A code of silence. Tradition forced this unlikely co-operation. The extent of which was determined by the organisational head. The Capo de Tutti Capi.

Silvio Delarno. He owned Don Nero. It was the only way that she was still alive. And Nicholas. And Silvio himself. A Capo would not tolerate the near misses. And the arrests.

Francesca breathed out deeply and with sudden awareness.

Nicholas wanted her to wear the medal, not as a gesture of his love but as a sign of her belonging. As a sign she was under mafia protection.

Francesca scanned the incriminating photographs taken in Rapallo searching for clues that would implicate other families. She didn't have to look too hard. Lucia and Mario Zanda's yacht, La Bianca Bella.

On the top deck a row of maritime flags and the Delarno crest caught the breeze. Different however because it lacked the heavy black Sicilian symbol. Francesca rummaged through the photographs.

Nicholas did not bear the ominous black markings on his chest. Perhaps he was distancing himself from the Nero connection. Perhaps he and Zanda were pushing to get rid of Nero. Contract negotiations.

Francesca pushed her hand to her chest. She all but grew up with them. Silvio was one of her father's closest friends. Did Stefano Salucci know too? Was her beloved father linked to this as well? She shook her head in disbelief.

"I should call Johnno." Francesca fidgeted with the keypad on her phone. Even Johnno would find it hard to believe she was an innocent party now. Once she provided him with the links she had discovered, her lack of knowledge of the family's activities would sound conveniently vague.

Surely it had not come to this. It was almost daylight. Left with no option, Francesca sent a quick text to Johnno.

"J, The cargo ship that customs has been tracking from Genoa Holdings, the one that docked in Fremantle yesterday is loaded with two containers belonging to Silvio Delarno. I know the delivery address for each. Secure that boat. I will explain when I see you. Delarno and Nero are working together. I bet my life on it. There is only one way to find out. Nic will talk to me. F"

CHAPTER 33

"She what?" Silvio exploded. Standing at the top of the home's sandstone staircase, he faced the orchard, his features contorted in rage.

"You imbecile." The old man reached for his revolver, aiming it at the bloodied man kneeling before him.

Nicholas rounded the corner. He needed fresh air and space to think after leaving the Commission's representatives to their deliberations inside the mansion. "Silvio! Christ, man! What are you doing?"

"This is none of your business Nicholas."

A desperate face turned to the son.

"I think it is. Who's this man?"

"He failed us." Silvio's frustration intensified.

"That may be so but see reason Silvio. For God's sake, Seta's breathing down our neck. We're in the middle of negotiations. You want to undo all my work with more irrational behaviour."

"Please. I will keep looking. I won't fail again," the man pleaded.

Nic faced his father. He was growing more irrational every day.

The son spoke calmly. "What's going on?"

Silvio looked at his son's set expression. "Perhaps I will tell you now."

"Yes, perhaps we should all know Silvio." Francesca stepped from behind the garage that had provided protection whilst she witnessed the sickening scene in front of her. "We'd all like to know the truth. Tell him, Silvio."

"Francesca? My God! Where the hell have you been? I've been looking everywhere for you…" Nicholas turned at her voice and the glock pistol pinning Silvio in her sights.

"Why don't you tell him Silvio? About me." She paused, her face taut with suppressed emotion. She briefly flicked her eyes over Nic in acknowledgement. "I know about your new business venture. Ares. Chi You. More importantly and somewhat more pressing, I know you're working to bring about closure to a family dispute between yourselves and Giovanni Nero."

The detective paused, addressing Nic, her eyes never leaving his father. "In Rapallo, you were asked to look after me in a certain way. I was to pass three tests to ensure admission to your little club. Submission. Trust. Loyalty. Does that sound familiar?" She looked briefly at her former lover, a distant coldness in her eyes.

Francesca motioned to Silvio with her pistol and a slight uplifting of her defiant chin. "Silvio Delarno, I'm arresting you on attempted kidnapping and organised crime related activities. I see that you have recovered sufficiently from your recent 'illness'. So, it shouldn't be a problem for you to come with me right now."

Nic instinctively positioned himself between Francesca's outstretched hand and his father. He recognised the turmoil in her eyes, despite her hard-set features. Their shared intimacy had tuned his mind and body to read her every thought. Every movement.

"Ha! Francesca. You have no proof! This is an insult to my family!" the old man shouted.

"Silvio stop!" Nic interjected, his voice smooth and silky. "Francesca, please. I don't understand this, but I see you're both angry. You realise that this situation is untenable. Who can talk with guns in their faces? Please, let's discuss this problem in a civilized manner."

Francesca was dumbfounded. "Nic, you're either blind or stupid. Perhaps you simply don't care. Your father was going to murder that man because he failed." She spoke with emphasis, lowering her tone. "Failed to get rid of me."

Looking firmly at his father, Nic demanded, "Is this true? Did you undermine me and order this action?" His eyes glistened with mistrust.

"My son, that's ridiculous. I'd hoped one day you would bring formality to your long affair. That this girl would be brought into our fold."

Francesca watched helplessly as a father worked his son. The old man looked at Francesca. "I think it's Francesca who has some explaining to do. Tell us Francesca, about this man Sinclair. He is your lover too, like my son. You're living as husband and wife. Tell me was it always your plan?"

Francesca glowered at him.

"You influenced my son in Rapallo. You pledged your dedication to Nicholas in Italy and at the same time took another lover. Your father would be disappointed to have raised such a whore. La puttana," the old man spat the final words, mocking her with his arrogant stare.

"I'm not a whore! How dare you," Francesca retorted angrily.

"Is what my father saying true, Francesca?" His voice was thin with emotion. "Did you deceive me? Another lover? Who's this man?"

Stunned that the situation was now twisted to something repulsive, Francesca blushed. "Nicci. Please. It's not what your father is inferring. You warned me, remember. I had to protect myself. To keep safe. I had no choice but to hide. And I certainly didn't take a lover."

Son glanced between father and lover.

She tilted her head in defiance. "Why would I lie? I have no reason to. Do you think this is easy for me? We've grown together since children. When you betrayed me I thought I'd die."

"I saved your life Francesca," Nic cut in. "Those men. Those photographs. They have nothing to do with me. I've been protecting you from them."

"Well," she responded, "whichever way you try to sell it to yourself doesn't much matter to me at the moment. I'm here to arrest Silvio. And you for that matter, if you continue to stand in my way."

"How can you say that?" Nic asked angrily. "My father has done nothing wrong. And for the record I was in Rapallo to sort out problems with a business contract. I have already given my statement to McCrae."

Francesca snapped. "Alright. You want to play games. Tell me, I'm curious, was it your plan to sort me out as well? I need to know Nicholas. Was my seduction in Rapallo your duty as directed by the Commission?" Francesca's voice rose in pitch.

His gaze dropped to her feet. She faced him in hurt and defiance. He couldn't bring himself to look at her, nor could he deny it. Francesca understood his silence and the realisation shattered her untested confidence.

"Francesca. We can do this. Just you and me. We can leave today and start again. Let someone else take over this police matter. Forget about all of this." His hand gave a sweeping gesture which took in his father, the house and the man still cowering behind them. "Remember in Rapallo, we could only think of each other."

Francesca stared at him, her vision darting from his hand to intense black pools of pleading emotion. Suddenly it dawned upon her why she had been given the history lesson in Rapallo. She realised what she was to bring to the family business.

"What do you mean forget?" Suspicion rang in her voice. "Are you asking me to make this case disappear? To betray my friends, everything I've worked for?"

He didn't respond. An emotional tear slipped along her cheek, she wiped it away with the sleeve of her outstretched arm. Nicholas stood silently defiant. He would not support her. He was standing by his family. He had taken sides.

"After all this time you don't know me at all," Francesca whispered, incredulous. Her throat tightened.

He softened at her distress yet spoke words of steely resolve. "Francesca, I understand you're confused. To understand me, you must realise that I won't let you come to my family in this way. Simply, you're wrong." His hand touched her face, gently wiping the tears, encouraging her to brush her cheek against his loving touch. And she did.

CHAPTER 34

Paul positioned himself behind Francesca, concealed by the extensive garden. When the mysterious tightly folded note, heralded in the Delarno family crest and addressed only 'Nicholas Delarno, Rapallo', had made its way to him, Paul became curious. How would a priest from the Basilica di Sant' Eufemia in Milan know he was the recipient's brother? How would such a note find its way to his chapel in Brisbane, Australia?

He turned to the Ministry for explanation. The ones who knew all the family business. And he was ashamed. That his family was involved in such despicable acts and that his own father would try to use Francesca in such a way. Paul's rage turned to fear for the young lovers last week when Antonio Nero visited his church.

Paul sat silently in the small timber-lined room listening as the heavy uneven footsteps echoed down the aisle towards the altar. They stopped at the confessional. Switching his phone to silent, the priest pre-dialled triple zero. In this parish, it helped to be prepared. As the heavy door opened, the tiny space was filled with the smell of stale wine and cigarettes. In the stuffy confines of the confessional, the putrid stench of the visitor took the priest's breath away.

His visitor clumsily slid the small timber covering back to reveal a gauzed area about fifteen centimetre square at waist height. Kneeling heavily in front of the gauze, his face unseen by the priest, the gentleman spoke in slurred Italian.

"Forgive me father for I have sinned. But it is for the sins of my family that I am seeking absolution. An innocent girl will be slaughtered like a lamb."

Paul watched in astonishment as the gentleman's hand came to rest on the bench in front of the gauzed window. He recognised not only the voice, but the very ring dominating the smallest of the puffy fingers.

"My son, wait here. Do not speak."

Paul exited the doorway to the confessional. He checked the church, locked the front door and opening the second confessional door, he helped Antonio to his feet, saying, "Cousin Antonio, let me get you some coffee and a comfortable chair. Then we can talk about this problem that is troubling you so."

In the vestry to the side of the church, Paul locked the second door. Here it was revealed to him the extent of the family's involvement in drugs and arms trafficking. A history of seething hate between families bound by a code that had lost relevance in a new country and a new order itching for establishment and control under the influence of Carlo Seta from Genoa.

Paul decided to read the note, its contents revealing a very distressed author, Francesca. Together, the two holy men turned to her police partner, Sergeant McCrae for guidance and help. Hours later the tactical response team headed to the Delarno home.

Paul may be a priest, but he was also a loving friend and brother. He would protect Francesca from his father, no matter what. He glanced at Antonio behind the small garden shed beside Detective McCrae. Heavily armed and kitted officers dressed in black stood in position at locations surrounding the majestic home. They waited.

CHAPTER 35

Francesca trembled slightly. If she backed down she was certainly dead, with or without Nicholas. *I need backup*, she thought. *I'm in over my head with this family.* The detective stepped forward slightly, searching for an outcome.

Nic spoke softly. "You do remember, don't you Francesca," he started. "I meant what I said. I want us. It's been my dream to see our children running amongst the groves and swimming in the cool waters somewhere in Italy. There's so much anger now and misunderstanding. You know it will calm. You are and have always been a part of our family."

Francesca listened. What if she had made a terrible mistake?

He reached for her hand, standing close. "Please Francesca." She must comply. The alternative didn't bear thinking about.

Francesca felt incredulous. This was it. She had spent her life waiting for this moment. It was so close to her now ... she could reach out and take it.

She slid her fingers along her forehead to ease the tension building in her temples. She pushed their coolness gently at the hairline before raking the lengths of her hair. As the emotion released within her, Francesca almost laughed. The scenario was ludicrous. That she even found herself considering his proposal was absurd. And yet the pull of him. The strength of his will to have her by his side. It could actually work. They could no doubt live a protected, happy life in Italy.

With a deep sigh Francesca made the decision. She would not squander her integrity. After today, it may be all she had left. The detective looked at him with wide-opened eyes.

Anyone can be strong when convictions are agreed upon. The test is born from difference. Facing the reality of opposing beliefs is when true grit and strength of character is determined. No matter how unpleasant the outcome. That was what she had fought so hard for in Wild Dog Creek. Francesca took a tentative mental step.

"Nicholas I have loved you my entire life. Once upon a time I wished so much for a life together. It will not work for us. Importing illegal firearms and drugs. For goodness sake. I cannot and will not be a part of this. I'm a sworn member of the Queensland Police Force. A cop. I've taken an ethical and moral oath to protect our state and this country. At present the evidence I have rests with your father. That makes me legally bound to bring him in for questioning." She finished with a heartfelt plea, "Please don't make this harder than it already is. Step aside and let me do my job."

Nicholas shook his head. "I'm sorry to hear that Francesca. You leave me with no other option. Perhaps now you'll be convinced that my father is innocent." He handed her a mobile phone.

~

"Hello?" Francesca held her eyes on the man standing directly in front of her. At the voice she stepped back, gripping her pistol tightly and pointing it at his chest.

"Francesca. You must listen to me. I heard you debating with Silvio and Nic. I know you're feeling confused between loyalty to your friends and your duty in the police. But, you must be true to yourself, no matter what. In the end it's you who decides what's right. Nothing else matters."

"Papa? Papa where are you? You can hear me? I can help you. Tell me where you are."

"No Francesca, you can't. You can only help yourself. And you must," he said gravely.

"Where is he? What have you done to my father?" Francesca screamed, glancing between the two men. A deep rage invaded her; she felt the blood drain from her face and wrap around her throat.

"Your father's safe. For now. What happens next depends on you, Francesca. You must make a choice." Nicholas spoke in a measured tone.

"You mean to trade my integrity for my father's life?" she accused in disbelief.

Her former lover's eyes turned cold. "How did you think this would end Francesca?"

She lowered her voice. "How can you make me do this? He's my father, for god's sake. You want me to sacrifice all my beliefs? To sacrifice who I am? How do I live a life knowing that? What type of person would I be?"

His face softened. "Francesca, my love. You'd be the girl who has given the gift of life to her father. The girl who would be my wife."

Francesca searched his face. Past demons threatened to tear her apart. Of course, she would save her father. But she couldn't trust that they would both live beyond today. There were too many unanswered questions. She wanted a solid deal. A deal where she would not stand in their way and her father would live.

She stalled for more time.

"Where is he? He must be here. He can hear me speaking to you. I want to see him. I want to know that he's safe. Once I give my answer I want to know what happens next," she asked, tilting her chin defiantly.

"Well, I see you're coming to your senses Francesca," Silvio sneered. "But you're in no position to make demands. I want an answer first."

"How do I know you're not just going to murder my dad or me

anyway? You can understand my caution Silvio. You've already tried to get rid of me many times."

Silvio mocked. "You'll have to trust me Francesca. You say you have a case against me. You can't prove a thing. We're victims. Victims of circumstances. However, my son believes that you can help us. Your father will always be a Salucci. You have the chance to change history. Your father, well … " Silvio shrugged menacingly as his intention hung in the air between them.

A sickening realisation dawned on Francesca. Her answer didn't matter. Silvio wanted her to say the words of a traitor before she and her father were both dead. Through the tears she yelled, "You son of a bitch Gino Castello. Don't shoot. Don't kill my father! Give me time to think."

It was too late. In the bunkhouse by the pool a dramatic scene was playing. Stefano Salucci sat in the chair, a gun pointed to his head. Horror on his face.

Be buggered if he would go like this though, without a fight. He tensed his body for the only chance he would get. He had to save his daughter. He made a decision. He would die in this beautiful setting. His blood would forever stain the Delarno floors, a reminder of his sacrifice and his daughter's integrity.

Stefano spoke quickly into the mouthpiece to his daughter.

"No! Francesca. I love you."

The old man struggled with Gino. He was no match for a gun but he was strong. The surprise attack caught the consigliore off guard. Three gunshots rang out.

"No! No! No!" Francesca screamed as they echoed through the phone. "Daddy!"

Her anguished cry filled the silence. It resonated around the complex in a tormented scream of pure, raw emotion. Francesca's wild eyes frantically searched the grounds. In the aftershock, the property was eerily quiet.

Nicholas froze. Shock resonated across his face.

Francesca turned to Silvio, her face full of revenge. "Your evil has no limits. My father was a brother to you."

She took a moment in the silence. Calmness stilled her hand and mind. Staring coldly into the old man's eyes, the detective's slow deliberate voice carried up the steps. "Pay for your sins Silvio!"

"Francesca! No!" Nic shouted.

~

In that instant Nic stepped towards her in anticipation of his father's wrath. He would not participate in this insanity. It should never have come to this. Instinctively, he used his body to shield her, pulling her to him, protecting her from his father.

The gunshot propelled him into Francesca. Simultaneously a second deafening shot rang close to his ear. They fell to the ground, his body protecting her as it always had.

Sound distorted from sight in slow-motion. A replay of events as they happened before her eyes. Fragments of exploding concrete and sandstone flew in all directions. Tiny stinging missiles blasted into Francesca's face and exposed arms.

"I'm sorry Francesca," he whispered. "The Commission could never trust a Salucci. Our love had proved them wrong. I'd never hurt you Francesca. I would die myself protecting you."

Nicholas drew a shaky breath. "I should have told you from the start. Silvio was wrong."

Loving eyes gently caressed her face. He breathed a shallow breath.

"I love you." His eyes closed and his beautiful mouth shaped in a half smile. "With all of me I love you. You've always been my beautiful flower."

Hot tears slid down her temples and she whispered. "I love you too Nicholas Delarno. I always have." She gazed at him. His smell, his warmth and strength. His arms wrapped around her in a defensive gesture as his dead weight pinned her to the ground.

She coughed slightly and her voice gained strength.

"Nicci. Wake up." She wriggled his hand free from under her hip and linked fingers. The pain made her cry out. He responded to her, a gentle pressure of reassurance. She focused on the top of his head. "Stay with me. Nicci. Come on my friend. Fight for us."

For the first time she noticed the flecks of blood covering his handsome face. She stroked his hair with her bloodied fingers. He didn't respond.

"Nic, open your eyes. Please ..." she whimpered, eyes now blurred with her own nauseating pain. "Stay with me. I can help you. You need to stay awake with me."

The sound of shattering glass echoed around the hillside. Dust and shouted commands filled the air. And then the sirens. Filtering through her nostrils, the smell of blood combined with the hot powdery stench of gunfire. An awful sound was coming from somewhere. It was persistent and growing louder. Francesca wished it would stop, until she realised it was coming from her.

"Stop!" she screamed in anguish at the sudden silence.

CHAPTER 36

Sinclair noticed the disturbance to the iron fence post about halfway along the perimeter of the extensive grounds. On the ground directly below, scuffed footsteps and trampled grass indicated trespass. A small clod of wet dirt hung on the edge of the whitewashed cement retaining wall. A sneaker print halfway up the iron fence marked the second foothold. Sinclair smiled to himself, Francesca's entry point.

Forensics waiting for Johnno's command were milling around the entrance to the great home.

Sinclair called their attention and continued on his way to recover Francesca's ute hidden in a surfer car park about a kilometre from the house. The frustration of not being by her side was manifesting in impatience. He needed to do something constructive. Finding the keys hidden behind the bull-bar he drove it to the front of the Delarno house. At least this way he would have independent transport.

Sinclair paced about. He needed to get closer.

Making his way to the guards at the entrance to the estate he waited behind the large granite gateposts. From here the concrete drive wound its way up the tree-studded parkland to the immense home. And that was it. The limits of his boundary.

Francesca's angry scream caught the breeze. Almost immediately the shocking sound of gunfire reverberated over the exclusive hillside. The cops scrambled for cover.

Amidst the confusion, Sinclair attempted to run towards the fight. Scowling openly at his thwarted attempt when a detective grabbed his shirt pulling him backwards to safety. Chief looked up at his master. *I'm right beside you*, his expression seemed to say.

In the eerie silent aftermath, the radios crackled with commands and a specific request. Sinclair McCrae was to stay at the entrance on gate duty. Seal the perimeter. No one in or out except emergency vehicles. He grumbled.

In the driveway of the Delarno estate, Francesca opened her eyes briefly as she felt herself being lifted into the waiting ambulance. "Sinclair?" Through the haze of pain she reached for Johnno's hand and placed it against her cheek. "You're here? You deserve better. I've let you down. Forgive me." She kissed his open palm and drifted off into blackness.

Johnno stood quietly and unmoving beside her. She released his hand, her faint words ringing about his head. He wondered if he'd imagined the whole thing as the ambulance left the scene.

Presently, an ashen-faced constable approached Sinclair. "Doctor Sinclair McCrae?"

"Yes. That's me."

"Detective Sergeant McCrae has asked me to come and relieve you. Detective Salucci has been shot. Sergeant McCrae said to wait for him and you can go to the hospital together."

"Thank you constable." The young man stood before Sinclair, eyeing the giant.

"Sir, I need to tell you." He bowed his head. "Her injuries are extensive. I'm sorry sir."

"Thank you." Sinclair slid against the pillar as his legs went out from under him. He buried his face into his hands, rubbing at his eyes. Absently he patted Chief's head. Yet another ambulance screamed up the driveway.

CHAPTER 37

"She's very lucky. The bullet deflected and entered Francesca near the front of her right shoulder. She's alive and we should focus on that, but she'll need more surgery and months of physiotherapy."

The surgeon paused for effect. "In my opinion, there's no doubt that the deflection saved her life. The angle of entry and exit indicates that whatever or whoever was in front of her acted like a shield. If it hadn't been there she would be dead."

Francesca heard the words and she faded into reality. Her eyes fluttered open and she focused on the familiar faces in the room.

"She needs plenty of rest. Don't stay too long." The surgeon turned and left the small room. "Ten minutes," he added looking back to Johnno and motioning for him to follow.

"Also, I thought you should know…she's pregnant. A matter of weeks. Possibly too early for her to be really sure, if she knows at all."

Johnno looked questioningly at the doctor.

"Blood tests. An ultrasound will confirm the dates."

He nodded, returning to the room. "Hey Movie Star, that was quite a performance. Glad to have you back for the encore." He was joking but his voice strained. He looked like he'd been to hell and back.

Francesca smiled faintly.

"Papa?"

Johnno swallowed hard and shook his head.

She nodded and swallowed down the tears.

"Nicholas?"

Johnno shook his head again. "I'm sorry Francesca. He was taken to another hospital. He passed away in the ambulance en route."

Francesca nodded and turned away.

"Francesca, Nicholas and Paul saved your life." He paused and his face saddened. "Your dad. We were too late. His injuries were too great. I am so sorry."

Francesca lay quiet and still, silent sobs caught in her dry scratchy throat. Ruthie moved in closer and sat quietly holding Francesca's hand, wiping the tears with a damp tissue. Her voice softly soothing.

Francesca shut her eyes. In the depths of her soul, a familiar melody returned. Her mind hummed the tune, singing softly the Italian words of comfort. The words that Nicholas had whispered the night of her dream.

"Nicholas," she whispered, drifting into grief. "I wish you had a second chance too. Thank you." A solitary tear slid across her cheek resting gently at her jaw line. "I'm sorry Daddy. I let you down."

~

Mel's hazel eyes watched the Hercules-like form of Sinclair McCrae. He was a man sure of himself and his abilities, yet a certain vulnerability when he spoke of Francesca warmed her heart. That he knew almost as much of Francesca's personal life as she did meant Francesca thought him pretty special too.

Francesca's description of her closest friend had left him in no doubt about Mel's place in her life. Sinclair recognised her straight away. He felt her warmth and the steely protective concern for her Francesca.

Mel was no pushover where her friend was concerned. She had grilled him on his intentions towards Francesca. Satisfied with his credentials, he was allowed into the fold. Her easy conversation style and the many hours of sitting and waiting had forged a strong friendship.

As Ruthie arrived, pale from yet another bedside vigil, Sinclair went in search of light refreshments, giving the girls a chance to talk privately. The bond of the three new friends grew to support each other as each breaking news reel showed reruns of the Delarno siege. The news feed continued with updates from eye witnesses and photographic stills of the victims.

Eventually, after the pictures of Stefano Salucci, Francesca and Nic could be witnessed no longer, Sinclair quietly rose to silence the noise. For hours now they had watched the images and stories. He looked around at the pale, tear-stained faces of Francesca's friends, gathered them to his arms and together they stood, embraced in sadness and relief.

At last, Johnno appeared. "You can go in now," he announced to the group.

The girls left immediately, holding hands for comfort. Noticing Sinclair's hesitation, Johnno pulled up a chair to talk. He turned the back towards the table and straddled the seat. By all accounts his brother had not visited her yet.

"You know Silvio was the main agitator," Johnno started.

Sinclair shrugged. He didn't really care about Silvio.

"Can you prove it?" he asked.

"I have enough to make a case against him. Francesca did some pretty incredible research. And it links nicely back to the old bastard."

Sinclair shrugged.

"Silvio was facing leadership pressure from the Commissions. That's why he brought in Francesca."

"I don't get it."

"Francesca is the key witness in the Chi You matter. By compromising her, the case is watered down, she's onside for future matters and Silvio comes out on top as the strongest contender."

Sinclair shrugged again.

"You know his plan had a number of flaws."

"Oh?" Sinclair raised his head to his brother.

"He was impatient. Bordering on senile. He didn't think Francesca would escape. And most significant of all, that her feelings towards Nicholas would change," Johnno concluded.

"Are you telling me that you believe this story? That it's all Silvio and Nic had nothing to do with it?" Sinclair asked.

"Of course not. That bastard was their key negotiator. But he would never have hurt Francesca. That's the key difference. It was the source of friction that led to disagreements and ultimately the mistakes."

Sinclair nodded. "Where is he now? The old man."

"In the cells. The Queensland cops want him first and then we can bring him to Sydney. He won't be going anywhere special anytime soon." Johnno crossed his arms over the back of the chair.

"And Francesca knows this. I mean about the conflict." Sinclair tried to sound nonchalant.

"She does. She figured it out last night. She went looking for closure and an arrest." Johnno shook his head in disbelief. "She needs support little bro. You know her better than any of us, even me. Is there something you want to tell me?"

Sinclair blushed and mumbled, "Not particularly."

"She also thought I was you when we loaded her into the ambulance."

"How do you know that?"

"She called me Sinclair. She said she'd let you down." He paused for effect. "The staff at the hospital told me she's been calling for you at night. They thought I should know in case it was important. You should go and see her."

"Yeah, I think I will." Sinclair leapt up and headed for the door. He'd deliberately stayed away so that she could recover. He didn't want to confuse the issue. To be honest, he was unsure of his standing in their relationship now that they were free of the river house confines and Nicholas Delarno was back in her life. This was the green light he needed and he couldn't get to her door quick enough.

Johnno chuckled quietly to himself. Not for him to interfere, but a gentle nudge in the right direction never hurt. Johnno reached for his phone.

"Yeah mate, I'd like to make a booking for two people for two nights. The most romantic room you have please. A bottle of champagne and chocolates on arrival sounds sweet. Next weekend. In the name of Jonathan McCrae. Thank you, I look forward to seeing you too."

Johnno wandered along the hospital corridor whistling Delta Dawn, searching for the coffee machine. Ruthie would be so surprised. She deserved a spoiling. Time for a bit of rest and relaxation with his girl before the next round. It was no trip up the coast, but chicks loved that whole romantic thing. He rubbed his big hands together and smacked them loudly. His work here was done. Well, for the moment, anyway.

EPILOGUE

Nicholas watched the white caps scatter as another squall blew across the vast Indian Ocean. The storm, whipped along by the water, gathered momentum as clouds merged with the black ocean and Nic couldn't tell where one began and one ended.

He stared at it for hours, the lonesome, wild beauty contrasting to the sumptuous interior of his bedroom. Caught between his memories and his recovery. Listless.

Alessandro Delarno's home was a sprawling manor made from local stone, steel and timber with three separate wings and views from every room. Sitting snugly within the landscape, it emerged from the hillside protected and exposed. A juxtaposition of harsh nature and comfort inside.

The contrast was not lost on visitors to the secluded retreat.

Inside, it was resolutely a single man's space, both luxurious and warm. Large sitting areas offset by private nooks added to the intrigue of the house. On display, ancient artefacts and modern artworks found a common passion: a study of shipping and maritime history.

Isolated on the gorgeous wind-blown property of his uncle, family members and friends were assured privacy and discretion. Since his arrival, visitors had been limited to a team of tight-lipped and well-paid medical staff, overseen by Alessandro himself.

He was alive.

But there was a cost. In the eyes of his family and the law, he was gone. Murdered in the cross-fire between his father and the police. Nicholas felt the pain. Again he thought of his mother grieving for her son and of course, his Francesca. He cried softly.

The nurse came again. She bent her pretty head to inspect the healing wound. He turned away. He was only interested in Francesca.

His mind turned again to the moments he'd hung in that place between life and death. A moment of absolute stillness. A place where time stopped. For an eternity there was silence. Clarity and understanding collided and he knew.

He knew all he would ever need and the only thing he wanted.

He breathed. Shallow and painful. It stung his chest. The young man gazed out the window and returned to that place on the steps of his father's house.

Pinned underneath him, Francesca whispered to him begging, encouraging, but most of all believing in him. He'd rested his head on her flat stomach. He refused to die. He would not die. Not like that.

Nicholas breathed again. Remembering.

"Francesca?" he had whispered, seeking assurance that she was still there; the difficulty to remain conscious distracted only by the assaulting array of smells surrounding him.

Blood. Its metallic sweetness filled his mouth and teased his nostrils. He spat it out, watching as the sticky red ribbons bound his body to hers.

Nicholas had closed his eyes to the distractions around them. He needed to sleep. Then he could draw upon his strength to move through the pain and help his lover. Nic let silence surround him, drowning slowly into the blackness.

"They're here!" Amongst the rubble of shot out concrete two bodies remained wrapped in each other. Nic heard them speak but his eyes refused to open. He listened. He had to protect Francesca.

He felt the hands around his neck checking for life and the pushing on his body to stem the blood flow. The hands were on his face, in his mouth.

Nicholas swallowed the panic.

McCrae had gasped when he'd seen them locked together, broken and bloody. His voice had shattered and stretched as he asked the medics for information. He remembered the detective being asked to help. That's when he lost consciousness, but not before he called for Francesca. A whisper and he felt his lips move to say her name.

He whispered her name again in the room, "Francesca."

A dream of broken images followed and then he woke. Here, with his uncle by his side and a team of experts on hand to help his body mend. In time, Nicholas would know the full story of his escape.

For now, he focused on Francesca. When the time was right he would find her. And make amends. Of this he was certain.

He breathed out slowly, his mind settling on the choppy sea beyond his bedroom window, and closed his eyes. One day. Francesca. Someday. Soon.

SERPENT SONG

ISBN: 9781925367805	Qty	.....
RRP	AU$24.99	.....
Postage within Australia	AU$5.00	.....
TOTAL*	$....	

* All prices include GST

Name: ....

Address: ....

Phone: ....

Email: ....

Payment: ❑ Money Order ❑ Cheque ❑ MasterCard ❑ Visa

Cardholder's Name: ....

Credit Card Number: ....

Signature: ....

Expiry date: ....

Allow 7 days for delivery.

Payment to:

Marzocco Consultancy (ABN 14 067 257 390)
PO Box 12544
A'Beckett Street, Melbourne, 8006 Victoria, Australia
admin@brolgapublishing.com.au

BE PUBLISHED

Publish through a successful publisher.
Brolga Publishing is represented through:
• **National** book trade distribution, including sales, marketing & distribution through Dennis Jones & Associates.
• **International** book trade distribution to
    • The United Kingdom
    • North America
    • Sales representation in South East Asia
• **Worldwide e-Book distribution**

For details and inquiries, contact:
Brolga Publishing Pty Ltd
PO Box 12544
A'Beckett St VIC 8006

Phone: 0414 608 494
markzocchi@brolgapublishing.com.au
ABN: 46 063 962 443
(Email for a catalogue request)